Praise for Lilah Suzanne

BROKEN RECORDS

"TOP PICK! This excellent take on the celebrity-and-normal-person romance moves at a fast clip while satisfying at every turn."

—*RT Book Reviews*

"Hollywood style meets Nashville charm in this sweet, sexy fling turned romance."

—*Publishers Weekly*

"4 1/2 Stars…The entire book has a dream-like quality that flows and ripples and it's the atmosphere of the book that stayed with me after the last page."

—*Joyfully Jay Book Reviews*

SPICE

"… Completely laugh-out-loud funny and the underlying romantic plot is the perfect backdrop for its sparkling characters, Simon and Benji, who are bound to induce a book hangover… Fresh, fun fiction at its best!"

—*RT Book Reviews*

"Suzanne keeps the humor warm and the sex real."

—*Publishers Weekly*

"Five Stars… The story is funny and sweet and almost painfully well observed. I loved it."

—*Inked Rainbow Reads*

PIVOT AND SLIP

"4.5 stars… Balancing laughter with touching emotions, this novella is a great first effort"

—*Carly's Book Reviews Blog*

BURNING TRACKS

BURNING TRACKS

lilah suzanne

BOOK TWO IN THE *SPOTLIGHT* SERIES

interlude **press** • new york

interlude 🧩 **press** • new york

"Storms make trees take deeper roots."
—*Dolly Parton*

1

"**The key to** a long-lasting relationship," Gwen says, hunched over on her knees to crawl beneath the gossamer folds of Clementine's dress, "is that you have to think of yourselves as a team." She grasps Clementine's ankle to secure the silk ribbon of her peep-toe, five-inch cork wedge shoe, just over the delicate protrusion of bone. "You have the same goals. You're working together, not against each other."

Gwen sits back on her haunches and hauls more of the dress over her head; the world goes a muted red with silky, gossamer fabric sliding and shimmering and catching with static on her neatly coiffed, platinum blonde hair. A garter belt strap dangles loose on Clementine's long, toned thigh. Gwen read once that Clementine's legs are insured for three-hundred K per leg, but she's never gotten more than a dismissive laugh in response to her questioning. They are quality legs. Certainly worthy of at least a general liability policy, protecting those at risk from the tight knot of her calves and the lithe power of her thighs. Gwen clips the first strap to Clementine's sheer thigh-highs and reaches around behind her to grab blindly for the second one.

"Thank you, oh relationship guru," Gwen hears clearly from under the dress; no amount of silk is enough to muffle Nico's sarcasm.

"Now wait a sec," Grady drawls in response. "I kinda like that. Sorta like a tandem bike ride?"

Gwen moves to the other leg and clips one strap, then the other. She fights her way out of the dress. "More like... a three-legged race, I think." She quickly combs through her short hair and runs a finger under both eyes to check for any bold black liner smudging. As she stands she adds, "There's a dirty joke in there somewhere, I just know it."

"Spare us," Nico snipes, and next to him on the plush king-sized bed, Grady grins.

They're gathered in a room in one of the high-rise hotels downtown; hair and makeup people have gone, leaving behind a vacuum of sounds and smells and gossip. Just a few final touches left on Clementine's outfit before her manager bangs down the door. Gwen nods to the mirror for Clementine to see the final product, then helps herself to some pistachios from one of the baskets on the table.

Clementine spins in front of the mirror; the dress flares out in a trumpet shape and her caramel-colored hair cascades in glossy waves over her exposed shoulders and down her back. When she walks, the folds of fabric part in a slit designed to go high up on her thigh and reveal the garter belt. Just a peek. A tease. An invitation to look, but not for long.

"Perfect," Gwen decides. "Nico?" She took the lead on Clementine's look for her new album and the upcoming tour's launch party concert, but Nico has such a keen instinct for what *works*. It's why she wanted to go into business with him in the first place; she may have the knowledge—years and bookshelves full of it—but Nico has vision. That can't be taught.

Nico doesn't reply. Clementine makes a face at them. Gwen turns and—

"Should have known better than to let them on the bed."

Nico and Grady are reclining now, dropped sideways in the center of the bed with their bodies curled and curved together, kissing: soft pecks with smiling lips that would be cute, sweet even, if it weren't for the location of Grady's left hand. Gwen exchanges a bemused look with Clementine.

"Hose 'em down or leave 'em?"

"The ice bucket would probably work," Gwen says. Then a pounding boom comes from the door. Nico and Grady spring apart.

"Showtime, Ms. Campbell."

Gwen gives Clementine an encouraging nod as she glides to the hotel room door.

"Wait, wait, wait." Nico hustles over, then stands with his feet planted wide, back straight, chest forward, shoulders set as if his spine were made of steel. Tipping his head to the left, he presses his thumb to his bottom lip. He hums, then tips his head to the right.

"Is it too much?" To hide the nervous wringing of her hands, Gwen tucks them behind her back. This is a major televised event focused on Clementine and Clementine alone, a big job for Gwen to have taken on by herself. "Not enough? I brought that silver and black diamond arm cuff, but I thought with the red dress and garter and those shoes—"

Nico holds up a hand. She closes her mouth. He lifts one perfectly arched eyebrow. "It's fantastic, Gwen. Well done." He sidles past her with a waft of expensive cologne and a nudge to her shoulder. "Have a little faith in your own abilities."

Call it imposter syndrome, or core wounds, or the ever-present yet impossible-to-achieve pressure to have it all. "I try to," she tells him.

There's urgent knocking on the door again; another call for Clementine to get to the stage right away.

"It's different," Clementine says, moving away from the door, "for women. We have to work twice as hard to get anywhere at all. And if you slip up, take a moment to breathe or be human, take your eye off the prize for *one second*—bam." She chops the air like the swing of an axe. "You're done."

Nico holds up both hands. He certainly isn't unaffected by prejudice and gatekeeping. But Gwen does enjoy how Clementine can deliver a pointed rebuke while she looks like pampered fairy-tale royalty. And she's not wrong: Most days Gwen can barely juggle relationship and career without failing at one or the other, or sometimes both.

"Not gettin' your pretty little behind on stage will probably end your career, too." Grady jerks his head toward the door just as more pounding thunders through the room.

Grady is in a gray suit, with the coat open and the collar of his white shirt undone and tie-free: casually, carefully disheveled. He's there as a guest, not the star of the show, so it makes sense for him to be understated. The fact remains that Grady Dawson is just one of those people who makes an entire stadium of people stop and stare. That can't be undone by a subtle outfit.

"I adore this dress. See if you can get more from this designer for me?"

"Well, Gwen did all the legwork, really. And the designer's based in Paris; I just got lucky when I was there on a family trip. But I'll see what I can do."

Clementine tugs Grady up from the bed and hooks her arm through his. "Was that the surprise family trip that Grady cooked up, when he flew everyone on a private jet—the one that secured his status as the favored son?"

Grady beams. "Yep."

Nico takes Grady's other arm. "I'd be jealous if I wasn't so happy to see my insufferable brother usurped."

"Aw, look at you guys," Gwen coos. "Aren't you a stunning threesome?"

Classic beauty Clementine, with her elegant, shapely body and perfect, shining hair. Grady, every bit the heartthrob and noted sex symbol, strong-jawed and blue-eyed, with his tousled golden curls. Nico, dark and striking, with sharp edges and hard angles to his features and body and something regal about the way he holds himself: confident, imposing, and sure. They really do look good together, the three of them.

"But enough about my fantasies." Gwen's wink is exaggeratedly salacious. "Get out of here before they resort to using a battering ram."

Clementine gives one last check in the mirror. "I always have them fetch me early." She runs her tongue along the front of her teeth, then dabs at the corners of her mouth. "You know what they say: 'On time is too late.'"

She air-kisses Nico, then Grady, then stops in front of Gwen and makes physical contact, pressing her satin smooth cheek to Gwen's. She hums a run of notes in Gwen's ear. Two years now Gwen has worked with her, and she has learned that Clementine is sweet and sharp and tremendously hardworking. She's also very private and nearly impossible to read.

Gwen is still shaking off the enchanting yet confusing moment between them when Clementine disappears from the room in a magnificent sweep of red satin dress and silken locks.

Nico frowns after her. "Who says that? No one says that."

Trailing Clementine down the hall is a group of people with clipboards and headsets, speaking frantic instructions, as well as Clementine's giant security guard and photographers and journalists jockeying to get closer.

Clementine calls to Gwen over her shoulder, "Sure you won't come along backstage, too? You can be my date."

"Nah, I'll clean up here, and catch some of the show from the wings like usual. But I should get home before Flora falls asleep. I haven't seen her all day."

"All right," Clementine says with a pouty little frown. "Be sure to tell that pretty wife of yours I said hey."

They say their goodbyes, the door closes, and Gwen packs away the unused jewelry and lingerie, the shaping undergarments, the sewing kit and steamer, the other dresses they'd had as backup, several pairs of shoes, and the discarded paper backings of the tape they used to keep everything in place and protect tender skin from blisters.

Gwen packs her car, flashes her industry badge to get back into the venue, and then watches from the VIP balcony area with a crowd of people she vaguely knows: other country stars and their entourages. She finds a spot near the railing. Clementine is a lot of fun onstage; she knows how to put on a show. Everything is in sync: the band behind her, the backup dancers, the blue and red and pink and yellow sweeps of light. She uses the whole stage, dances and shimmies and jumps and sings. She looks amazing, and the crowd clearly adores her.

Gwen watches one more song, a slow, emotional one. Melancholy for people and places left behind. "Burning Tracks," the host calls it, and reminds everyone that the concert is streaming online and to be sure to use the hashtag #burningtracksreleaseparty when they tweet or Instagram.

Gwen does neither, but she does text her wife.

OMW. Wait up for me?

2

Their house is that bland style known as foursquare, and looks like a cube with square windows, an idyllic, flat, square yard, and a wide, square front porch. Gwen had been drawn to Victorian architecture: the gingerbread houses with fairy-tale spires and brightly colored exteriors. Or the new, modern condos downtown, like the one Nico bought: upscale, urban, right in the heart of all the action.

But in the end, they liked the huge amount of square footage after being crammed in overpriced apartments in L.A. for so long, and Flora loved the charming, historic family neighborhood, the proximity of a farmer's market and good schools, while Gwen liked its eclectic collection of turn-of-the-century houses. The house seemed like a blank canvas, too, like a spiral-bound notebook with heavy textured paper just waiting for her to fill the pages.

And that gorgeous claw-foot antique bathtub in the master bath.

Mostly, though, it was the price tag. Gwen is still convinced they robbed the sellers blind and then rifled through their pockets just to shake them down a little more. Tennessee real estate prices are a unicorn-prancing, rainbow-hued dreamscape compared to California. Or: really fucking cheap.

She pulls into the driveway, parks behind Flora's four-door hybrid sedan, cuts the headlights and the engine, and leaves the jewelry and extra dresses and shoes in the locked car instead of hauling it all inside and then out again in the morning. It's a safe neighborhood. Safe to the point of tedium.

It's dark inside; the yellow glow of the porch light falls on the wide wooden staircase in the foyer, and a sliver of light comes from beneath the door of their bedroom upstairs. The front door creaks closed.

Gwen heats up leftover pesto tortellini, gives Cheese—their giant, lazy orange tabby—another serving of food that the cat really does not need but begs for anyway, and then creaks and squeaks her way out of the kitchen and over the old oak floors past the living room, dining room, and foyer—all politely and quietly set in their respective corners—and up the stairs.

"Hey, you're up."

"You said to be." Flora looks up from her book. Raven-black and thick as velvet, her hair is unbraided and twisted up onto the pillow behind her. "A reminder, however, that I'm used to getting up at six a.m." She yawns so wide her jaw cracks. "I can't educate twenty-seven second-graders and keep up with your schedule."

Gwen leans over the bed for a quick peck. "I know. I'll be quick, promise."

She washes up, brushes, flosses, and changes into a slouchy T-shirt and bikini briefs. Then she checks her phone while still in the bathroom: reminders for tomorrow, meetings to attend, emails to be sent. Hand on the doorknob, she thumbs open a brief social media indulgence.

On Instagram, Clementine has just posted a picture of herself at a burger place, flanked on either side by Nico and Grady, giant, messy chili-cheeseburgers heading toward their open mouths. The caption reads: *After-party grub with my two favorite boys! Yummy and yummier.*

It has a wealth of likes and comments. Thousands and thousands.

Gwen feels jealous—not stabbing, chest-clawing jealousy, but a pang. Jealous of the burgers or the boys or Clementine, she's not sure. Once upon a time, this hour on a Saturday night wouldn't mean a face scrubbed clean and a schlubby old T-shirt and bedtime.

She tells Flora as she climbs into bed, "Clementine invited me to be her date."

"Oh?" Flora doesn't look up from her book. "Does that include a goodnight kiss?"

And because she tells Flora everything, Flora gets to mercilessly tease Gwen about her *former* silly, harmless crush on Clementine. Gwen flops on the bed and groans into her pillow, "No."

"It's a good thing I'm not the jealous type, hmm?"

Gwen spent quite some time under Clementine's dress to fiddle with her underwear, so yes, it probably is a very good thing. "I don't even know what her deal is. If she's even dated any of those people the tabloids say. If she likes girls or boys or both or neither. Maybe she's only into people dressed in furry animal costumes. I'd never know."

Gwen flips onto her back, and Flora finally sets down her book: *Ina May's Guide to Childbirth.* It goes on top of the ever-growing stack of books about pregnancy and babies on Flora's nightstand.

"Her deal?" Flora asks. From this angle the light falls just right, casting contours and shadows over her full, plush lips, big dark eyes, and round, short nose. "Naturally beautiful" is a term that was made for Flora.

"Gosh, you're pretty," Gwen says, craning her head back to flash a playful grin.

Flora looks down and away, as she always does when someone compliments her. "Thank you. And what does that have to do with anything?"

"Just noticing." Gwen walks two fingers up the gracious curve of her hip and sets her hand where Flora's waist dips in. "Right. Clementine. You know, what she's into. What's her deal?"

"You could ask her." Flora settles into her pillow, rests a hand on the nape of Gwen's neck, and strokes Gwen's buzzed short hair there with the pads of her fingers.

"I have. She just says something like, 'Sugar, I'm married to music.' Or: 'I got bigger fish to batter and fry, hon.'" Gwen's twangy, Southern-belle Clementine accent is spot-on, she's sure.

Flora's face is patient. "Well, maybe she doesn't need to have a deal. Maybe she really does want to focus on her career."

Again, the myth of having it all. It's not unreasonable for Clementine to drop out of the relationship race entirely. "Okay," Gwen says. "But why not be up-front about it? Why let people think she's dating this singer or that actor or this athlete… or Grady. People would be less curious if she was like: 'Banged him, not her. Had three crummy dates with her; oh god, no, not him.'"

Flora's fingers scrape higher up Gwen's scalp, where the hair is longer and flopping over to the side. "Her life seems complicated," Flora points out. "Perhaps it's easier to just go with it. At any rate,

G, it doesn't really involve you, hmm? I mean, your relationship with Clementine is strictly professional."

"Yes. Blah." Gwen pokes her tongue out between her teeth. "Fine. I know. Why are you so practical and smart?"

"One of us has to be," Flora teases. "Now are you gonna finally make a move or can I go to sleep?"

Gwen hums and drops a kiss on Flora's lips and on the side of her neck, gets her fingers under the hem of Flora's nightgown where it's bunched up on her thigh, and—

Flora lets out a huge yawn, then throws an arm over her eyes.

"Flor—" Gwen says, with a laugh-groan. "Am I boring you?"

"Mmm, no. I'm in the mood, I swear."

Gwen leans over Flora's covered face, her lax body, and deadpans, "Really."

Hovered over her with Flora quickly losing the battle to stay awake and Gwen hesitant, she wonders, have they hit that point? Where watching a depressing documentary on TV or finishing a chapter in a book or *sleeping* is more appealing than sex or going out? Is this what they have to look forward to till death do them part? Half-assed attempts to get off before one of them starts snoring?

Flora breaks her from despair, and the thought that she should have gone out with Grady and Nico and Clementine after all. "Hey." Flora lifts the arm flung over her face, presses her thumb to Gwen's pout and pouts back at her. "Really. I want to."

"You can sleep. It's okay," Gwen reassures her. It's not Flora's fault, Gwen's recent discontent and itchy need to *do something, be somewhere else.* She hates when she gets like this, with her own clashing desires for stability and commitment, excitement and freedom, at war.

Gwen blinks down at Flora: her partner, her wife, her best friend. The person she's inexorably twined her life around, like restless climbing ivy to a sturdy, sure oak. The girl she saw across a dorm room that teemed with bodies and alcohol and smoke. She had felt a tug, a physical pull, toward her, shy and quiet and beautiful. *It's you.*

Flora's soft lips quirk up, her hand reaches down, and she guides Gwen's hand up her thigh, over her hip, and down into the front of her panties. "Hey," she says again.

Gwen hears without words: *I'm here. I'm with you. Always.* Flora kisses Gwen with a kiss that starts like smoldering tinder, then burns to life when Gwen strokes the slick heat of her, and Flora gasps.

"Oh." Gwen breathes the surprise into her sternum, moves out of the way so Flora can shimmy her nightgown off. She's wet and warm and swollen; she really was in the mood. Gwen cranes down, circles a perked nipple with her tongue, then sucks and bites and hums while she strokes the protruding nub of Flora's clit.

"I—" Flora breathes in, sharply. Spreads her legs and arches up. "I was thinking about you."

Gwen has no need to coax an orgasm out of Flora tonight, no long lead-up with her mouth or a toy; she just pushes two fingers inside and moves them with the cant of Flora's hips, back out to the spot that makes Flora moan and scramble to grip the pillow behind her. Close.

"Yeah?" Gwen is always happy to hear that she turns Flora on. She hardly believed it the first time it happened, and still hasn't quite recovered from disbelief that it has happened at all.

"Was, um—" Flora starts, losing focus when Gwen lavishes attention on her other nipple. She whines, and her thighs start to tremble and splay. "Thinking about—making a baby—"

Gwen looks up and pauses, hand stilling. *Making a baby?* "Honey, I have some difficult news for you."

Flora smacks at her arm. "Hush. You know what I mean. *Ungh.*" She gasps and rocks her hips. "Being together. Planning... *God.* You know I like that stuff."

"Yeah." Gwen redoubles her efforts, pressing in and in and out, circling and stroking with tight flicks of her wrist, swiping her tongue flat, then in pointed flicks. Flora grabs her wrist and the back of her head and comes with string of gasps and shivering snaps of her hips.

Gwen watches Flora's chest rise and fall, rapid and heaving at first, then slowing, even and measured. Her arm is flung over her face again.

Lips bitten and brow furrowed, Gwen shoves her hand into her own underwear. She gets to stare at Flora while she's still coming down and out of it. She's trying to hurry; Flora still makes her ache and flush and yearn with every luscious bared bit of her. The tension builds and builds. Gwen rocks into her own fingers, pinches her nipple under her shirt, until Flora peeks out from under her elbow and asks, "What are you doing?"

Gwen grunts. "Getting off so you can sleep."

"No need to martyr yourself, G." Flora pushes up and crawls over Gwen's body on all fours. Flora's fingers replace Gwen's, and her breasts hang heavy, brushing Gwen's. "I'm here," she says, and thoroughly takes Gwen apart, like someone who knows exactly how.

3

Gwen wakes the next morning to two texts from Nico and an empty space beside her in the bed. She stretches and untwists her T-shirt from around her waist, then grabs her phone and heads downstairs.

> **Nico:** Have I mentioned lately how great you are? I'd be lost without you.
> **Nico:** Unrelated... Can you come in for a few? Need help shipping.

"Morning. I made muffins." Flora is in her Sunday gardening clothes: a floppy straw hat, old cargo shorts, a yellow T-shirt with holes and patches of discoloration, and polka-dot rain boots that go up to her knees. The outfit is horrible and yet very cute.

"We could go full-on English countryside garden chic," Gwen tried to tell her when they were first digging up corners of their yard for garden patches and raised flower beds. "Like the Duchess of Cambridge."

"Buy four hundred-dollar boots to spread manure?" Flora said, wiping sweat from her brow with her arm and smearing dirt across her face.

Gwen conceded the point and went back to hoeing and making jokes about hoeing.

"Muffins from my muffin," Gwen says, this late, lazy morning, and takes a blueberry poppyseed from the basket on the kitchen table.

Flora gives her a fond shake of the head before going to the backyard.

It's sunny and not too hot. Gwen can eat her muffin and sip her strong Irish breakfast tea and watch Flora pull weeds and dig trenches and tenderly place plants with newly budding flowers and delicate roots.

"Hey, Flor?" Gwen calls through the window when Flora comes closer to fill her tin watering can. "Nico wants me to come in for a few hours, is that okay?"

Water spurts from the spout next to their deck, mostly getting into the watering can but also dripping onto Flora's boots and puddling in the thick grass. "Okay. Just not too long? I wanted to look at donor bank options."

Picking a donor; are they that far along in the process? But that's the next step. That's the plan. What Flora wants. What she...

That's the plan. She finishes her muffin; it feels like a rock in her stomach. "Sure. Shouldn't take too long. I don't know why he needs me to ship things back anyway. We've been making Spencer do that."

Flora turns off the water, and the pipes make an ungodly screeching noise. She hauls the can up and stumbles and sloshes her way back to the new row of flowers; water splashes everywhere as she goes.

"You need help?"

"I got it," Flora answers, even as she nearly loses her grip on the can. She's soaked with patches of wet from the waist down; her shorts cling to her legs.

"If you say so." Gwen tips back the last syrupy dregs of her tea and calls out before she goes off to shower, "By the way, those galoshes are super sexy. Wear them for me tonight?"

Flora waters her flowers in the sun and says with a laugh, "Go to work, Gwen."

After a quick shower, Gwen stands in front of her closet in only her black boy shorts, considering her options. It's Sunday, which means comfy casual. But she's heading into the office downtown, which means on-trend professional. It's the end of summer, not quite fall. She doesn't like to browse; she likes to go with her gut. Her gut says: high-waisted black leather skater skirt; white T with *Thanks for Nothing* printed across it; heeled black ankle boots; thin silver choker. She grabs a lightweight red blazer as she darts out the door.

Walking into their office in a restored brick building in a once-blighted, now historic and hip part of town, Gwen drops a cruller from the bakery downstairs on Nico's desk and asks, "Why isn't Spencer doing this?"

Nico ignores the cruller. He probably had tofu-and-kale scramble for breakfast. Or two cups of coffee and nothing else. A man of extremes. "Spencer has flounced."

"Flounced?" Gwen scans the office. Moving their home base from L.A. to Nashville meant more than just packing up and carrying on as usual from a new city. The vibe is different here: downtown Nashville has a Southern-gothic-meets-art-deco style, so their studio changed accordingly. The L.A. office was cool and chic, but this one has a polished vintage feel, with its exposed brick walls and refurbished honey-colored floors. They did bring along their chrome desks and clothing racks, which complement the industrial wire lighting and exposed wood beams. Add the white leather couches, the new chrome ceiling fan, and they certainly *look* as if they fit right in.

Gwen's desk is across the main floor from Nico's, separated only by wide open space. The racks of clothes and shelves of shoes and hooks with bags are organized in a loft above the reception desk, which is, indeed, abandoned. Flounced from.

Nico goes on typing, his expression neutral. Gwen has known him long enough now to read the *told you so* implied in his breezy dismissal. "You missed all the excitement."

Gwen sits across from his desk, crosses her legs, and takes a bite of her cruller. "Well, don't hold out on me."

Nico finally looks up, head titled and chin jutting. He's in slim lightweight mustard yellow chinos, a thin blue sweater with the sleeves pushed up, and gray suede loafers. A perfect Sunday at the office look.

Flora teased her about having a crush on him, too, when she and Nico worked together at the salon in Beverly Hills, before they made the leap to personal stylists working with D and C-list Hollywood celebrities, then climbed their way up to attending to the reigning princess of country music—but Gwen feels more admiration than crush. Nico is so confident, even when he's not; he carries himself in an assured, effortlessly cool sort of way. Something about him makes people take notice.

"I knew hiring Spencer was a bad idea."

"Oh, you've been a waiting a long time to say that, haven't you?" Gwen licks sticky icing from her fingertips.

Nico sighs and scratches a hand through his dark hair, which is still trimmed close on the sides, but has a new, meticulously messy sweeping part. "I didn't want to be right about him."

"You sure?" She has to give him credit. He really did try to find ways to help Spencer learn the styling business, and if he came off as brusque and blunt, well, that's just how Nico is. It's how he got to be so successful in the first place: Diplomacy, politeness, and hesitance have no business in Hollywood. Or, mostly Nashville, these days.

Nico's face goes soft with that far-off, dreamy look he gets only when he's thinking about one thing, one person. "Yes, because Grady cared about him. And I hate when Grady cares about people who aren't worth his kindness."

Gwen props her chin on both hands, her elbows on the cold edge of Nico's desk. "Aw, you guys are almost as a disgustingly sweet as me and Flora."

Nico smiles softly. "Almost."

Gwen flops back in her chair. "Okay, eat that doughnut and tell me about Spencer's epic flouncing." She pauses and cocks her head. "You know, I was right in the middle of teaching him the subtle yet important differences between shawls, capes, cloaks, and mantles, and how to achieve the perfect drape. Now he'll never know."

"Tragic," Nico says with a lift of one eyebrow. "It happened out of the blue. Maybe not for him, though. I called him early this morning. I was up because Grady was up and certainly he remembers how irritatingly early Grady gets up, he was his assistant for over a year. Anyway, the designer of Clementine's album release party dress wants her to keep it, so I didn't want it shipped off. And he said—"

He squints as if trying to gather his thoughts, presses his hands flat together and rests them beneath his cleanly shaven chin, and breathes in slowly through his nose.

"He said: 'Fuck you fuckers, I'm fucking out of here'?" Gwen guesses.

"No." Nico laughs. "I mean, essentially, but, oh, something about how he's outgrown us, and he's not going to lower himself to being our *errand boy*. He wants to make it on his own. I suggested he wasn't ready. He suggested, well. Let's just say he didn't take my opinion under advisement."

Gwen pulls a face, annoyed. Spencer was an intern, and an intern only for a year and half or so at that. *Everyone* has to start with grunt work. It took her several years to make full partner, and that was with busting her ass to the point of nearly ruining her marriage. But clearly not everyone can hack it. "*Can* we get an errand-boy? That sounds nice."

"That does sound nice." Nico stands, and she mirrors him. He's almost a foot taller than she is, but he's on the willowy side, slim-muscled and sharp-boned. "But until we find an errand-boy to do our bidding, we have clothes and jewelry and shoes to pack and send back to their designers."

Gwen fetches last night's unused items from her car, Nico eats his cruller, and they go up to the loft.

"So did he say where he was flouncing off to?" Gwen asks, putting a jewelry case in a box and dumping packing peanuts on top.

Nico checks the inventory slip and marks off the item. "Hollywood."

"Ah, the seductive call of Hollywood." She closes the flaps and holds them in place while Nico tapes the box closed. "Do you miss it?"

"I do, yeah." He examines a pair of shoes, then takes the protective tape off the sole and heel. "I miss the hustle, sometimes. It's so sleepy and slow here in comparison."

"I miss In-N-Out Burger," Gwen says, taking the shoes and finding their box.

Nico groans. "Yes, oh god. A Double-Double at one a.m. after hitting the after parties in WeHo. No burger here can compare."

"The beaches."

"The mountains," Nico counters. "California mountains are better."

"Outdoor concerts."

"The sun."

"A decent Asian market." Nico sighs. "Or fresh seafood."

Gwen folds and tapes, marks off items, prints packing slips. "Decent produce, too. The avocados here are appalling."

They stack the boxes by the front door, ready for delivery first thing in the morning. It's not that she *dislikes* Nashville. It's fine. Quirky and cute and pleasant, overall. Unlike Nico or Flora, however, she was born and raised in Los Angeles. She fits there. Here, she's still waiting for the day when she pulls up to her house and it feels like home, instead of that place they bought recently.

She misses L.A. as she would a missing limb, an essential part of her; she feels a constant phantom twinge. She's not unhappy, but she aches with an emptiness she doesn't know how to fill. And the thought of putting down roots here and not in L.A., raising her child here, being *stuck*, is a constant itch in the back of her mind, an agitated churn in her stomach, a restlessness under her skin.

"When does Clementine have an event out there next?" Gwen wonders as they walk down the concrete stairs of the building. Spencer was keeping up with the scheduling, too.

"I'm not sure. I'd have to double-check."

"Maybe..." Gwen pushes open the door to outside, where it's still early afternoon, still mild and breezy. "Maybe I can take the lead on it, go with her."

Nico flashes her a quick smile. "Yeah. Maybe Grady can book something, too. We'll all go out and visit."

"Sure, yeah." Only, to Gwen, going back to L.A. doesn't seem like a visit. It seems like going home.

4

"So, this is the bank we already looked at in California." Flora tilts the desktop screen to look at yet another sperm bank; every free moment this week has been spent on baby planning. They are shoulder to shoulder at the desk in the office, soon-to-be office and playroom, if everything goes according to plan. Because a baby is the plan, the logical next step in their lives. And something Flora wants with her whole huge, kind, nurturing heart.

A few days ago they'd looked at a local sperm bank, even stopped by for a quick tour, but it seemed to focus on infertility issues in straight couples. It was fine, but didn't seem quite right. The California bank was recommended by friends who had used it successfully to have adorably rambunctious twin boys.

"Is it weird that I like knowing the donor is from California?" Gwen says, scanning the list of sperm donors: no names, just numbers.

"No, I don't think so. If helps you feel more connected, that's not weird." Flora scrolls past the first few rows of listings. "Elaine and Hattie chose a donor who listed an interest in sports. Not athletic ability. Interest. That's weird."

Donor number 5673: Green eyes. Brown hair. English, Chinese, African, Irish, and German descent. Add Flora's half Colombian, one-fourth Italian, and one-fourth Portuguese ovum and this kid could have the whole world covered.

Flora scrolls on.

"Is an interest in *Monday Night Football* genetic?" Gwen had always found Elaine and Hattie a little off-putting. Sometimes they put the whole family in matching T-shirts—and not even for outings, just for the hell of it. Twins or no twins, that's not right.

"I hope not." Flora pauses. "Here we go: blond hair; blue eyes; Polish, Russian, and Danish descent."

Oh. Like her. Only—Gwen brushes fingers through her white-blonde hair. "You know this is from a bottle, right?"

"Yes," Flora says, turning to Gwen with a patient smile. "But you are still blonde. Ish. Just darker now. It was closer to that color once upon a time." Her smile slips then, unsure; the corners of her mouth turn down. "Don't you want the baby to look like you, too?"

It's not really something she's thought about, but her instincts say no. It doesn't matter. The conversation about who would be pregnant was easy: Gwen had no desire to host a baby inside her body for any amount of time, and Flora very much did. A biological tie never felt essential. The people Gwen shares blood with barely tolerate her, and the people who mean the most to her, whom she loves completely, are no blood relation at all.

If the baby doesn't look like her, she doesn't think it will bother her. At least, not enough to prioritize it over a donor's health history or the number of kids he already has running around in the world. Or whether he has an interest in men in spandex playing professional grab-ass.

She feels outside of the whole thing anyway. She's just here for Flora, who has to do the hard part and grow the kid. Gwen glances at the time in the corner of the computer screen. Flora is home from work on the early up, early off schedule of an elementary school teacher, but Gwen still has to do a fitting with Grady, then finalize jewelry for Clementine. So, more than anything, she doesn't want to fight about sperm when it really doesn't matter that much to her.

"Well," Gwen finally says. "Do *you* want the baby to look like me?"

Flora's expression shifts to impassive; her mouth is a straight line, her eyes trained on the computer screen. She pulls her braid over a shoulder and twirls the end around one finger. She's upset. Gwen has to act fast. "You know what. Yeah. Let's go with the blond guy. I mean, his baby picture is adorable. He's healthy. His family is healthy. I want him." She pauses, makes a sour face. "I want his spunk?"

"Gwen, gross." Flora hovers the cursor over the *request donor* button, hesitates, and then takes a breath and clicks. "It's not quite official. I still have to get a physical examination."

The clock ticks to three forty-five. "I'm sure it'll be fine," Gwen says in a rush, hopping up and giving Flora a peck. "Text me the appointment time, and I'll make sure I don't have anything else scheduled, okay?"

"Okay," Flora says, and Gwen is gone, stopping by the hall bathroom to check her makeup: thick black liner, smoky shadow, dark burgundy lips. Check. Purple lace-up dress with thick black belt and knee-high black leather boots. Check.

Happy wife. Check.

She barely gets one foot inside the office when Nico asks, "Did you make the final call on the gala dress for next month?"

"Hello to you, too." Gwen makes a show of setting down her bag and settling into her chair as if she can't quite get comfortable. Nico gives her a *ha ha, very funny* look but does amend his greeting.

"Hi, how are you? How are things? Did you pick a gala dress or not?"

Gwen pulls up a picture of the dress, sent by the designer: an amazing, strapless bias-cut gown with gemstones that morph from blue to purple to pink depending on the lights and the curve of Clementine's figure. It's a showstopper. "Check it."

Nico squints from his desk when she turns the screen, then glides over in his office chair. "Hmm," he says with a dismissive flick of his head. "Let's go with the Armani we talked about." He scoots away again.

"You told me to trust my instincts," Gwen protests. This dress screams at her instincts.

"I never said they'd always be right." Nico gives her one of his patented, critically arched eyebrow looks. "It's way too daring for this event. There is a time and a place for a dress like that, and a thousand-dollar-a-plate art gala is not it. Think dark, understated, classic."

Nico is a great friend and even better business partner. They're doing incredibly well, thanks to their dedication, and she knows he appreciates her. But he can't tell her to take the reins more often and then hold them in a death grip high above her head.

Gwen swallows her irritation; Nico's probably right about the dress not quite fitting the occasion, but she chose it for exactly that reason. What is style if not daring? What is the point of making a statement if that statement is: *I look just like everyone else here?*

She's taking out her frustration on a pile of invoiced shipping receipts—every few whacks of the staple she imagines flattening the arch of Nico's perfectly groomed judgmental eyebrows—when the studio door opens and Grady comes in like the sudden slant of a golden sunbeam.

"Hey, y'all!"

Nico's whole demeanor changes when he's around Grady. Gwen has often thought of Nico's personality as a warm, tender heart surrounded on all sides by jagged barbed wire: incredibly kind, yet sharply guarded. She had watched him date with all the enthusiasm of a day spent waiting in line at the DMV, and while she had Flora all along for the ups and downs, Nico's life was this job. His passion was devoted entirely to making other people shine, never himself, until falling in love became as improbable as a lightning strike; it just wasn't happening, so why worry about it?

And then came Grady, who was so obviously never just a client—even when Nico denied it to himself. Gwen saw it, she knew.

Grady cups Nico's face and kisses him so tenderly that Gwen has to look away. She staples the rest of the piles with gentle pushes instead of angry slams. With Grady, all of Nico's sharp edges disappear, and Gwen knows true love when she sees it.

"Are you going to the art gala, too?" Gwen asks, after Nico and Grady have parted but not before they've stopped grinning dopily at each other. Honestly, they *live* together now; all this would be annoying if she weren't so happy for them.

"Um," Grady says.

"Yes," Nico answers for him. "In fact, let's go look at some jackets. It's standard black tie, so nothing too exciting, unfortunately."

Gwen follows them to the loft, debating with herself about suggesting they do something different: perhaps a deep-purple velvet coat, or a textured pattern that would catch the flash of a camera just right, like the rejected dress she'd picked for Clementine. She says nothing; the words are trapped on her tongue by the fear of getting it wrong again.

"Let's start with a peak lapel," Nico says, after Grady has changed into black trousers. They'll need to be hemmed, Gwen notes, crouching to measure. She writes: *pants, three-quarter-inch hem.* From the floor she takes more notes, writing down the date and a description as decisions are made: *Ferragamo belt, black, double buckle. Shoes: Ralph Lauren, monk strap, black.* She misses having Spencer here to do this crap. Full partner, and she's sitting on the floor waiting for Nico to call out his decisions as if he's ordering lunch at a drive-through.

"Or should we do the shawl lapel?" Nico smooths the sleek material with both palms. "Yes," he says, answering his own question immediately. He drags his hands up and down the lapels fit snugly to Grady's chest. In a huskier tone he adds, "Yes, that's nice."

It's Gwen's turn to narrow her eyes. "Right."

"Turn," Nico says in that same husky voice. Grady looks at Nico with heavy-lidded eyes and a lusty smirk before turning slowly, his fingers twitching at his sides. Gwen shakes her head and writes: *hem sleeves.* The air is so thick with pheromones that people passing by outside are no doubt flummoxed by their own sudden horniness.

Nico checks the fit of the coat, making sure it lies flat without any creases from pulling too tight or bubbling from the cut being too loose, by slowly and very thoroughly dragging his hands across Grady's back and shoulders, then over the seat of his pants.

Grady's restless fingers clench. She can hear Nico breathing heavily, and that is quite enough.

"Boys," she says, and they both look at her with wide-eyed expressions, as if they'd completely forgotten about her existence. She hops up, caps her pen, and closes her notepad. "I know I tease you a lot about your sex life, but I do not actually want to be part of your weird, tuxedo-fetish foreplay."

Grady and Nico start to speak at the same time, then stop at the same time, and then start talking over each other again. Gwen waves off their flustered babbling. "Relax. I'll go get lunch." She remembers those days with Flora, being so gone with heady new love they couldn't even brush by each other without making out a little.

But Grady shakes his head as he carefully removes his tuxedo jacket. "No, I'll go. I have a meeting with my manager I'm late for anyhow. I'll be back to try on stuff for the other event... the, uh..."

"Charity fundraiser," Nico supplies.

Grady changes back into his snug black T-shirt and jeans and gives Nico a parting kiss that isn't tender like the first one, but an obvious promise for later. He winks at Gwen as he leaves. No shame, that one, and she loves him for it.

Nico, however, looks mortified. "Sorry about that," he says, hanging up clothing.

"No worries." Gwen rolls up the belt to pack it away. "I'm just glad you didn't get as far as measuring his inseam."

"Yes, all right. Can we drop it?" He strides down the stairs with his chin lifted, and Gwen scurries to follow.

"Hey, if you're gonna involve me, I have questions." She hops up on his desk and kicks her heels against a metal drawer. "Do you do that at home? Slowly dress him instead of undressing him?" Nico pretends to be reading something on his computer screen.

"Do you like to stay clothed the entire time and just wiggle around on top of each other like oversexed walruses?"

"Okay." He pushes her off the desk. "That's enough now."

She slides off, giving him space before she pokes too much and he gets snappy; but he is actually chuckling. "Aw, look at you," Gwen says. "So happy."

He smiles widely, without turning away or hiding it. "I am. I really am. I do miss California, but I'm happier than I thought I would be here."

Gwen nods and sits at her desk. One of these days, she hopes, Nashville will finally feel like home for her, too. Until then, she pushes the feelings of disconnection and restlessness away.

"Shit," Nico says, jumping out of his chair. "I forgot the cuff links at my apartment. Can you take over Grady's fitting when he comes back?"

"I was going to anyway," she replies to his already retreating back, raising the volume of her voice when he opens the door. "Since you were ten seconds away from jumping him right in front of me!" The door clicks closed, which she takes as confirmation that he heard her, and she heads back to the loft.

5

When Grady returns, she's in the loft setting his options out on their own rack for easy viewing.

"Hi Grady, come on up."

He grins and takes the stairs two at a time. She does enjoy his happy, hyper energy, the way he seems to bring sunshine with him when he enters a room. She likes that he's growing his hair again, too. Ringlets and spirals in golden chaos, eyes of sparkling—

"Hey, you have blond hair and blue eyes."

Grady gives a confused smile. "Yes..."

"Hmm," she says, then shrugs. "Anyway, I have three suits for you; peruse at your leisure." She plops down on one of the white leather ottomans, then rests her chin on one fist. He *is* very handsome. Healthy. There is the family history of addiction, but... hmm. "Do you want kids, Grady?"

Grady pauses with a gray suit against his chest. "Um. I don't know." He puts it back on the rack, then thinks for a moment. "I spent a lot of time as a kid gettin' left behind. You know what my life is like, here and there, doin' this, that and the other thing all the time. That's no life for a kid."

"Yeah, I get that."

"I don't think Nico wants kids," Grady adds, picking up the black suit with cool pin-striping. She picked that one. "He says they're sticky."

Gwen chuckles. "That sounds like him." It makes her happy anyway, knowing that when she asks Grady about his future, about his family, he thinks of Nico.

"Where is he, by the way?" Grady pulls aside the last suit, a more daring skinny-fit mauve. Gwen was planning to talk Nico into wearing that one; it suits his frame better. Grady is too beefy, but Nico's enjoyment of Grady in tight, tight pants clouds his judgment sometimes. That's why Gwen is here. "I think the black," Grady adds.

"Agreed." She pulls it from the rack and puts it on a hook on the wall. "And Nico said he forgot some cuff links, so he ran back to the apartment to grab them. He should be back any minute."

Grady twists around, eyebrows low and eyes narrowed. "What apartment?"

The air in the loft has gone heavy and tense, she's not sure why, and she doesn't know what to say. Was Nico supposed to be somewhere else? Does Grady think he's *with* someone else? Because Nico would never—

"His apartment," Gwen reassures him. "Just by himself. Okay, let's pick shoes."

But Grady stands rooted next to the garment rack of suits, his hands balled tight at his sides, his jaw clenched. The door opens, and Nico rushes in.

"Oh, good, you're still here. Did you pick the mauve suit? Because I..." He trails off when he reaches the top of the stairs and sees Grady's face. "What's wrong?"

"You didn't sell your apartment," Grady says, without inflection.

"I—" Nico looks to Gwen, who quickly spins around to *very carefully* inspect the shoes for any scuffs or improper lacings.

"Why did you tell me you sold it when you moved in with me? What are you doing there that I can't know about, Nico?"

"It's not—Grady, I'm not—" Nico releases a frustrated breath, then says lamely, "I was going to tell you I—"

Behind her, Gwen hears the rapid footsteps of someone thundering down the stairs. A door slams, and she flinches. Then silence. She turns to find Nico slumped on the ottoman with his head dropped into both hands. "I didn't realize, Nico. I'm sorry." She feels terrible. If she'd had any idea that Grady didn't know, of course she would have kept her mouth shut. Why does she never keep her *mouth shut?*

"No, it's not your fault. It's mine." He looks up, one hand still gripped in his own hair. "It wasn't selling, the apartment. So the realtor said I should take it off the market and do a few upgrades, then put it back up and..." He shrugs helplessly. "I just didn't."

Gwen says nothing, but sits on the couch near him.

"Is it so crazy to want to keep it? It's a great location."

Gwen lifts her eyebrows.

"I know, I should have told him. I know, okay." He groans and drops his head again.

"Nico, listen." Gwen takes pulls his hands away, holds his wrists. "You wouldn't be you if you didn't consider all angles before making a huge, life-changing decision. Moving in with someone is a big deal."

"Yes," Nico says with obvious relief. "It is."

"But, you can't run a three-legged race alone." She releases his wrists and smacks at his knees. "Not enough legs."

"We're a team. I know." He sighs, loud and dramatic. "I'll go find him."

Nico helped her when she and Flora were going through a tough time, and she wants to help him—not to be some relationship guru, but because she wants to see her friends happy. "Why don't you let me go," she offers. "I'll smooth things over a bit. I have to finish his fitting anyway."

On the drive out to Grady's house—or, Grady and Nico's house—or, like, *sort of* Grady and Nico's house—Gwen is on Nico's side of the issue. The place is way out in the boonies, just farms and forest, the occasional gas station and lonely curving street with little squat houses. She understands why Grady would want to be secluded, somewhere with a little solitude and peace and quiet, but in a setting like this, she always half expects to be hauled off by some banjo-playing redneck who emerges mysteriously from the woods and disappears just as quickly. Not that she has a problem with banjo-playing rednecks.

She drives all way over the river and through the woods, down the winding dirt path driveway to Grady's huge country cottage set on acres of trees, and he's not even there. The house is dark and locked, and when she peeks in the windows of the garage, his various vehicles are parked, silent, and covered. The space where his pickup truck usually is and the spot next to it for Nico's zippy little red Miata are both empty.

Gwen scoots up onto the hood of her orange Mini Cooper, thinks, and then reluctantly calls the one person who will no doubt know where Grady goes when he doesn't want to be found.

"Listen. I'm pissed at you, so let's just put that out there. A heads up, maybe? I thought we were semi-acquaintances who mostly tolerated each other, Spencer. You don't just throw that away. I'm hurt." She kicks the front bumper and switches the phone to her other ear. "But this isn't about that. I was hoping you could help me find Grady. He's... upset about something. I can't find him. Just call me back, I guess?" As she gets into her car, she asks herself: *Did Grady go to Nico's apartment?* Probably not.

"Oh, and by the way," she adds before cranking up the engine and ending the call, "I was just about to teach you how the Industrial Revolution was a total game-changer for fashion, *and* about the complex feminist history of corsets, so I hope you feel bad about missing out. Because you are."

She's on the highway, just a few exits from the center of downtown, when she gets a text, interrupting The Lunachicks blasting from her sound system.

Spencer: Try Ray's in Edgefield

Ray's in Edgefield is a rough-looking, gray cinderblock dive bar in an even rougher-looking part of town. Half the windows are covered with plywood, and Gwen makes her way through a pothole-riddled dirt parking lot and along a cracked, weed-lined sidewalk. A neon sign reads OPEN, and under that, handwriting on a scrap of cardboard adds CASH ONLY. Inside, it's dark. The floors are brown-stained cement. There is no stage, no music, just one TV loudly playing *Sportscenter*. It reeks of cigarettes and sour beer and is the sort of place Nico would call "charming" with pursed lips.

Yet, with his back turned to the door, hunched at the bar with a sweating clear glass set in front of him, Grady doesn't look out of place. It's as if he spent a lot of time in places just like this once, before he was famous, before he was rich, before he met Nico. The bartender is like the leader of a biker gang: big, bald, bearded, and tattooed.

"What do you think would happen if I ordered a Cosmopolitan?"

Grady turns to face her as she sits on a stool, her legs dangling high off the floor. His face is still drawn and sad, but less angry now. Resigned.

"Can't be worse than trying to drown your sorrows in a club soda." He picks up the glass and shakes it, ice cubes tinkling and condensation dripping on the scuffed surface of the bar.

He's not drinking alcohol. Gwen's shoulders relax a little. The bartender comes by, and she orders a club soda with lime in solidarity and because she never has a great grasp on how to deal with the minefield of recovery and sobriety and addiction. Gwen sips her drink and looks around.

The bar is fairly empty; it's still early afternoon on a weekday. A guy drinking at a table is around their age, late twenties or early thirties or so; a group of college-age women play pool at the one warped pool table; and a man in his seventies, possibly younger plus decades of hard living, keeps unsuccessfully hitting on the girls.

Gwen sends a look of disgust his way—he could be their *grandfather*, for fuck's sake—before turning back to Grady.

"For what it's worth, I do think he intended to tell you."

Grady spins his glass in damp circles. "You know what they say about good intentions."

"Wait, I know this one. It's something related to penis size, right?" She watches Grady bite down on a smile and knocks his knee with her own. "I may be mixing up my idioms."

The joke seems to work the way she'd hoped; Grady's protective posture opens a little, the crease disappears from between his eyebrows, and he sits up higher. "You know, I never really understood that one. I mean, if the road to hell is paved with good intentions, then where do bad intentions lead you?"

Gwen takes a sip of her club soda and jerks her head in the direction of the creepy old guy openly leering at girls who are barely of legal age.

Grady glances over, scowls, and says, "True." He takes one last swallow of his drink, then pushes it away. "This place is too depressing sober; let's go."

As they leave, Gwen slows, worried about the young women. She's sure they're smart and capable and perfectly fine, but this weird nurturing instinct takes over and she can't help it. She just wants them out of there and safe. So she detours to the pool table, leans close to the girl with shoulder-length brown hair, and takes a chance. "Hey, do you want to meet Grady Dawson?"

The girl just looks at her blankly, and okay, not *everyone* knows Grady, not even in Nashville, and that's likely the anonymity Grady was hoping for here. But then the tall one with curly black hair smacks the short one with long brown hair and hisses, "I told you that was him!"

By the time Grady is finished chatting and charming and taking pictures in the parking lot, the creep is gone, and all three girls head home safe and swooning. Gwen is pleased enough with herself to indulge in saccharine pop radio in her car; then Grady leans into her open window and asks, "Have you ever ridden a dirt bike?"

She has never ridden a dirt bike and after a dozen attempts and a dozen graceless tumbles into the dirt, she apparently never will. Grady is a good sport about it, helping her up and only teasing her a little every time she falls, but his attention shifts constantly to the riders zooming past, and his body language is tight and impatient. Gwen gives up and sits on the bleachers to watch so Grady can blow off some steam. It's too bad; the biking gear and constant roar of engines appeal to her inner Evel Knievel. She could also create some interesting looks with the brightly colored leather and heavy black padding.

Among the other riders, Grady is indistinguishable, taking the steep cliffs and sharp turns at increasingly breakneck speeds. When he nearly wipes out after flying off the highest hill, Gwen decides to call for backup. She's out of her depth with Grady here; they're friendly, they have a solid working relationship, but Grady came into her life via Nico, and that's how she thinks of him, mostly: one half of Grady and Nico.

Gwen takes a short video and sends it to Clementine with a message, *Should I be concerned about this?* She doesn't hear back until Grady has blasted around the course three more times, so recklessly that it may be time to give in and call Nico. It's not worth giving Grady space from Nico if he's going to break his neck in the process. Clementine gets there first.

Clementine: Maybe. Where did you find him? I got the 411 during fitting

Gwen texts back, *a bar*, and the reply is immediate.

Clementine: I'll be there just as soon as I'm done with this meeting.

6

"**Hey, G. Would** you mind stopping by the store for a loaf of bread. Something crusty, you know the kind."

Gwen hesitates. "Well, I *can*."

Flora's frustrated puff of air crackles through the phone. "Are you not coming home for dinner? Because I made a huge pot of stew and I hate when you don't tell me in advance—"

"No," Gwen interrupts, before she can get too upset. "I just..." She turns away from the back corner and toward the folding chair where Grady is being treated for some scrapes after an epic wipeout. Clementine is hovering over him, fussing about the gash next to his eye.

"Your *face*, Grady. Of all places."

Just outside the closet-sized first aid-slash-concession stand-slash-gear shop stands Clementine's enormous bodyguard, Kevin. Inside it smells like motor oil, popcorn, and antiseptic. And yet this is not the weirdest client situation in which Gwen has found herself. Close, but not quite.

Grady is more than a client, though, or he should be, and not just to Nico.

Gwen turns back to the corner. "How do you feel about having Grady over for dinner?" She just can't shake the feeling that Grady shouldn't be alone, even though he claims to be fine and is clearly annoyed at Clementine's worried fluttering about. She tried to get him to call Nico, but no dice, so she feels a little guilty about contacting him, but if she were Nico—

Gwen: Found him. Thought you would want to know. He's okay.

Nico: Thanks, Gwen. Where are you now?

She glances back when the metal folding chair squeaks and scrapes across the floor as Grady stands and brushes a cascade of dirt from his racing jersey and pants.

Gwen: Dirt bike track.

Nico: Thought he might be there. Or out in the woods.

Gwen: Come to my place. 45 mins?

Grady's truck, Clementine's Town Car and the black security SUV follow Gwen to the store and park in a circle around her tiny car as if they're all participating in a spooky celebrity séance ritual. Only Gwen goes inside, fidgeting in front of the bakery counter with her phone ringing and ringing in her ear with unanswered calls. She doesn't know what kind of crusty bread Flora wants. And will she care if Clementine tags along? And Nico shows up later? And does Clementine's bodyguard even sit down to eat? Is he a cyborg, as Gwen suspects?

Flora doesn't pick up any of Gwen's calls. She must have left her phone somewhere after their first conversation, so surprise asiago cheese bread and extra guests it is.

"Do you want to fill me in here?" Flora asks when they all arrive, taking the bread and glancing toward the unexpected guests in the dining room.

Gwen stretches up on her tiptoes to get out five bowls and five plates, and says in a quiet rush before Grady or Clementine come into the kitchen, "Nico didn't sell the apartment, but told Grady that he did, and Grady was at a bar, but not drinking, and then at a dirt bike track which is potentially worrisome? And then he crashed and looked like an injured sad puppy, like look at him, and Clementine—"

She snaps her mouth closed when Clementine glides into the kitchen and gushes, "This place is just darling!"

Flora ladles out a serving of stew, rich and steaming and mouthwatering. "Thank you." She smiles at Clementine, then gives Gwen a wide-eyed, *this is seriously strange* look.

"And look at you two, in your precious little kitchen." She claps her hands. "Oh, I just *adore* it."

Gwen wonders when superstar Clementine Campbell was last in a regular home with a regular kitchen. Judging by the way she's exploring the photographs of Flora's nieces Nyla and Evie on the fridge, the whiteboard with reminders about vet appointments, bills due and the number for a plumber as if she were an anthropologist discovering an unknown primitive society, probably a long time.

"Uh. Let's eat," Flora says, after filling the bowls and slicing the bread. "Should we wait for—" She glances down the hallway, where Grady is sitting slumped at the table, and mouths, "*Nico?*"

"He's tied up with a designer right now; it's fine." Gwen turns her face up for a kiss. "This smells amazing, Flor. Thank you." She's laying it on thick to make up for the celebrity guests, and they both know it, but Flora indulges her with a smile and a kiss, and then instructs her to get everyone something to drink.

The minutes tick by slowly, with a few brief conversations, but mostly in silence. Flora is characteristically quiet, Grady is uncharacteristically quiet, Clementine is still enchanted by the house, and Gwen can only natter on about nothing to herself for so long.

"So, how did y'all meet?"

Grady is still quiet, polite and sweet, but mostly tearing off chunks of bread and swirling them around the thick gravy in his bowl. Clementine switches her wide-eyed fascination from their home to them, wanting to know what Flora does, then talking excitedly about her favorite teachers, the ones she had before her first hit single at fifteen. After that she had favorite private tutors.

"In college." Flora says.

"At a party in college, the week before I flunked out," Gwen adds. "One of those dorm room gatherings where you just sit around getting high as a kite." She winces. "Sorry, Grady."

Grady swirls his bread and sits with his cheek smushed on his fist. "I've been high as a kite plenty of times. Don't bother me."

"Anyway. At a party..." Clementine says.

Gwen takes the prompt. She squashes a carrot into mush with her fork. "I couldn't stop staring at her. I mean, can you blame me?"

Flora scoffs at that, shakes her head, and stares at her bowl. Grady pipes up with, "She's right. You're an incredibly beautiful woman, Flora," in that gravelly purr of his. Flora's cheeks glow a deep red.

"But," Gwen continues, giving Flora time to recover, "she had a girlfriend. So I didn't talk to her at all. Stared at her like a creep instead. We had some friends in common, though, so I'd keep seeing her at gatherings, at bars, at parties. Always with the girlfriend. What was her name, Flor?"

"Imani."

"Imani, that's right. She was this brilliant, dreadlocked goddess, double majoring in—"

"Philosophy and poetry."

"And here I was. A college dropout who looked like I'd just busted out of eighth grade detention—"

"She had blue hair and a tongue ring," Flora says with a soft smile meant only for Gwen. "I noticed her. So when Imani and I broke up and I ran into Gwen, I was intrigued."

"Yeah, by the tongue stud." Gwen gives her a smirk. She had some good times with that tongue piercing. "I chipped a tooth with it right after we started dating, so it had to go."

"And I stayed."

"And then they lived happily ever after." Gwen tucks a lock of hair, loose from her braid, behind Flora's ear.

"Aww." Clementine's cooing breaks Gwen from a spell; she'd almost forgotten other people were in the room with them. She'll never forget that night, when shy, quiet Flora approached *her*, when she first really looked at Gwen with those huge dark eyes. Flora's hair was a curtain of black around her face; a summery blue dress hugged every gorgeous, thick curve of her body. And when she haltingly and breathlessly asked if Gwen wanted to *hang out alone*, Gwen went dizzy with rushing blood.

"She was way out of my league," Gwen says. They're fast approaching a decade together, and Flora still makes Gwen tilt-a-whirl woozy. "She still is."

Flora frowns and shakes her head, and Clementine says, "Hey, don't sell yourself short. You're hot. Like a hot little pixie."

Before Gwen can even begin to process *that*, there's a knock on the door, and Nico's voice calls, "Can I come in?"

At her other side, Grady goes stiff. Clementine hops up to kiss both of Nico's cheeks, and Flora stands, picks up the only bowl still full of food and makes for the kitchen. "I'll heat this up for you."

"Grady, I—" Nico stops, halfway into the chair on Grady's right side, then grabs Grady's chin and frowns. "Your *face*."

"That's what I said," Clementine tells him.

"He wiped out." Gwen makes a dramatic wipeout motion with both hands.

Grady jerks his chin away. "It wasn't that bad."

It looked that bad; he hit the ground after flying off a hill so hard his helmet popped off and he went skidding like a rag doll across the dirt. Her instinct bubbling up, sudden and urgent, Gwen didn't remember standing but was at his side in a flash. Not even Clementine got there as fast as she had.

The dining room is silent and tense. Flora is taking her sweet time heating up the pot roast, and the rest of them are finished with their food, floundering for something, anything, to say. Gwen shifts uncomfortably in her chair; Clementine glances, unfocused, around the room; Grady scowls at the floor; and Nico frowns at Grady's scowling.

The microwave beeps, and Clementine's phone chirps with a reminder. "Shoot, I'm sorry, y'all. I have a phone interview soon. I forgot."

"No problem." Gwen hops up, relieved at the excuse to scurry from the room and walk Clementine to the door. Behind them, Nico and Grady talk in terse whispers.

"Keep an eye on him for me, okay? And tell Flora I apologize for eating and running and thank you both for the dinner. My place next time?"

"Sure." She'll find some way to cope with eating a professionally catered dinner at Clementine's mansion. *Somehow.*

Clementine, her body slim and rounded with pert, toned curves, hugs her. She always smells so good, too; like honeysuckle. Looks like a lingerie model, sings like an angel, smells like a flower, nibbles pot roast like a hummingbird.

They say goodnight, and then Kevin the bodyguard appears to walk Clementine to her waiting Town Car. The door clicks closed, and the conversation in dining room is steadily increasing in volume.

"... has nothing to do with wanting to be with other people, Grady," Nico is saying. "As if *you're* the one who should be worried about cheating."

"The hell is that supposed to mean?" Grady says, his voice verging on a shout.

She doesn't want to hear this, she doesn't, she—there's no escape; her back is pressed to the closed front door as if she's hoping to fuse with it. The open floor plan they loved so much when they bought the place means there is no way to get anywhere unnoticed. Maybe she could creep along the far wall and dash up the stairs. They're so creaky, though. *Why does this house have to be so old and open and creaky?*

"I didn't mean it that way," Nico says, backpedaling. "You know I—the bi thing doesn't bother me, you know that."

Grady gives a humorless laugh. "The bi thing."

Nico groans in frustration. "I mean that I, I am *here*, for you. I left my family and I left my career in L.A. I moved to *your house* in the middle of fucking nowhere, Grady, in a town where I'm afraid to stand too close to you in the grocery store because this godforsaken state has to be dragged kicking and screaming into the twenty-first fucking century, *for you.* I came here for *you.* I am *sorry* that I didn't tell you about the apartment. I just didn't think it was that big of a deal."

There's a long beat of silence, and maybe it's okay, maybe they're hugging or kissing or gazing lovingly into each other's eyes, or making out on the table; at this point she'll be happy with any of those. She breathes out and pushes off the door. Then Grady speaks again.

"Well, if you're so miserable, maybe you should leave."

"Leave what, Grady?" Nico's voice sounds thin, helpless. "This house? Your house? The state? You? All of it?"

"Yes. No. I dunno." Grady mumbles, just as lost as Nico.

"Okay. I will be at the apartment then. For when you do know."

At the sound of rapid footsteps, Gwen jumps, picks up an umbrella from the stand by the door and tries to be really enthralled by the Velcro strap keeping the folds tightly closed.

"Thanks for having me over, Gwen," Nico says, forcing niceties with his jaw tight. "See you tomorrow."

"Goodnight!" she calls, with way too much enthusiasm. Nico gets in his little sports car, guns the engine, and peels away so fast his tires screech.

Still, even with the palpable hurt on Grady's face that makes Gwen's stomach sink, even with the way he lets himself be gathered into Flora's arms when she rushes back into the dining room—still,

Gwen gets where Nico is coming from. To give someone everything and still believe it's not enough, that nothing will ever be enough because *you* are not enough—Gwen knows what that's like.

7

Eight years ago...

Their first night together, Gwen took her to a clump of tan stucco apartment buildings: one of those complexes with a name that sounded exotic but didn't really mean anything at all.

"The Apartments at Casa del Capri," Flora read, following Gwen through the entrance, up the sidewalk past metal mailboxes, a green-tinged pool, and a sparsely landscaped courtyard. At every step her heart pounded; rasping quick breaths made her throat dry. And not for the first time, she wondered what the hell she was doing here, with *her*. Adrenaline, uncharacteristic recklessness, and desire spurred her on; misgivings were tucked away.

"Well, if they called it something true, like The Apartments del Roaches and Black Mold, I bet they'd have to lower the rent." Gwen cut across a scrabbly patch of grass to apartment 127-C. "Watch out for dog shit."

Right. This little blue-haired punk girl had caught Flora's attention and refused to let go. At that party Flora had sat, bored with her girlfriend, who was having a very intelligent discussion about Duchamp and his theory of art: Is art subjective or just a result of context? What is art? Can art be defined? It was the sort intellectual stimulation Flora had hoped to find at college, only—

God, it was so *tedious*. Everyone trying to out-clever the others. And Imani—Imani was beautiful and tender both in bed and of heart. Everyone thought Imani was great. Flora thought Imani was great. Imani was just *great*. There were no sparks with Imani, but perhaps sparkless love was what mature, sensible adults had. *Everything is great, great, great,* she told herself. Until Gwen.

"Here we go." Gwen opened the door, flicked a light on, and pulled her bottom lip into her mouth. Sparks, and sparks.

Flora stepped past the threshold into a dim studio apartment that smelled of damp, smoke and lingering incense. She imagined Gwen sitting cross-legged on the thin mattress that had been placed carelessly in the center of the space, reading the books stacked along the wood-paneled walls, and blasting her bulky over-sized stereo that had speakers larger than the mini-fridge rattling away beneath a hotplate in the corner. The carpet was dingy brown; the lone kitchen countertop was covered in unpleasant orange laminate. Still, it thrilled Flora to think of Gwen in this space, and even more to be there with her.

Gwen fidgeted. She did that a lot: never still, always moving, always thinking. *Is Gwen art?* Flora had watched her at that party when Gwen had turned away, talking excitedly with her hands, laughing, shifting up to her toes. The rest of the room, the music and smoke, Imani and her counterparts, had all faded to a drone in the background.

She had rings and studs punched through her nose and her eyebrow, and curving all the way up the shell of one ear; they glinted with silver and stones of green and black and purple and pink. Her hair was like a swath of blue sky, and she had round, curious eyes to match. Was art in the context of Gwen the delicate turn of her prominent clavicles, the slope of her pale throat, the pink bow of her curving lips, the slight upturn of her nose? Was it her small breasts, her flat stomach, the gentle hill of her hips, the shift of her thighs, the rise of her ass?

Or maybe it was her laugh that was art: high and loudly uninhibited, the wild cackle of someone who gave zero thought to what people may have thought of a laugh like that. It was what Flora noticed first about her, that laugh. That zeal. That metal bulb in the center of her tongue.

Gwen rocked up and down on her toes as Flora looked around the apartment. She crossed one arm across her stomach, dropped it, tucked it behind her back, and then bit her lip again. With every passing second she was less and less the dangerous, sexy rebel Flora had first pegged her for with a glance and a knee-jerk judgment based on blue hair, black clothes, and so many piercings. She liked both options: sexy rebel *and* cute and nervous. She liked the idea of all of the unexplored facets of Gwen. Every time they crossed paths, Flora could only think of exploring all of them.

"Did you move in recently?" Flora asked, moving to a corkboard pinned with magazine scraps, the only decoration in the place.

Flora could feel Gwen watching, her heavy gaze lingering on Flora's shoulders, bare beneath the straps of her sundress. On the sweep of her body as she moved around the room. On her fingers as they traced a picture pinned to the board.

"Yes," Gwen said. She was quiet, and though Flora knew her mostly as a peripheral friend of friends, she at least knew that Gwen was not usually quiet. Flora looked over, and Gwen fidgeted and frowned. "I, um… left school… pretty recently, so."

Waiting for judgment, Flora could see. She hummed and turned back to the board. "Is this what you want to do instead?"

On the board were pictures of clothes torn from magazine spreads, arranged into outfits: Headless torsos draped in gorgeous designer gowns, shirts and pants pieced together in interesting combinations, shoes and jewelry arranged with deliberate thought and care.

Gwen shook her head and wrinkled her snub nose. She was so cute, with her blue hair, long on one side and shaved up the other. All black clothes and black combat boots every time Flora saw her. Flora wanted to feel every perky inch pressed against her. It was new and exciting and intriguing.

Sparks.

"It's just for fun," Gwen said of the inspiration board. "I like putting outfits together." She shrugged one shoulder, sharp and thin as a sparrow's wing. "Sometimes I watch people and think about what outfits I'd put them in."

"Oh?" Flora turned from the corkboard and made her way to where Gwen stood. "And what would you put me in?"

Impish was the only way to describe that answering grin: slow and teasing, doe eyes nearly twinkling with mirth. She laughed, and Flora did, too. "I see."

Gwen lifted up on her toes, bit her bottom lip, and stared at Flora's mouth before pressing a hard, eager, off-center kiss there. Flora stumbled back. Her thighs hit the top of the huge stereo speakers; they wobbled and thumped against the wall, and Flora grabbed Gwen's hips to steady herself. Heart pounding, head spinning, knocked off balance, Flora turned her head, parted her lips, and took control of the kiss.

Sparks, yes. From her mouth to her skin to the hot pit of her stomach to the twitch between her legs. But it also felt... right. In a way that Imani never did. She should be right here, in this crummy studio apartment with no furniture, with roaches hiding behind the crumbling plaster. She should be kissing Gwen now, later, forever.

Gwen's boldness made Flora feel bold; her eagerness made desire gather tightly in Flora's belly as she pushed her hands up beneath Gwen's T-shirt. She found the warm, taut skin of her heaving stomach, thumbed the ridges of her hipbones, the inward slope of her pelvis, skimmed a lingering brush just above the button on her jeans. Gwen's breath caught, then rushed out across Flora's lips.

Flora swayed back against the speakers again when Gwen lunged in for another fervent kiss, sliding her tongue across Flora's. The speaker thumped, Gwen sighed, and Flora moved her hands to Gwen's ribs, widening her legs to get a sturdier stance as her back twisted at an odd angle. Gwen wriggled immediately into the space between Flora's thighs so the line of her body pressed into Flora. Flora's hands slid higher; the firm mounds of Gwen's breasts brushed Flora's knuckles, and she explored the shape of them with her fingers: high and round and small. And when Flora teased lightly over the pebbled nubs of her nipples, Gwen gave a high, sweet moan and rocked her hips hard, nearly sending Flora toppling backward.

"We should—" Flora pulled away from another heated kiss to push off from the sharp edge of the speaker. She laughed lightly at the awkwardness, cutting off when Gwen's mouth simply moved on to Flora's neck as if there had never been an interruption.

She moved her way down with quick pecks, then sucked at the juncture of Flora's neck and shoulder, dropped the strap of Flora's dress away and nipped at her collarbone.

"Oh." Flora was knocked off balance just by the heat of Gwen's mouth. She held one hand steady on Gwen's shoulder, one on the buzz-cut back of her head. Gwen had both straps pushed down and was mouthing the rise of Flora's breasts over her bra.

"You're so beautiful," Gwen said, her bottom lip dragging on the newly exposed dark circle of Flora's areola. "I don't even care that you have a girlfriend."

"Actually, I—" Flora started to say, and then Gwen's tongue and the hard metal bead of her tongue ring dragged a circle around Flora's nipple. Flora gasped, hand spasming on Gwen's head. "*Oh.*"

Flora's legs went wobbly and her quick breaths came out as soft moans. She barely remained upright as Gwen licked and sucked and bit down with gentle tugs of her teeth. Flora could feel how slick she was between her own legs, could sense the tight pulse of heat, yet if she collapsed onto this speaker she would crash to the ground and ruin the moment.

"Can we—" Flora said with difficulty, as a fresh pulse of heat shuddered through her when Gwen looked up and flicked her tongue ring against one spit-slick, sensitive nipple. Words escaping her, Flora gestured to her uncomfortably twisted position and the speaker behind her.

"Sit," Gwen said with a jut of her chin. "It's sturdy."

Flora gave the speaker a dubious look, but Gwen's mouth returned to its task and Flora lost the battle with gravity. The speaker tipped a little, then settled against the wall, holding her weight just fine.

"See?" Gwen said with her impish smile. She stood between Flora's legs again, gaining a height advantage that she seemed to find delightful. "You ever sit on a speaker like this and crank the bass up? Feel it thump against you?"

Flora looked up at her. "No."

Gwen leaned down for another kiss. "Maybe next time," she whispered against Flora's mouth, before capturing Flora's tingling, tender lips between her own.

Who was this girl? This reckless punk-pixie girl who sang to Flora like a siren? It wasn't as if Flora had been asleep and was now woken gently by the kiss of a blue-haired girl in combat boots; this was a jolt, a sudden, shocking flare of awareness.

Flora's dress was shoved up to her hips; Gwen's hand drifted over the inside of Flora's thighs, slowly making its way to the aching wet heat in her pussy. Two fingers slipped beneath Flora's underwear to rub over her swollen clit. Flora's knees parted wider; she arched back against the wall, and Gwen's fingers worked in quick, small circles, then long, slow drags. When Flora cried out and scrambled for purchase on the speaker's edge, Gwen stayed focused on that perfect spot. She kissed her again with a clack of her tongue ring on Flora's teeth, and the pleasure climbed and climbed.

Gwen was not a slow sleepy awakening; she was a searing burst of energy.

Still floating down from her climax, Flora fumbled the buttons of Gwen's jeans with weak, uncoordinated fingers. She pulsed with heat anew when she found the front of Gwen's red boy shorts damp and clinging.

Flora pushed Gwen's pants and underwear down as Gwen tugged her own shirt off. Everything about her was so small and tight and pale and pretty. Flora fanned her hands across Gwen's stomach, liking the way it jumped and clenched beneath her fingers.

Flora leaned up to lick across one tiny, pink nipple, then used the wetness to roll it between her thumb and finger.

Gwen breathed out harshly through her nose. "Please."

Flora obliged her by pressing the heel of her other hand against her clit. Gwen's hips jumped forward, Flora's middle finger slipped inside her, and Gwen threw her head back and groaned. She planted one hand on the wall behind Flora's head, riding Flora's hand and biting her lip with her face scrunched tight.

Flora crooked her finger at different angles until she found a spot that made Gwen spit a loud curse, then sat back to watch Gwen's face with two fingers crooked inside, her thumb flicking Gwen's clit, Gwen's hands on her own breast pinching her nipple hard, much harder than Flora liked. Flora filed that away for another time just as Gwen came with a series of colorful curses and convulsions that sent her sinking down to the floor.

Flora craned forward, curious now about the bass thumping against her, as she was still aching, still so turned on.

Gwen leaned back on her hands with her legs bent at the knees, gave Flora a dark, lusty look, and asked, "Wanna try the bed out this time?"

It was much too soon to think that she'd follow this girl just about anywhere, so Flora just replied, "Yes."

"Can I take you out?" Gwen asked later, handing Flora a lukewarm glass of sulfurous water. She fidgeted, looked away, and then blurted, "Unless this is like, a one-time thing, which I totally get. Because you have a girlfriend and I knew that, and this is definitely a hookup, okay."

Flora pressed a smile to the rim of her glass. Oh, that's what she meant to say before they got carried away. "Actually, Imani decided she needed some time to fully embrace her *transcendent self.* Which she naturally had to be single to achieve."

Gwen scowled. Adorable face scrunched indignantly. "What the fuck?"

Flora hummed. "Yes, essentially."

It was just as well. They'd barely even been a couple these past few months, and one of them had to work up the nerve to end it eventually. Flora had felt guilty that she'd waited so long and not done it herself, particularly when she'd spent more time thinking about the girl with blue hair than her own girlfriend. Her guilt had shrunk, however, when Imani informed Flora that she was "ruled by her id." Flora knew enough about philosophy to recognize a pseudo-intellectual insult when she heard one.

"What a *douche,* I mean—" Gwen's eyes widened. "Sorry, that was—my mouth gets ahead of my brain. I shouldn't..." Her creamy-pale cheeks blushed prettily.

"You can take me out," Flora said, pleased at the turn of events. She hadn't expected Gwen to be interested in dating—hookups, but not dating. *How many more surprises did Gwen have in store?* Flora's stomach fluttered at the thought. "I'd like that."

8

It's a week later—seven days filled with thoughtful silence and vague hums and far off gazing, of Gwen asking, "What?" only for Flora to reply, "Hmm? Just thinking"—before they talk about the awkward fight between Grady and Nico after the awkward impromptu dinner party.

"Are you happy?" Flora finally asks, halting and hesitant and in the dark of their bedroom.

Gwen considers her current position settled between Flora's legs, a hand on the sumptuous curve of her ass, her mouth dragging kisses up the warm, generous swell of one breast, the other hand pinching and rolling and circling the hard, peaked nipple of the other. "I am pretty damn happy, yes."

"I don't mean right this second." Flora's fingers fall from the nape of Gwen's neck to pick at a crease on the bedsheet. "I mean. Generally. In Nashville. In this house."

I came here for you echoes in Gwen's head. The conversation with Nico about missing L.A. The tickle in her brain that she's stuck, trapped, being dragged along on this baby plan. How she can never let on, because it would devastate Flora.

"I think it's been good for us," she says, catching her bottom lip on Flora's nipple so things don't get too far off track. "I don't work as much. We can afford this huge house where you can garden. The bathtub is rad." All true things, all good things. Gwen closes her eyes, settling with a sigh in the soft give of Flora's cleavage. Certainly, things could be much worse. She could be Nico, alone in his bachelor apartment, iced out, untouched and frustrated.

Gwen moves down, lips and nose and tongue tracing the downward contour of Flora's torso, the inward ebb of her ribs and waist, the outward flow of hips and softly rounded stomach, and down between her thighs.

Flora sighs and shivers. She is propped on mounds of pillows with her knees bent and dropped open. "But—" she says, exhaling, "—are *you* happy?"

"I'm happy if you're happy," Gwen says easily, because she is. Because... that's enough for her, isn't it? There are more pressing matters at hand—or mouth—and anyway, what does it matter? She's here, and they're settled. She's never been one to dwell on what could be or should be or might have been. She was defiant and rebellious in her youth, but she's an adult now, doing adult things.

She has everything she's ever wanted and things she never expected to have. The nagging itch is something she'll just have to ignore.

And *right now* she's not really interested in talking. Gwen ducks down, licking with pointed laps until Flora's clit swells hard and glistening from its hood, and Flora inhales sharply as her fingers scrape restlessly against the back of Gwen's head.

Gwen hums against the hot, spread-open center of her, drags her tongue in long, flat passes up and down Flora's labia, and then fits her lips over her swollen clit and sucks.

"*God.*" Flora groans and gasps and bucks her hips when Gwen gets the pressure just right in just the right spot.

Gwen pulls back then, not meaning to tease but not wanting it to be over just yet. She knows Flora is close by the quick, greedy lift of her hips, by the way her free hand is clutching and scrabbling at the headboard behind her. Gwen loves this, loves the taste of her lingering on her tongue, how responsive she is, and how after nearly ten years it's no less incredible than that first night, in Gwen's shitty off-campus apartment with a mattress on the floor her only furniture. Flora, so sweet, so beautiful, had looked at Gwen with her dark, serious eyes, and Gwen had never felt so understood before. She didn't know then what they would become, of course, she just knew that she had to see Flora again. Had to keep her, somehow, in her life.

"*G*," Flora says, sharp and breathless. She's never very commanding, not aggressive with what she wants. She doesn't need to be. Gwen knows.

Gwen smiles, tilts her head and darts her tongue to either side and just underneath the swollen bud, slides two fingers inside her and crooks them. Flora arches and moans and drops her knees wider. Gwen works her up until she's twisting, moaning brokenly, and gripping at the sheets, the headboard, the pillows behind her. Then finally Gwen moves to lick one spot, staying there, letting Flora ride her tongue and clamp her thighs around Gwen's head and come, arched high and tight off the mattress.

Flora eases down with happy hums and a satisfied smile, her eyes heavy with love and lust. Gwen hovers over her; this beautiful, smart, kind, nurturing woman that Gwen gets to keep 'til death do them part.

"Come here," Flora says huskily, making the heat in Gwen's belly spread low, pulsing between her legs. Flora is happy, and that can be enough for Gwen.

A few days later, Flora is the same position: lying prone but propped up, legs parted wide and fingers in a white-knuckled grip. Only this time it isn't Gwen's head settled between her thighs, but Dr. Anisha Alapati and a syringe full of their donation sample from Mr. Blond-Haired Blue-Eyed Number 3876.

Flora is anxious on the examination table; the sterile paper beneath her crinkles as she shifts and breathes in calming patterns and adjusts and readjusts the shapeless gown that covers her from neck to knees. Gwen sits on a stiff plastic chair next her, holding her hand.

"Okay." Dr. Alapati wheels back her stool, stands, snaps off her gloves, and goes to the sink to wash up. She's slight and short, with a dark blunt bob, a slim face, and a crisp, lilting accent. "Stay in this position for five to ten minutes, and I'll be right back." She lowers the inclined end of the table so Flora's hips are elevated above her head.

"This is weird, right?" Gwen wanders around the room now that her hand has been released from Flora's vise-like grip. She picks up a 3-D model of a uterus, ovaries, and fallopian tubes. "Little spermies, just swimming on up there." She demonstrates with a finger along the model.

"I'm trying to not think about it," Flora says. Paper rustles beneath her as she shifts in her unnatural position.

"I bet we have a front-runner already." Gwen plops the model back on the desk. "We'll call him Steve. Steve the Super Swimmer Sperm."

Flora laughs and shakes her head. "You're ridiculous."

To distract Flora from her obvious discomfort, Gwen starts to reply with further details of Steve's continued race to the ovum, but her phone rings in her pocket. She lets it go to voicemail, then checks it and wishes she hadn't.

"What?"

Gwen bites her lip, releases it. "It's Nico."

Flora looks up at the ceiling and folds her hands on her stomach. "It's fine. It's not like I'm going anywhere."

"Okay." She pulls her phone out, hits call, then says, "Go Steve, go!" before ducking out into the lobby.

"Oh, good," Nico says when he answers. "Are you busy?"

"Trying to get my wife pregnant, but other than that." After a hugely pregnant woman gives her a funny look, she goes into the main lobby.

"Shit, sorry. I forgot that was today." He sighs loudly. "Okay, never mind."

"Nico, what is it. Just—hop to it already."

"Fine, okay. I was thinking about heading back to L.A. for a while. Hit some shows, meet with some new designers. I know we decided on everything for Clementine's next tour and press blitz, but I was thinking I'd like to do some different things."

"And you can run away from Grady," she points out.

Nico is quiet, and she can just see him, at his desk with his head in his hands, the coif he tries to keep so artfully disheveled ruffled into haphazard spikes from running his fingers through it so much. "Maybe we both need space."

"Maybe," Gwen agrees. Maybe not. "You know that's not really going to solve anything, though. Like you have to deal with it eventually."

"I know. I—" He releases another frustrated huff. "He's doing the thing now where he pretends everything is just super-great and wonderful. Like he's over-the-top manic happy right now, and honestly? It's worse than him being angry and silent. I don't know how to reach him. I don't know if he *wants* me to reach him." He pauses, and she can hear him shift, can hear the muted *swish* of him scrubbing his hand through his hair again. "If you think I should stay... I mean, you can go to L.A. instead."

Of *course* she wants to go to L.A. But it doesn't matter just how badly she wants to or how much Nico really should stay and work things out with Grady; she can't leave Flora right now. "No, you go. Take a little time. I'll keep an eye on him for you."

"Thanks, Gwen, you're the best."

It still warms her heart every time, even when they disagree. "I know," she says.

"Everything okay?" Flora is sitting up when Gwen gets back to the room, and Dr. Alapati is filling out a check-out form at the desk.

"Fine." Gwen smooths the flyaway hairs that came loose from Flora's braid when she was lying on the table. "How do you feel?"

Flora smiles, then ducks her head. "I have a good feeling about Steve."

9

Gwen spends the next two weeks hip-deep in meetings and phone calls and fittings and all of the drudgery and administrative duties that Spencer abandoned. She checks on Grady from time to time, though he's spending most of his time in the studio "exorcising his demons," as Clementine claims. Gwen is back and forth with Nico on the looks he's putting together, nudging him to go with his more daring choices: yes to sheer skirts, yes to gingham, yes to a slouchy pastel trench; no to parkas, no to culottes, no to whatever that fringed and feathered thing is supposed to be.

"It's couture," Nico says. "You love that crap."

"It's not couture, it's hideous," she replies, while inputting a backlogged stack of shipping receipts into Excel.

"Same difference," he sniffs, like the snotty pain-in-the-ass that he is. She misses him like crazy.

And in those two weeks Flora changes. They don't know if the insemination took, but Flora acts as if it has. She switches from black tea to one made of alfalfa and nettle leaves that smells like steaming cut grass; she eats dark greens and lentils and handfuls of walnuts and pumpkin seeds for zinc and omega-3 fats. She stops drinking wine and eating sushi and taking hot baths. Gwen takes over scooping the litter box to avoid toxoplasmosis and microwaves their lunch meat in case of listeria.

They don't know if they have so much as blastocyst, a mere blob of cells, and already this potential baby is taking over their lives.

Gwen gets *the* call when she's facing down a stack of FedEx boxes nearly as tall as she is, waiting to be opened and organized and steamed and prepped.

"I threw up this morning!"

"Oh." Gwen searches her desk drawers for the box cutter, then pauses. "Are you taking a sick day?" No way she can go home early and tend to Flora. It's going to take her *forever* to go through all of the clothes and accessories by herself. And she cannot afford a stomach virus right now.

"Gwen, this is a good thing," Flora says, drawing the words out. "Think about it."

She tugs her mind out of work mode. *Throwing up. Why is Flora happy about—*

"Oh." Gwen blinks and blinks and then widens her eyes. "Oh! Oh my god! Did you take the test yet?"

"No, I wanted to wait for you. Can you come home?"

"Of course, yeah. I'll be right there."

The boxes can wait. She won't be able to focus now anyway, and the most pressing items are for Grady, whom she hasn't been able to track down all day. And Clementine will understand. She races home, parks crooked in the driveway, races upstairs, races into the bathroom with Flora, helps her fumble the little purple box open and then waits.

"I never thought I'd be excited about you peeing on stuff."

Flora wrinkles her nose. She's perched on the edge of the bathtub, staring down at the little white stick in her hand. Gwen kicks her feet in the air, up on the counter next to the sink. Gwen makes a ticking sound with her tongue and checks the timer again. Only thirty seconds have passed. Time is going slower. Soon they'll be frozen, stuck in this moment, this place, their lives still and unchanging.

One minute.

Flora stares at the plastic stick, and Gwen stares at her. She's fresh from work and still dressed "teacher-mode" in an A-line skirt and colorful blouse. Soon she'll change into something more free flowing: a gauzy dress or a gypsy skirt or wide-legged patchwork pants. Flora claims to know nothing of style, says that's Gwen's deal. But she has one, has presence and grace without even trying.

Two minutes. Gwen smooths her hands over her outfit of red and black and leather, buckles and heavy chains. She's a punk rock wild child all grown up, and it hits her for the first time. She's going to be a mother. Like, really, for real, a mother.

Not as if she didn't know; every step of the way she's been aware, of course, of the path she's on. And yet as long as she was wholly focused on one step a time, she could forget where they were leading.

She's going to be a mother.

The timer dings, Gwen jumps, and Flora flips the stick over. Gwen doesn't need to read the test stick to know the results: the elation and relief on Flora's face tells her everything. She jumps up and hugs Gwen so hard that she slides off the counter and into Flora's body. If it weren't for Flora holding her up, Gwen would collapse right onto the hard tile floor.

She allows herself one day to panic. Then after that it's easy enough to get swept up in Flora's happiness. That's all Gwen wants, to make Flora happy; that's enough.

Then it's back to work.

"Hey! Gwen!"

Grady and Clementine are performing together at the star-studded charity event downtown tonight. Usually Nico would dress Grady the day of, and keep tabs on Grady the night of, but he's still in L.A. So Grady is hers, and Grady is—

"So happy to see you! Come on in!" He hugs her tightly and then moves aside so she can enter his house. Once she's inside he hugs her again, his big strong chest and big muscled arms engulfing her. The clothes she brought are crushed between them; her face is pressed to Grady's defined pecs as she says, muffled, "Hi, Grady."

"Oh! Is this for tonight? Awesome! I love it!" He takes the garment bag and tosses it on the bench in the entryway.

"You didn't even look at it," Gwen points out, trailing him into the living room.

"I'm sure I'll love it. You're amazing, of course I will." He turns and flashes that charming sly grin. *Manic happy,* Nico had said.

The living room is littered with instruments and food wrappers, balled-up sheets of paper and fast food napkins with illegible scraps of sentences in bleeding ink. There are cans and bottles of soda on the floor and side tables and nearly covering the hammered steel coffee table.

Gwen can see Nico's touches all over this house: new, modern furniture; commissioned local art on the walls and shelves; new, textured wallpaper in a deep rust color; a huge bamboo plant withering in a corner; a neat stack of celebrity and fashion magazines piled next to the couch, buried under the soda cans; and a shelf with board games and well-loved books taking up nearly an entire wall, now that the study upstairs has been converted into an enormous walk-in closet. It certainly doesn't appear as if he's been keeping a secret apartment downtown.

"So, do you want me to come by before the event? I can meet you at the office or you can come by Clementine's house."

"Nah." Grady hops over a discarded electric guitar and kicks a soda can with a sharp *ping* in the process. It clunks against the opposite wall. He brushes candy wrappers and pillows off the couch, pulls something up and turns back to Gwen with a huge grin. "Check it out!"

It is a purple knit scarf roughly the size of a boa constrictor. "Wow," Gwen says, because, *wow*. "Did you make this?"

"Yup." Grady drapes the scarf over her shoulders, wraps it around once, then again. And still the ends dangle past her knees. "You're so tiny," Grady says with a laugh. "All tiny and cute."

"Like a squirrel?" Gwen says from beneath the many thick folds of the scarf. She pushes it down and away from her face.

"No, no," Grady says, tugging the scarf where it's pressed up to her ears. He tips his head, leans down and holds really intense eye contact for a long, charged moment. "Huh."

"Wh—" Gwen can't stop noticing how soft his lips look. She should ask him what kind of lip balm he uses. "What?"

"Your eyes," Grady says in a low, soft voice. He tilts his head in, so close she can feel his warm breath. "They're blue, but more of a blue-gray. It's really stunning."

Why can't she stop watching his lips move? How is his jaw perfectly square? And who smells that good, just naturally?

Grady wets his lips, flashes one more crooked grin, and then steps away. "Keep the scarf. It looks good on you."

Gwen nods, still a little dazed. "Yeah okay." She presses the soft material to her flushed cheeks. When Grady Dawson turns on the charm, he really turns it on; she both envies and pities Nico. Gwen shakes her head and starts to shed the scarf. "I'll see you tonight, okay? Call me if you need anything."

He's already walking away, off to the kitchen to fuel up for whatever insane extreme sport or hyperactive shenanigans he's heading to next. Just as long as he's finished by eight and doesn't maim himself, it's not the worst way to deal with feeling betrayed.

"You should come tonight!" he calls from the kitchen.

Gwen finally manages to unwind herself. "Uh, Flora's been having a lot of morning sickness, which they should really call all-day sickness; it's awful. I should probably be there to hold back her hair and rub her feet. You know, fun Saturday night stuff." She makes a jazzy sweep in the air with her hands.

"Oh, that's right! A baby!" He's got a half of a sandwich crammed in his mouth, but Gwen gets the gist of it. Grady swallows. "That's heavy. A *baby*."

Gwen leans against the kitchen island. "Yep."

"Mmm," Grady mumbles around another bite. "But you guys are settled. You're ready to give up your life for a kid. I admire that. My parents just—" He takes yet another huge bite, then flaps his hand in a dismissive sort of way. "Took off."

"Yeah," Gwen says. Are they talking about his parents or Nico? "I guess we know what we're getting into here."

Grady smacks his hand flat on the marble top of the island. "Commitment."

"Right."

Grady spins around, flings the refrigerator door open so hard it crashes into the counter and all the bottles and jars inside rattle loudly, yanks out another can of soda, plunks it on the counter and snaps open the tab. Soda spurts from the top; he doesn't notice. "Because you know, if you say you'll stick around, you stick around. Like you don't have a secret apartment, I bet. Right? I bet."

Talking about Nico, then. Grady chugs the soda, belches, and then goes to the fridge again. When he spins back around, Gwen gently takes the can from his hand. "Hey, hi there, why don't you take it easy on the Mello Yello before your heart explodes?"

Grady gives the can a look of longing, but nods. "Yeah. Right. Yeah."

"Also? You should call Nico and tell him how you're feeling. Honesty, same team, three-legged race, remember?" She pulls her phone from her pocket, picks up a discarded piece of paper from the floor, and a finds a pen. The paper has the words *rock opera? timpani?* written on it in Grady's messy scrawl.

"Is that what you would do?" Grady asks as she writes down the address and time of the event. "Total blunt honesty, even if it might upset him and make things worse?"

She taps the end of the pen on the table and pushes the paper toward him. "I don't know," she answers. She's struggling with that herself right now, and as much as she hates to admit it, "It'll come up one way or the other, eventually."

And sometimes, late at night when Flora is curled up, softly beautiful and fast asleep, Gwen watches her in the dark and thinks about the baby growing inside of her, and the prickling itch of doubt turns to full-blown panic.

She's has eight more months to make it go away. The itch turns into the steady tick of a clock counting down.

10

Clementine's place is no mere house, no simple building of rooms and furniture and appliances, but an estate. A spiked iron gate surrounds a Tuscan villa-style mansion: three floors, pale stone exterior with arches and sweeping spiral staircases, intricate iron balconies, columned front entryway, stacked tile roof, pool, guest house, greenhouse, stables and a studio, all on acres of perfectly manicured grass and sculpted hedges lining the long, winding driveway. Gwen parks next to the burbling courtyard fountain, carefully unloads the gown, shoes, and jewelry, heaves her travel case onto her shoulder, and hobbles to the double-arched front door.

She had to buzz in at the front gate, and now has to buzz in again at the front door. She gives a salute to the camera when it whirrs and chirps at her from above, and then she's escorted in by Clementine's mountain-sized security guard.

"Thanks, Kevin," she says, directing it up to the outer ozone layer where Kevin gives a perfunctory nod.

She's tempted, as always, to curtsy here in the marble-floored foyer, with its double-spiral staircase and ornate chandelier swinging from the cavernously tall ceiling. Instead she fidgets.

Clementine saunters in, hair in a messy bun, wearing low-slung yoga pants and a tank top and eating butterscotch pudding from a plastic cup. "Hey, girl."

She still looks magazine-ready gorgeous, somehow, and she hasn't even had hair and makeup done. "Hey." Gwen hikes the garment bag up higher. "Ready to get started?"

"You know I'm always ready for you, sugar," Clementine says with a wink, sauntering up the stairs, narrow hips and toned ass swinging.

Gwen trips over her own feet to follow.

"So, I hear congratulations are in order." Clementine eases down on the vanity bench in the second floor bathroom, which is done in marble and gilded mirrors and high arched windows. To the right is a large closet, and on the left a whirlpool tub, spa-style shower, and steam room.

"Wow, word travels fast," Gwen says from the closet. She hangs up the garment bag and unzips it to reveal the lace and tulle lavender gown.

"You're in the South now, sugar. Gossip is our native tongue."

"Yes, well." Gwen goes back into the bathroom, sets her hands on her hips, and looks at Clementine, who is eating her pudding and humming. "Yes. Thank you. Uh. Go change."

While Clementine is changing, Gwen sits on the vanity and eyes the shower. It has one of those waterfall shower heads and massaging jets. It looks like bliss; she'd probably never leave. Of course, Clementine didn't get here by lounging in the indoor salt water pool sipping merlot. Like Grady, she's barely around at all. She works her ass off. Works her ass off to *have* that ass.

"Zip me up?" The dress is artfully tiered with swaths of frothy tulle; it has a deep neckline of embellished lace and a nipped-in waist.

"I love this gown." As Gwen tugs the zipper up, her fingers brush Clementine's smooth skin and angled bones. Clementine makes a vague noise of agreement. Gwen crouches to fluff the hem out, then pulls her bag over to find the double-sided tape. "No?" They'd agreed on it just two days ago, but she's had clients do a total flip-flop on an item two seconds from stepping out on a red carpet or stage; two days is nothing.

Clementine brushes her long, delicate fingers down the puffy skirt. "I know I sound like a jackass, but—" She pauses to scrunch her nose up. "Sometimes I get sick of fancy gowns. Not like…" She drops her voice, "Like, 'ugh, gross, a designer gown again.'"

"But maybe we could change it up a bit?"

Clementine taps her forehead and points at Gwen. "See, this is why I like you so much, G. You get it."

Gwen's stomach goes a little funny when Clementine uses Flora's nickname for her, not that she knows or is doing it to be pushy. Hell, it's on their business letterhead, so that's why, she's sure. Still. "Uh." Gwen stands, plucks off a square of tape used to ensure everything stays where it should, and tugs the right strap over Clementine's shoulder. "We could put you in a suit next time. I can schedule a fitting." White, the pants tapered skinny and snug, nothing underneath the fitted blazer, which would be buttoned up to her sternum, showing just enough cleavage and skin. She'd look divine. Gwen goes a little woozy just thinking about it.

She works on keeping Clementine's dress in place, securing it over the ridge of her collarbones and along the firm round outline of both breasts.

"What would Nico say about a suit?"

"Nico is not here," Gwen points out. She pulls the shoes from their box and opens earring and necklace cases. She has to believe in herself and her abilities with or without Nico's approval.

"Speaking of Nico not being here—" Clementine flaps her hands at the offered shoes, "Those look painful. I'll put 'em on in the limo."

"I talked to him," Gwen says, setting the pointy-toed pumps aside for now. "He's pretending he's too busy to think about anything but work."

Gwen moves back so Clementine can sit at the vanity and put on the jade earrings while looking up at Gwen through the mirror. "Sounds right. Meanwhile Grady is jumping out of airplanes and trying to drink his body weight in Mello Yello."

Gwen laughs, then frowns. "Wait, seriously?"

"Yeah, he must go through a case a day. Gonna rot his perfect teeth at this rate." She reaches for the necklace.

"The other thing. Jumping out of an airplane?" Gwen helps her with the delicate clasp, lays it just at the nape of her neck.

"Mmhmm. Skydiving instead of working in the studio. Talked to Billy and Brad from his band, and they said he's been going on about rewriting the entire album, making it a concept album, which of course he doesn't have time for and the record company is going to shit a brick about." She turns the green jewel to face the right way, so it rests just inside the scooped hollow of her throat, then shrugs in an *oh, well* gesture.

"Should we? I don't know… do something?" What, Gwen has no idea. Get Nico back here, for a start. Make those two talk and stop being idiots.

Clementine stands, and from the front of the house the buzzer sounds. Hair and makeup probably, the whole terrifying bunch. "Sometimes it's best to let him get it out of his system for a while. As much as we may want to, we can't make him be okay. *He* has to want it."

"I know. I just feel helpless, I guess." Gwen gathers up her things, puts the tape away, and puts the empty garment bag, the shoe box, and jewelry boxes in an easy-to-reach spot for later tonight. "I'm just worried he's going to do something stupid. Or Nico will do something stupid. God, love is stupid." She huffs a laugh, shakes her head, and thinks about Flora at home, expecting her. *Expecting.* Her stomach lurches again.

Clementine tugs the elastic band from her hair. Waves of soft brown cascade down, and the scent of honeysuckle fills the air. "Why do you think I stay the hell away from it?"

Gwen wants to protest that she's kidding, mostly. That love is wonderful, in fact—usually. She wants to ask if Clementine really stays away from love or if she doesn't talk about it, and she wants to ask *whom* Clementine falls in love with. If she's been hurt before, if she's just afraid of getting hurt again. Or if she just really, really has no interest in romance at all.

But her hair and makeup team descend upon the bathroom—three people, each louder and more demonstrative than the next—in a whirlwind of hairspray, curling irons, blending brushes, and gossip; so Gwen makes her escape, only quickly reminding Clementine with her usual parting words:

"Call me if you need anything."

11

She gets a blast of texts on her drive home, all from Nico.

I miss him.

I miss him so much Gwen.

How do you just COPE with loving someone this much? I can't cope with it.

I'm such an idiot.

The things I put up with for him.

The tabloids and paparazzi and crazy fans and constant travel and of course I'm not taking off OBVIOUSLY.

I'm such an idiot.

Gwen only texts him back once he's gotten out what he needs to say. She sits in her driveway in the dark to type: *Probably time to come back then.* And at the front door, with the key in the still-locked deadbolt, adds, *I don't know how to cope with loving someone that much. If I ever figure it out, I'll let you know.*

Then she goes inside and feeds Cheese, even though Cheese has food in her bowl, but no, not *that* food. She heats leftover shrimp stir-fry and eats it by the lone white light of the open microwave, then heads up the creaky stairs.

Flora is awake, but not sitting against the headboard reading and waiting for Gwen, not lesson-planning or filling out her grade book, but curled up on her side, awake and slowly breathing in-out, in-out through her nose.

"Hey, are you okay?" Gwen eases onto the bed, careful not to bounce too much. The slightest thing seems to set Flora off: strong food smells, moving too quickly, the sight of dirty socks. Even TV commercials with food make her face go ashen.

Flora breathes, in-out, in-out. "Yeah."

Gwen rubs soothing circles on her back. "Can I get you something?" She hates being helpless to make things better, and doesn't really know how to be okay with the way this pregnancy is making Flora so miserable. It's normal, good even, the doctor says. She still hates it. Gwen rubs up and down and around the hunched bend of Flora's back. Flora breathes, in-out, in-out, in-out. Then finally says, shakily, "I think it's passing."

From her bag dropped on the floor, Gwen's phone chirps with a text, then another. She glances at her bag, but keeps rubbing. It's probably just Nico, but she is still on call for this event, all on her own out here.

Flora gives a relieved gust of air, then flips over. "Hi."

Gwen's chest floods with warmth from the sweet, soft look, from the way Flora's hair fans out around her face with locks and strands covering her forehead and one eye. Flora tips her chin for a kiss, and Gwen brushes the hair aside. A chaste peck, then Flora's lips part, inviting Gwen to pull the flesh of the bottom one between her own, and they are sucking and licking, mouths moving together. Flora whines, high and wanting, and Gwen slides her tongue against Flora's. She's just starting to think this is going somewhere wonderful—Flora's fingers stroke and scrape her scalp, Flora wiggles beneath her, heat pulls and builds—when Flora pulls away suddenly, turning her head to the side and covering her mouth.

"What?" Gwen blinks, hazy, and touches her own tingling lips.

Flora says from behind her hands, "It's just—you taste like shrimp."

"Sorry." Gwen frowns, then covers her mouth to keep the lingering shrimp scent contained. "I'll go brush."

Flora shakes her head, squeezes her eyes closed, and then bolts out of bed and into the bathroom. Gwen collapses onto the bed with a frustrated sigh, calling out between retching noises to make sure Flora is okay, though of course she can hear for herself that Flora is not okay. Fantastic.

On her way back from getting plain crackers and a glass of water, Gwen digs out her phone to check the messages she missed.

Clementine: Dress tore. Used some tape but not sure how long it's going to hold up. I'm on in thirty!!!!!!!!!!

Clementine: Also Grady is MIA.

"Fantastic," Gwen says, out loud this time.

Flora emerges, pallid and weak, taking the water and crackers with a shaky, "Thanks, G."

Gwen braces for impact, holding her phone up as evidence. "I have to go back out. Fashion emergency. Possible Grady emergency."

Flora perches on the bed and nibbles one tiny corner of a cracker. "It's fine. I'm calling it a night anyway."

"Are you—?"

"Yes, I'm sure." Flora offers a wobbly smile. "I'd rather not have any witnesses to all that anyway." She gestures to the door with her glass. "No sense in both of us suffering."

Gwen lifts her bag, deposits her phone inside it. "I hate when you're sick. It kills me." She would suffer for her if she could, and still a selfish part of her is so grateful she *isn't* the one suffering.

Gwen tries for a goodbye and goodnight kiss, but Flora holds up a hand.

"Shrimp breath, right." Gwen blows her a kiss instead, and Flora pretends to catch it and press it to her heart. "I love you."

"I love you, too."

Back out again, circling the block outside the venue: a two hundred year-old pioneer feed store made of brick and ancient wood gutted and redone as an upscale restaurant and event space and decorated with wooden barrels, bales of hay, and old burlap sacks.

She has to flash her industry badge and ID to the bouncer at the front, wind and duck and shove past a densely packed crowd of well-dressed, well-to-do patrons in the foyer, and then dash upstairs and through a crowd of local personalities, international music stars, and the entourages of international music stars, along with the lucky few regular folks who are goggled-eyed and mingling. Enchanting fairy lights are strung from the ceiling. Waiters in tailcoat tuxes and black bowties are carrying trays of hors d'oeuvres and fizzing flutes of champagne. The back wall is taken up by a long, cloth-covered table carefully arranged with auction items.

Gwen gets her bearings and spots the stage: low, set up in the center of the room and currently occupied by an emcee in a cowboy hat announcing the next bid and the next artist to take the stage. Anxiously waiting in the wings is Clementine.

"My hero," Clementine says, miming a swoon, with her hand fluttering to her forehead.

"I know you're not serious, but I like it." Gwen unearths her mini sewing kit, threads and knots a needle with purple thread, and fixes the strap right there in the shadows of the stage. She glances around to the group of singers and musicians milling around, all dressed to the nines. Some of them nod at her, or wave, or make aloof but intentional eye contact. She's been in Nashville long enough now to be part of this group, to be recognized herself. A life has built up around her without her realizing it was happening.

"Okay, crisis averted." Gwen pats her shoulder. "Now, what's happening with Grady?"

"We're on in ten now, and he's still not here. We're the final auction of the night: A duet serenade and meet and greet." Clementine exudes calm as she says this; she seems unconcerned, and smooths the ruffles of her dress methodically. But there's a crease between her eyes, and her mouth is pressed thin as she looks over to the entrance. "I called. I had my assistant go by his house, I—"

They're interrupted by Grady's manager, Vince, a round, balding man in his late fifties, currently red-faced and frantic. He usually operates by phone, preferring to manage from afar. This must be serious. "Did you find him?"

Clementine gives a curt shake of her head. The poor guy looks distraught to the brink of panic attack, or at the very least an ulcer.

"I'm sure it's fine. You know Grady when he gets his mind on something. Probably he's in the woods writing his next chart-topper." Clementine touches Vince's elbow lightly and flashes a wide white smile, a photo-ready, smile-through-the-chaos look, but Vince buys it. He nods, frets, paces, then hustles away again.

Clementine bends close, her voice low and her breath warm at Gwen's ear. "Truth be told, I'm worried. He hasn't pulled something like this in a long time."

Gwen's response is lost because there's a sudden flash of light, then several more in a blinding pulse. Clementine turns it up to ten, posing and smiling and shifting close to Gwen. Gwen shields her eyes and turns away, but Clementine pulls her by the hand and says through a plastered-on grin, "Smile, sugar. Don't let 'em see you sweat."

It's insane, the lights from the cameras and the reporters calling Clementine's name, asking her questions without waiting for an answer, demanding she "Look this way" or "Over here, Clem" or "Are you alone tonight, Clem?" and "Who are you wearing, Clem?"

Serene and elegant and poised, she handles it all like a pro, all while Gwen clings to her hand and feels like a deer standing frozen in the oncoming headlights of a truck.

"I'm blind. I'm actually blind." Gwen blinks and blinks; spots of purple and white and blue crowd her vision. "What does the world look like? I've forgotten already."

Clementine laughs and drops her hand. "Give it a few, you'll be all right."

A stage manager gives Clementine her signal to perform. Still no Grady, but the show must go on. Gwen packs up her sewing kit, then slides back into the crowd to leave. She hesitates. *Should I look for him? But where? That skeevy bar? The dirt bike track? No, it's nighttime.* She takes a tall glass of champagne and munches on polenta-mushroom diamonds, blue crab beignets, and goat cheese tarts. *Who else knows all of Grady's hiding places?*

"My good friend Grady Dawson sadly couldn't make it tonight. He sends his deepest regrets and double the donation instead."

Clementine's voice in the mic is honey-sweet and lilting. She flashes a smile into the harsh stage lights. "So I'd like to play for you all a song from my new, not-yet released album." She pauses while the crowd cheers, surprised and delighted. "You can catch it on my *Burning Tracks* Tour. This one is all about living your life while you've got one to live. Hit it!"

Clementine Campbell is at the top of the heap for two reasons: hard work and honed instincts. She's talented, sure. A star on stage, that much is easy to see. Less easy to see is that she's sacrificed everything to have the career she does, and how few people understand that. Gwen gets to be one of the lucky ones.

So she stays and forgets about anything or anyone else and watches Clementine shine.

12

Clementine has to do the meet and greet, take photos, do interviews, and then mingle. Gwen is having fun, sipping her skinny flute of champagne and chatting and perusing the auction table. Whatever this Foster Hope organization is, they made out like bandits tonight. She picks up a pamphlet but drops it when Clementine pops up behind her, tugs her away by the elbow, and not-so-gently pushes her to the back exit.

"Keep walking, keep walking."

"Clem, what are—do you owe someone money and they came to collect? Why are we making a break for it?" They weave through the crowd, and just as they reach the exit, Clementine wobbles—those heels really are killer—and Gwen slings an arm around her waist to steady her.

"Thanks, sugar." Clementine leans her weight into Gwen, and a series of lights flash around them just as she's hauling open the heavy back door. "See? That's why. I'll never get out of here with them snapping at me and I've had enough. I want to go find Grady."

Inside the metal and concrete stairwell is Clementine's security guard.

"How the hell—" Gwen starts. *How did he know? Bat-signal? Pheromones?* Kevin falls in behind them. Clementine kicks her heels off, hooks them with two fingers, and takes off down the stairs at a fast clip.

"This isn't like him," she says, spinning around a landing to the next set of stairs. "Not anymore."

Gwen follows as quickly as her shorter legs will allow. "Should I call Nico?"

Now on the basement parking garage level, Clementine pauses. She works her jaw; her eyes dart. "Let me find him first. I should have—you were right to try and stay with him, I—" She shakes her head and opens the door.

"Hey, this isn't your fault." Gwen follows Clementine, and Kevin follows Gwen. "I bet he just forgot. He never hired another assistant, and Nico is usually with him before, during, and after..." Gwen's voice echoes in the darkened garage.

He was acting erratic yesterday, all alone, and Gwen knew that. She *knew* he wasn't okay and she did nothing. If Nico ensures that Grady is where he needs to be, and Nico is not here, then that falls to her. She failed at her job. She failed as a friend. She's failing as a partner. Soon she can add failed mother to the list.

The pretentious hors d'oeuvres spit bile up her throat.

"I'll find him." Gwen catches up to Clementine and the limo waiting with its engine running. "I did last time."

Clementine considers, her face drawn; even worried and in this terrible lighting she manages to look ethereal, like a softly glowing angel. Whatever Clementine is paying her aesthetician is not nearly enough.

"We'll both go," Clementine finally declares, getting into the limo and scooting over to make room for Gwen. She shakes her head. "Time to call in the cavalry on that boy."

Just before Gwen ducks into the limo, there's yet another flash of light.

"Can we head to DisChord, please?" Clementine says, while Gwen presses her face to the window to find whoever followed them. She should sic Kevin on those creepers. But they pull away and out of the garage too fast. Kevin is behind them in his black Navigator, and Clementine seems undisturbed, as if being stalked and photographed everywhere she goes is normal, because it is.

"Want some water, hon?"

Gwen flops back in the seat, takes a water, and enjoys the admittedly luxurious ride to the music store in a decked-out limo.

DisChord is in one of Nashville's many square, flat buildings; it's not the trendiest or most well-known vinyl record store in Nashville, but it's been around for decades with its streamlined shelves of vintage records in pinewood boxes, squeaky gray floors, and harsh fluorescent lighting.

"Grady's favorite," Clementine says, ridiculously out of place in her designer gown and bare feet, dramatic makeup, and elaborate updo. "He doesn't buy often. Just likes to 'be with the music.'" She arcs her arms out dramatically.

The cute girl with a nose ring and neck tattoo watches them from behind the counter, then pretends she isn't watching them. They don't find Grady, but Gwen does snag a 1979 copy of *The Buzzcocks: Live at the Palladium*, one of the best punk bootlegs around.

"Nice," the cashier says. She rings Gwen's purchase up and can't stop glancing at Clementine, then away, then back, the whole time.

Gwen wants to pat her on her sweet little Mohawked head. Gwen had once hidden her guilty pleasures, too, until she met Flora, who saw right through her. Flora, who loves boundlessly and with conviction. Grady, too, loves unreservedly and without fear, even after so much loss and heartbreak.

If Nico finds out she lost Grady or let him get hurt, he may never forgive her. He *shouldn't* forgive her.

"We could check Nico's apartment?" Gwen suggests, back in the limo. Grady must miss Nico as much as Nico misses him and could have wanted to feel close to him somehow.

But the apartment in the sleek steel and glass high-rise is dark and silent; two stickers from missed package deliveries days ago are stuck to the door.

Down on the street, they pass upscale restaurants and bars and high-end stores; enough is happening in this area even late at night to make it hip and young. The limo is double-parked in front of one of those overpriced hipster-magnet thrift stores.

"Hey, Clem." Gwen pauses and takes two steps backward. "Want to slip into something more comfortable?"

They browse shoulder to shoulder, pushing aside shapeless sweaters and puffy-shouldered rayon blouses, acid-wash jeans and neon T-shirts, babydoll dresses, halter tops, super low-rise jeans, and velour tracksuits. *Everything old is new again,* Gwen thinks, and checks a cute 50s-era shirtdress for any tears or stains.

"How about this?" Clementine shows her a hideously frumpy floral print dress with a wide Peter Pan collar, long puffy sleeves, and a hemline down to the ankle. Shaped like a deflated rectangle, it's the sort of dress that is worn by someone who has no other choice. It makes Gwen's soul feel sad.

"Although," Gwen muses, handing Clementine the adorable powder-blue shirtdress, "If anyone could pull that thing off, it's you." She takes the offensive frumper and shoves it back on the rack. "In fact, within the week it would be the next hot fashion trend, thanks to Clementine Campbell."

"Keep flattering me like that and I'll never let you go home." Clementine's eyebrows lift and fall and she grins, flirty and teasing.

Gwen's neck goes hot. "Go change, we're on a mission. And careful with that gown!"

"Whatever you say," Clem says, her voice dropping low, and then she's off to the tiny changing room. Gwen pushes the clothes on the rack back into place, and in the few seconds she'd looked away, Kevin had appeared next to the changing room with his arms crossed and his intimidating glare firmly settled into place.

"How in the fuck..." Gwen mutters, walking, bewildered, to a bin of shoes.

They try Grady's favorite chicken restaurant, his favorite barbecue place, the diner that Gwen knows he and Nico like to go to late at night when Nico gives in to junk food after a hard day or an imploring look from Grady. They hit a few music clubs and, after that, some bars, usually in and out fast enough that no one should notice Clementine, but she gets stopped for pictures or autographs or stared at everywhere they go.

It's seeping into early morning by the time they end up at a park. The air is light and cool; rustic lamps puddle light on the trails. They walk together at a tired, meandering pace in the fading dark beneath a hushed canopy of trees, and eat frozen custard from Grady's favorite late-night custard place—naturally.

"Okay. 'Burning Tracks.'" Gwen scoops a bite of chocolate custard. "Angsty song about heartbreak. What was that line? *Leaving shattered pieces of me on the other side for you to see.* Who did it? I need to know."

Clementine pokes at her strawberry cheesecake custard. "Not all of my songs are autobiographical. Sometimes they're just stories."

Their feet swish on the dirt trail, crickets chirp, and something rattles the leaves high in a towering oak tree. "So all those love songs are lies? I feel betrayed, Clementine Campbell. Betrayed. I thought you understood my unique pain."

Clementine laughs, steals a scoop of Gwen's custard, and says, "Love is for chumps."

Gwen clucks her tongue at the custard theft and the sentiment and teases, "Who hurt you?"

Clementine doesn't laugh, and a heavy silence pushes between them on the dark and empty walking trail. They don't talk again until they reach the bottom of the long stretch of steps that Grady likes to run for an early morning workout once or twice a week, and sometimes just to blow off steam.

Clementine stirs her melting custard, hangs her head, and confesses quietly, "There was this girl..."

"Oh, there's always a girl." Gwen sits on a bottom step and pats the cold, dirt-dusted space next to her.

Clementine sits and stretches her long, long legs out in front of her. "I was young. Real young. But I've never felt..."

Heavy silence again, until Gwen prompts gently, "What?"

"I was gonna say that I've never felt that way about someone, but that was before. I was fifteen when my first single went gold, you know. My life is not normal. I've never had the chance to see how I feel about anyone. I can't just date, go out a few times and see how it goes. I can't fall in love. Can't just... have that. Not with everyone looking, watching and waiting. I loved her, you know?

And she didn't love me back. But sometimes I wonder if it only hurts so bad because she was the only one."

Gwen's chest aches, and her eyes prickle. She sets down her custard cup and gathers Clementine close. It hadn't occurred to Gwen that never getting the chance to love and lose can hurt just as badly as heartbreak.

"You're so lucky, you know? To have Flora. The life you two have." The sun is rising between the trees; the tips of the leaves are bathed in gold. "I wish I knew what that was like. Just to see. Even for a little while."

Gwen puts her arm around her shoulders in a comforting gesture. "You will, Clem. I promise."

13

Eight years and *two weeks ago…*

"Shit, I'm so sorry. Shit."

The first minute of their first date, and Flora was wet. She pulled her skirt up from her lap where the light blue embroidered fabric was now blotched with a dark puddle. "It's okay."

Gwen hovered over her, up on her knees and moving her hands over Flora's damp lap frantically. "No, it's not. Oh shit, I didn't even bring any napkins. What kind of fuck-up doesn't bring napkins to a picnic?" Her face was crestfallen.

"It's fine. It'll dry." To prove her point, Flora shifted the wet patch of fabric into a spot of sunlight on the bridge where they'd set out their picnic. Where *Gwen* set out the picnic. She'd planned this whole thing, tugged Flora by the hand the entire way—like a kid showing off her super cool tree fort—to this little footbridge over a pond surrounded by ferns and shrubs and thick trees, where a weeping willow stooped, its branches dragging, while sunlight flickered through it along with a caressing breeze.

Gwen had dressed in her usual all black: jeans with a hole in the knee and a black shirt ripped at the sleeves, neck, and midriff, showing her concave stomach and belly button ring, the notched ridges of her ribcage beneath her pale skin, and the clear protrusion of her hipbones. Her heavy combat boots had thumped across the bridge to show Flora what she'd prepared: a white wicker basket with a red checked blanket; two champagne flutes; strawberries and roasted chickpeas and finger sandwiches of cucumber and vegan cream cheese.

"I'm considering radical veganism," Gwen had said, laying out the food, then popping the champagne. "I'm having a hard time kicking bacon, though."

"Are you twenty-one?" Flora had to ask, because she could have sworn Gwen was a sophomore. And she didn't really look much older than twelve. Flora couldn't imagine that anyone would buy the fake ID Gwen must have used. "Because I am," Flora continued, gently chastising. "I could have gotten the champagne."

"What fun would that be?" Gwen had wiggled her eyebrows mischievously, handed Flora a glass, and poured the champagne with trembling, overexcited hands. She'd poured it everywhere but in the glass.

"I really am sorry," Gwen said again, picking at a sandwich, feet swinging off the edge of the bridge. "This was supposed to be romantic. The girls I date aren't usually into—" Gwen seemed to change her mind halfway through the confession and finished with a mumbled, "romance."

Flora picked up a strawberry and nibbled the end. "I'm not like the girls you usually date?" She casually crossed her legs beneath her, trying to look more indifferent toward the girls Gwen usually dated than she felt.

"Am I like the girls you usually date?"

Flora smiled. "That's fair." Something moved in the water below them; a fish or a turtle, it was hard to tell through the murky water. Ripples passed over the surface, and the shadow in the water moved on. "I haven't dated that much," Flora confessed. "I like monogamy, I guess." She shrugged, finishing her strawberry. She'd really gone from relationship to relationship without casually dating much at all.

That was what seeking Gwen out was about, that night, trying for a one-night stand. And yet, here she was anyway.

Gwen pressed her lips together, put down her sandwich, and brushed crumbs from her hands. She nodded at Flora's champagne-damp skirt. "Silk brocade can be touchy. You should hand-wash it in cold water, then lay it flat to air-dry when you get home."

"You know a lot about silk brocade," Flora said, but Gwen just shrugged. The mood had shifted, though Flora didn't know why. They ate in silence. Flora was comfortable with the relative silence; it wasn't awkward between them, though it really should have been. There was an occasional rustle in the bushes, more flickers of movement on the water. The botanical gardens were tucked away right in the middle of the UCLA campus, and every once in a while sirens or jackhammers or particularly enthusiastic honking broke through to the oasis.

Gwen, however, was restless: she tucked one leg under the other, then switched, rested on her haunches, crouching, then plopped back down to kick her feet off the edge. She tore off bits of bread to feed a turtle that popped briefly out of the water. Something was on her mind, and Flora decided to give her space to say it when she needed to, if she needed to, instead of pushing.

"I flunked out," Gwen finally said, her gaze darting to the water, her mangled sandwich, her black scuffed combat boots. "I didn't quit, like I said."

Flora leaned back on her elbows; sun warmed her upturned face. "When?"

"A week ago? The night you came..." She paused, a very pleased grin tugging at her lips. "... over. That was my second week in that apartment. I'd been ditching class to take extra shifts at work and finally had too many absences. I don't know, I just—" She tossed more breadcrumbs to a turtle that was no longer there. "None of this was ever what I wanted. My parents chose this school. My guidance counselor recommended business administration. I don't even—" She whipped her head around. "What are you majoring in? What's your plan, Flora?"

"Teaching," Flora answered right away. "I'm getting my masters after this and then I'd like to teach elementary school. First or second grade, ideally."

"See? That's exactly it. I don't even know what I want, because I've been pushed into a school and a career I don't want to be in, and I went along because..." She gestured helplessly. "It was easier, I guess. I didn't want my parents to be disappointed in me. Again. But here I am. A dropout working at a salon, though at least yesterday they moved me up from receptionist to this *intern-stylist* thing or whatever."

Flora sat up, crisscrossed her legs, rested her hands between her knees, and turned toward Gwen. "So wait. In two weeks, you got an apartment and a promotion. Clearly you have tenacity and a good work ethic. You put together that awesome inspiration board. And this picnic." Gwen looked up, tipping her head curiously. "Pretty impressive, I think," Flora said.

"It sounds like more than it is."

"You should give yourself some credit, Gwen." Flora moved closer again, clasping their hands, needing to touch her. Flora bent to look up at Gwen. "There's more than one path to success. And you have... gumption."

Gwen burst out in a loud laugh, an echoing *ha.* "Most people just say 'obnoxious,' but let's go with gumption."

Flora smiled. "You go after what you want; what's wrong with that? I mean, I knew you wanted me. It was pretty clear."

Gwen shook her head. "I thought you had a girlfriend and slept with you anyway. That's exactly the sort of thing I *do* and then only think about later. I couldn't even drop out officially. Just got up one morning and got ready for class and just—" She flicked one hand, discarding something imaginary from her fingers. "I stopped going. Didn't even tell my parents, and they're going to flip the fuck out. I have no plan. I never have a fucking plan, you know?"

"Okay, so." Flora pulled her spine straight. "If you channel all that energy into something that you're really passionate about, then you could make a plan."

Gwen sighed. "It's not that easy."

"Why not?"

"I don't..." Gwen started, then her face shifted into a sly grin. "I mean, the plan for today was to wine and dine you and then get you back in my bed."

She was clearly trying to change the subject, but Flora flushed hot anyway. "Okay, and after that?"

Gwen's grin faltered; her gaze went far off and unfocused. She pulled her legs up, tucked them against her chest, wrapped her arms around them, and set her chin on her knees. "I don't know what comes after that. I don't know how to look down the road and see what might be coming. Could you really picture yourself with someone like me? I mean, long-term. *Monogamous.* Like, what I can possibly offer you, Flora?"

Flora reached out, daring to touch her, daring to make another first move, and scratched her fingers through the buzz-cut right side of Gwen's head. She tucked the longer blue fringe behind Gwen's ear. "Well, I have to say I like your plans so far."

14

Gwen still has Clementine snug against her in the park with the dim early morning brightening around them. Her long limbs are curled in, her silky honeysuckle hair against Gwen's cheek. If she could do more, could tell Clementine that love is waiting for her, that it will appear when she least expects it, that it will feel so easy and right she'll hardly believe she ever felt alone, she would. Clementine's life just isn't that simple, and hasn't been for a very long time.

Clementine sniffles and pulls away, wiping at her eyes, and then, out of nowhere, a giant dark figure looms in front of them. Gwen reacts on instinct, yanking Clementine behind her. She's ready to kick and bite and fight; she's so glad she wore her heavy steel-toe spiked boots. The huge shadowy figure moves closer, reaches out; Gwen tenses, rears back and—

He holds out Clementine's phone.

"Holy shit, Kevin." Gwen's heart slams against her chest; adrenaline and relief flood her veins. Clementine's ever-present security guard slips away like an apparition. "You should really get him a bell."

Clementine shoves the phone in Gwen's face. "I got a message from Grady."

Gwen pulls at Clementine's wrist. "What is it? Is he okay? Where is he?"

Clementine shakes her head, then pulls up Grady's message, which is a forwarded video of a monkey buying a drink from a vending machine.

"Okay," Gwen says slowly. "Maybe. Maybe it's a coded message. He's been kidnapped by monkeys who are holding him hostage in..." She plays the video again, squinting at the symbols on the vending machine. "China?"

Clementine huffs, taps at her phone, and jams it against her ear. "He better hope it's a coded message begging me to not kick his ass—Grady! Where the hell have you been?" Her voice carries through the park. "Yes, that was tonight," Clementine says, and then in an imitation of Grady's slow, deep drawl, "'Oh shoot' is right... Double would be a good start... Make sure you call Vince; you probably shaved ten years off that poor man's life... Yeah, why don't you go to bed; that way when I come over it'll make it that much easier for me to *smother you in your sleep,* Grady." She listens for a while, and her face eases by increments away from angry and worried: her eyes relax and cast downward, her mouth goes from a tight line to a frown, her jaw relaxes, and her shoulders drop. Her voice goes soft. "I know, sugar. I know."

She hangs up the phone, clicks a button so it goes dark in her hands, and then looks down at it and sighs.

"Well?" It's been a long, stressful night and Gwen is exhausted and relieved and just a little irritated. Flora will be up and starting her day in just a few hours now.

"He says he forgot. He was out with some friends. And now he's home." Clementine gives a little lift of her shoulders and a brief raise of her eyebrows. "I'm just gonna swing by his place and make sure he's all right. Let's get you home first."

They toss their cups, in which the frozen custard has melted to a thick goo. Somewhere in the trees, Kevin follows as they walk back through the park to Clementine's waiting limo.

"This was kind of fun," Clementine says at the tall stone entryway to the park. "I mean minus the wild goose chase."

Gwen hasn't had a night like this a long time, not since she and Flora moved to Nashville to settle down, buy a house, and start a family. Her days of hitting a show, then a party, then a pool hall or head shop or greasy diner are over.

"It was fun, even with the goose chase." Grady is safe and sound, and she got a night out, a rare bootleg record, some hot chicken and frozen custard, and maybe not just a client in Clementine, but a friend.

Back at home she feeds Cheese, then strips to her underwear, brushes her teeth, and falls asleep as soon as her head lands on her pillow. She sleeps through Flora getting up, sleeps through her own alarm, and bats Cheese away with a groan when she begs for more food. She sleeps through a phone call, through a few texts.

Waking is abrupt and unsettling, though she can't figure out why. The backyard is bathed in afternoon light and speckled with the shadows of dancing leaves. The house is quiet but not silent;

pipes groan, the freezer clatters a deposit of ice cubes, and Cheese meows next to her.

Cheese. Staring down unblinking from her perch on top of the headboard. "You're worse than Kevin." Gwen sits up and tosses the covers aside to pull a baggy T-shirt from her dresser. "At least he lurks around for protection and not just food."

Cheese meows again, then runs ahead of her down the stairs and into the kitchen. Gwen feeds the cat, starts water in the teakettle, and settles down to a bowl of cereal. The doorbell rings as the kettle whistles.

"You're awake now, good." Clementine is on her porch looking rested and radiant and perfectly put-together in a red pencil skirt with a yellow silk tank tucked into it, black heels, and black scarf tied high on her neck. Her hair is twisted up and her makeup is flawless.

Gwen is wearing an oversized Grumpy Cat T-shirt that Flora's mother bought her for reasons Gwen has not been able to figure out. Her hair is flattened to her head here and standing up in spikes there and she's got on no makeup.

"I just woke up," Gwen says. "Uh. Come in?"

Clementine enters, revealing Kevin's black Navigator parked at the curb. Gwen leads her into the kitchen and offers her some tea, since the kettle is still hot.

"Do you have oolong?"

Gwen picks up the boxes of tea in the cabinet. "I have black Irish breakfast tea or pregnancy tea." She looks over her shoulder, to where Clementine has settled at the table by the window. "I'll just give you breakfast tea."

"Good call," Clem says, and adds, as Gwen is pouring the water into two mugs, "Oh, I didn't know you had a cat!"

"That's Cheese. She doesn't like people usually, so consider it an honor that she's isn't hiding from you in terror." The cat is sprawled in the sun smack-dab in the middle of the kitchen, too full from her third breakfast to move.

"Her name is Cheese?"

Gwen sets down the mugs and sits across from Clementine at the little table. "Mmhmm. She had a brother named Mac, but he died a few years ago. Now her name is just a sad reminder of what once was." She sips her tea. "The Cheese stands alone."

Clementine smiles and picks up her mug. "It's hauntingly poetic."

"It is, isn't it?" Gwen finishes her cereal, and Clementine sips her tea, and this time it doesn't seem odd having Clementine in her house, sitting in her kitchen. It feels comfortable. Friendly. More than friendly.

"So there's been a development," Clem says, breaking the companionable silence. "I thought you might want to know."

Gwen swallows one last bite of Cheerios and drops her spoon. "All right, give it to me."

Clementine gives her a slowly spreading grin. "You're too much. Okay, it's about Grady. And us."

15

"**Clementine wants me** to go to Vegas." Gwen is slicing carrots for the salad, while Flora sprinkles fresh oregano from the garden into the sauce bubbling on the stove.

"Okay."

Gwen pauses with her thin-bladed knife raised in the air. "Really?"

"G, I'm beyond accustomed to you taking off at a moment's notice. I'll miss you, of course. But yes, really." Flora taste tests the sauce, licks it from her lips, then adds another pinch of minced garlic. She's changed into a long cotton dress. The material ghosts along the curves of her body; her hair is loose from her usual braid. Gwen has had trouble focusing on dinner prep since she got home from the office about thirty minutes ago.

"You should come," Gwen offers casually, knowing the answer but feeling the need to ask for the sake of her own conscience.

"To Vegas? Pass. Hey, could you slice some bread while you're at it, please." Gwen finishes cutting carrots, adds them to the salad bowl, and then grabs the loaf of Italian bread while Flora continues to tinker with the sauce. She takes another taste, smacks her lips and asks, "Is it a show or party or?"

It's none of those.

Me and Grady do these weekend getaways, just forget about the rest of the world. Indulge.

"Um. I'm still sorting out the details." She doesn't mean to lie or withhold information, but how to tell her some of it without telling her everything?

That Grady is spiraling out, maybe, possibly, probably, and needs to get away. How Clementine smiled and batted her eyelashes and asked Gwen to come, and Gwen agreed without stopping to think about Flora at all. How there's a picture of Gwen and Clementine on the front page of a prominent tabloid, backstage at the charity event holding hands and leaning together, and inside the magazine one of Clementine bent close to whisper in Gwen's ear—and another, of them leaving the event together with the caption:

Clementine Campbell's date to the Hope for Children fundraiser fuels suspicion. More than a gal pal? Close source confirms: "There has always been something between them."

How does she even begin to explain any of that? She deflects instead. "How are you feeling today?"

Flora checks the pasta, then turns off the back burner. "Better. I've kept everything down so far, and I didn't almost fall asleep at my desk during a math test." She drains the pasta; clouds of steam rise, making her cheeks flush and her hair coil into wisps at her temples. Gwen piles the bread into a basket, moves behind Flora, and kisses her neck.

"Are you feeling *better* better? Because it's been a while." Gwen kisses her way over the bend of Flora's neck, then slips a hand around her side and drags it up to the swell of her breasts and down the bow of her waist and the arch of her hip.

"One day without puking and you're all over me." Flora trembles as she says it, which lessens the impact of her chiding.

"Can't help it. You're extra sexy lately." Gwen slips her middle finger into the low bodice of the dress—the fabric gives easily—and lightly circles one erect nipple.

"I think you just want what you can't have," Flora teases.

Gwen smiles against Flora's warm skin, drops a hand in a passing brush along Flora's waist, and teases lower. "*Can* I have you?"

Flora inhales quickly, then grabs Gwen's hand and kisses her palm before stepping away to serve the pasta. "After dinner."

Gwen pouts.

"And I wanted to talk about a theme and color scheme for the baby's nursery."

Gwen sighs.

"Oh, and this bill from the insurance company. I was confused by it. I need you to call; I don't have the energy to deal with them."

Gwen groans, carrying the bread and salad bowls to the dining room like a woman heavily burdened by life's unfair treatment. "Then can I touch your tits?"

Flora dips her head and presses a smile into her hand; her ears are red at the tips. "You're too much, you know that?"

"So I've been told." It makes her stomach squirm when she remembers Clementine giving her a similar look and saying the same thing. She's walking a razor's edge, here; she feels a recklessness in her coiled, poised, and ready to strike. Gwen pushes it down, ignoring the rattle of warning.

"The sauce is perfect, Flor. Better than your mom's."

Flora's ears tinge red again. "When are you leaving?"

She's not sure. Clementine had meetings and a casual appearance and radio interviews and—Gwen's not sure what else, aside from safely depositing Grady at the studio first and foremost. She said she'd call with details, which she does when Gwen is in a lukewarm bath, settled snug inside the perfect cocoon of Flora's body, with her back against Flora's chest and her legs dropped wide inside of Flora's.

Gwen's phone trills from the bedroom as Flora rubs tight, smart circles against her clit while the water gently sloshes with the churn of Gwen's hips.

Gwen gets distracted for just a moment, then Flora finds the right rhythm and pressure. When she comes, Gwen accidentally kicks a bottle of shampoo off the ledge of the tub. "Oops." Gwen sinks, blissful and satisfied and sleepy-warm, back into Flora's arms. "The hazards of bathtub sex." She fucking loves this tub.

Flora laughs, kisses the damp crown of Gwen's head, and then pulls the plug so they can get out.

Clementine: Got Grady. Ready to go tonight?

Gwen responds in the affirmative after checking with Flora and promising she'll get her all tucked in and cozy before taking off. She gets another message immediately after that.

Nico: I'm at the airport. Heading back tonight. I need to see him.

Gwen towels off, pulls out clothes, and reaches to answer. Flora emerges still naked from the bathroom, looking for her nightgown. Gwen forgets all about Nico when she gets Flora spread and panting and pulling at her hair. She doesn't give anyone a second thought while she's got her face buried in the sweet part between Flora's thighs. It's not until Flora is wrung out and satisfied and tucked into bed that Gwen remembers to let Nico know what's going on.

Gwen: You still there?

She packs quickly, and drives to Clementine's house. From there they all take a Town Car to the airport, check in and board, and Gwen looks one last time before shutting down her phone for the flight. Nico never replies.

16

They're only in the air for about fifteen minutes before Gwen can no longer stay quiet and still, and jumps out of her oversized leather reclining chair to wander around. The private jet is so upscale it makes her house look as if they slapped some old moldy cardboard together and picked up roadside litter to decorate it. And her house is nice.

She moseys to the front and creeps on the captain until the lone flight attendant closes the door and asks pointedly if Gwen needs something. Then she shuffles all the way to the back, past the thick curtain, leaving Grady and Clementine in the center cabin where four chairs face each other with pull-down wood tables and individual flat screen televisions on hinges are angled to the side.

A bar in the back offers a selection of gourmet snacks, juices, and seltzer water in snazzy little bottles. "Don't mind if I do." She twists open a water, leaning back against the counter to slug it down.

"Oh! Hi, Kevin." She startles, but she's accepted now that she always will jump when Kevin slithers in like fog.

There's a couch in the back, too, along with one large TV screen and the bathroom. It's just as swanky as the rest of the plane, but even so Gwen recognizes it as the area for the celebrity entourage and not the celebrity. It's where she usually spends her time, the back of the jet. Metaphorically, anyway.

And now she's a... guest? A friend? A friend that Clementine touches a lot.

She should be home with Flora, a voice nags in her head. She should not be on this luxurious private jet with a woman who touches her a lot and looks at her like that. Logical, grown-up, married, soon-to-be-a-mother Gwen shouts in her head about *responsibilities* and *maturity* and *professionalism* and god, she is such a *fucking drag*. This is why she likes *doing* and not thinking; thinking is too stressful.

"Let me ask you something, Kevin. Have you even woken up and realized you have everything you ever dreamed of? The career and the girl and the house and the baby on the way? And thought—" She shrugs. "Well, I guess that's it then. This is my life. This is *it*. And now what? I look ahead and there's *nothing*."

Kevin inclines his head *just so*. Gwen takes it as encouragement to go on.

"Flora is the best thing that ever happened to me, bar none. I don't even know where I would be. Nowhere, probably, I..." Kevin's eyes track her as she paces in the little carpeted walkway between the couch and bar, and she deflates after a few passes and leans over the couch's armrest. "She is the reason I work so hard. She makes me want to be a better person because she is kind and generous and caring, and sure, she hogs the covers at night, and yes, she puts her dirty socks next to, but not in, the hamper even though it's like two centimeters farther away, and she couldn't parallel park at gunpoint, and her idea of a crazy night is using two bath bombs, but I'm glad. Because if she were actually as perfect as I think she is, I couldn't do it. I'm already terrified of disappointing her. Even though I feel like I *am*."

Kevin leans back, crosses his arms, and blinks twice.

Gwen sighs. She's aware of her own patterns. She hates letting anyone down, and when she realizes she has, despite her best efforts, she turns to sabotage instead. If she's gonna screw up, she may as well do it thoroughly. "You ever feel outside of yourself, Kevin? Like you're watching yourself head for imminent disaster but it's too late. You're helpless to your own neuroses. Like the more irrational you are, the more it makes you irrational?" She can't be the only person who sees a potential for disaster and decides to go ahead and throw a grenade at it just to get it over with.

Kevin's eyes close.

Gwen walks backward to the main cabin. "Okay, good talk."

She plops back into her seat. Grady is curled to the side in his, reclined with his eyes closed and breathing slowly. He could be asleep, though the chair rocks back and forth in a steady *tick-click, tick-click,* and his right leg jogs restlessly; for all Gwen knows, he's coiled tight with constant, humming energy even while sleeping.

Hunched forward, glossy waves of hair falling over her face, Clementine is on her laptop, typing and clicking away. She's dressed down, in slouchy gray cotton pants and a loose black tunic, deceptively simple for their steep designer price tag. Whatever she's working on has her full attention; her eyebrows are drawn in and her mouth is pulled down.

Gwen unearths her tangled earbuds from a corner of her carry-on, and puts on a little relaxation music. After spilling her guts to Kevin, maybe she can sleep. He's such a good listener. She's halfway through the third song when one earbud is forcibly popped out of her ear.

"Whatcha listening to?"

"'Suck My Left One.'"

Clementine narrows her eyes and tips up her pointed chin. "Sorry?" Gwen laughs, nods to the earbud in her hand so Clementine can listen, and starts the song over.

"It's Bikini Kill," Gwen explains as Clementine slides the earbud in.

She bobs her head. "Okay, like a girl punk band."

"More like *the* girl punk band," Gwen clarifies. She takes the earbud back and is just settling in to listen and relax when Grady pipes up, eyes still closed, still turned on his side toward the window.

"That's debatable."

Gwen blinks at him. "Uh. I don't think it is."

He cracks open one eye; the whites are shot through with snaking rivulets of red. He looks comfy in a soft blue Henley and wool slacks, his hair in a chaos of curls and several days' worth of sandy blond facial hair just on the edge of becoming a fully realized beard. He also looks as though he hasn't slept well in days.

"Patti Smith. I mean—" The eyebrow over his one open eye lifts. "I mean, *really*."

"Okay, but we're talking bands," Gwen argues. "Bands exclusively made up of women."

Grady shrugs and opens both eyes, but turns to look out the window. This is what he's been like, Clementine had told her when they first boarded and Grady hit the bathroom before takeoff:

manic highs and deep, drowning lows; and she's afraid that one of these times he's either going to soar so high no one will be able to reach him, or drop so low that it will be impossible to drag him up again.

"Who would you pick, Grady?" Clementine closes her laptop, shifting to set her chin on her fist. "Battle of the girl bands, go."

Of course. Pick something Grady loves to talk about, something that he uses as a salve on his tender, easily fractured heart, something that's always there for him: music. Gwen slides her a quick smile. Clementine winks and presses her ankle to Gwen's. Gwen sits frozen at the contact. It's friendly. Friendly ankle touching, which is completely fine and normal and friendly.

Grady is silent, looking blankly out of the dark window. Gwen sets one of her trusty Doc Martens on his seat and shoves him into a sitting position. That snaps him to attention, and casually puts Gwen's ankle out of Clementine's reach.

"Okay, okay. Well, The Runways were a pretty early contender, but whether or not they really fit in with the punk movement musically—"

"Debatable," Gwen fills in. She spends a moment enjoying the thought of a young, defiant, leather-decked Joan Jett. If they're naming 70s punk bands, though—"Siouxsie and The Banshees."

"Oh yeah." Grady perks up, just a little, eyes brighter and mouth nudging into a smile. "How about X-Ray Spex or The Slits?"

Gwen lifts her eyebrows. "All right, I'm impressed. You get street cred points for that, Grady."

He smiles crookedly, that charming, self-assured, not-quite-but-almost cocky grin he usually wears, and drawls, "Darlin', I had street cred. Finely honed in my years as a juvenile delinquent." The smile goes full-on cocky then. "And a not-so juvenile delinquent."

Gwen hasn't heard much about his wilder past, just what the tabloids claim and the little bits Nico has mentioned. It doesn't make sense to Gwen, why everyone tiptoes around Grady's life before he turned it around. Part of what makes him so great is that he overcame it, used his mistakes and pain to be a better person and make art that inspires other people. And anyway, she's curious, why not, it's late at night, and they're stuck in long flight on a private plane and the more engaged they keep Grady, maybe the less likely he is to slip away again.

"You name something crazy you did when you were younger, and I will, too."

Clementine lifts her laptop and opens it again. "Oh, I'm staying out of this. My misspent youth was performing at state fairs and talent shows."

Gwen pushes up in her chair to get her legs crossed beneath her and rubs her hands together. "Okay, I'll go. Snuck out to see a concert when I was fourteen."

Grady shakes his head. "I snuck out so often my Memaw was shocked when I *didn't* sneak out."

Oh, it's like that then? "I can do better," Gwen says. "Spray-painted an abandoned house."

Grady leans in, smirks. "Spray-painted a church."

Clementine, who is working again but apparently listening in, gasps. "*Grady.* You did not." Her face is the picture of scandalized.

"Oh yeah." Grady laughs, then shakes his head again, at himself this time. "It was uh, I believe, a very tasteful rendering of..." He looks at Gwen and wiggles his eyebrows. "A giant pair of boobies."

Gwen bursts out in laughter, then glances over at Clementine and tries to get it under control. "I'm sorry, that's—" She chokes on a laugh and finishes, "terrible. Just awful," in an entirely unconvincing way. "Okay, I... shoplifted a bunch of stupid shit."

Grady leans back, crosses one leg at the knee and waves a hand in dismissal. "I was stealing in elementary school. Come on now."

Gwen wiggles in her chair and thinks. It's exciting, in a stupid, immature way, reliving the times she was a rebellious punk, not tamping it down and expressing it only through fashion and being kick-ass at her job, but admitting how *fun* it was being stupid and carefree and untamed.

"My senior year, some friends and I would take off at lunch, go to my house and smoke weed and break into the liquor cabinet, and just do the dumbest shit. Jump off the roof and prank call people. Once we found some fireworks in the basement. It's a wonder I still have all of my fingers and both eyebrows." Gwen laughs and looks around, waiting for Grady to one-up that anecdote.

But his face has turned somber again, and he looks away to the window. "If we're gonna talk about the terrible things I did when I was drunk or stoned, that's a whole 'nother game, darlin'."

Gwen's body goes cold all over. "I'm sorry, Grady, I didn't—"

Grady doesn't respond, and when Gwen looks over at Clementine, she gives Gwen's hand a pat. She leaves her hand on Gwen's hand for a little too long, then goes back to working.

It's very late now, and if Gwen wants to get any sleep before they arrive in Vegas she should probably try soon. Clementine shuts down her computer, calls the attendant over, and asks her to bring blankets and pillows and turn off most of the lights. The chair is comfortable and leans back far enough to feel like a bed, and with the white noise of the plane slicing through the sky, Gwen starts to drift quickly.

Then from the dark, Grady's voice comes, slow and sleep-slurred. "Breaking into the liquor cabinet, though. That's cute."

Gwen glares at him, though it's too dark to see. Her totally justified, fury-fueled rebellion was not *cute*. "I had really strict parents," she defends. "Nothing I did was ever good enough and their love was conditional on me being who they wanted me to be."

Grady's voice is thick with sympathy. "Sorry, Gwen. I was just teasing." He yawns and adds offhandedly, "I guess there's more than one way to mess up your kid."

Gwen huddles in her seat and lifts the window shade to stare out at the black sky. "I guess so."

17

Seven years ago...

Gwen's hair went through many different looks after Flora started hanging out with her regularly: blue to pink, then a short purple Mohawk; green spikes, orange spikes, black spikes; a bright red, old Hollywood heartthrob style, sleek and slicked in a severe part; a shaggy, messy purple always falling into her eyes. Then she shaved it all off and started over. Her natural hair color was a dark dirty blonde, Flora learned only after several months and countless hookups.

"I like this," Flora said on one of the last nights in her dorm, when all of her stuff was packed to move in a few days, after graduation. Gwen had changed her hair again, to a short, stark platinum blonde that framed her angled face and round eyes.

"Yeah?" Gwen smirked, flipped over in the small bed, neck and ears and cheeks blotchy pink as they always were after sex. "You into blondes?"

Flora ignored the response on the tip of her tongue, the part that wanted to define this, whatever it was, but she smiled tightly instead. "I guess." What she was into was Gwen. Gwen no matter what her hair looked like: red, black, purple, rainbow. Blonde. But she didn't want to ruin it, didn't want to push until Gwen felt smothered by her and disappeared.

Flora could be laid-back about it all; she was too busy to fret much anyway, what with finishing school and preparing for grad school and finding an apartment near Pepperdine. And when she did see Gwen it was fun. Easy. They saw shows: Gwen's punk bands, where people slammed into each other, and the band spit on the audience, and someone always wound up with bloody nose or in a fight. Gwen took her shopping, to the beach. Flora took Gwen on hikes, to the farmer's market, to swap meets, to botanical gardens and art exhibits. Later, they wrapped up in each other, drinking red wine and laughing until their sides hurt on Gwen's lumpy mattress. It was as if they were expanding each other's worlds, breathing new joy into everything they did, together or apart.

It didn't need to be defined. Flora knew what they were, where they could go, what they could be, even if Gwen never would.

Flora didn't see her on graduation day; Gwen was working. She was full-time at the salon now as a hair stylist, and she also had a part-time gig at a department store as an assistant buyer. Flora's parents and sister flew in from Virginia and Maryland. She was glad she'd left home for college, glad for the people and experiences she never would have had back there, but she missed her family desperately.

"So proud of you, honey." Flora's mom engulfed her in the comfort of her soft, squeezing hug so tightly, Flora's graduation cap flopped off.

"Cecilia, Flora, let me take a picture," her dad called, snapping a photo of them together outside of the pavilion where crowds of graduates and their loved ones were still streaming out.

Her sister Selene jumped in for a few pictures, and then they hugged, and then her dad couldn't stand it any longer.

"With honors!" Flora's dad joined in the hug and said in a quivering voice, thick with emotion, "That's my girl. So, so proud."

The sunlight beamed so hot Flora sweltered in her gown, the crowd was loud and pushy, and Flora soaked up her family's love and support and belief in her. She was lucky and she knew it.

"Okay, Gabriel, if you cry, I'll cry, and the girls will cry, and we'll all be a mess." Her mom wiped at her eyes when she pulled away, though, fooling no one.

More pictures, until Flora couldn't see through the floating orbs in her vision; then they went out for dinner until her parents called it a night. "We're heading back to the hotel before your mom turns into a pumpkin."

One more hug, with her mom's short, plump frame on one side, her dad long and lanky on the other. Her sister stayed, moved to the other side of the booth, ordered more drinks, spun her wedding ring and gave Flora a significant look.

"I love the dress." They'd moved on to cocktails now that their parents were gone. Selene poked her straw into her Long Island iced tea. The crowd in the restaurant was giving way to younger, louder patrons.

"Gwen picked it out." It was seafoam green and came to mid-thigh, with bell sleeves and crochet accents. "Upscale boho," Gwen had called it. "Fits in with your overall aesthetic." Flora didn't even know she had an overall aesthetic. She tugged the skirt toward her knees beneath the booth she and Selene shared in a dim corner and smiled at the memory of trying it on, at how Gwen had insisted she needed an accent belt and the sleeves needed hemming, so Flora took it off and then—

She kept her head ducked as her face burned hot.

"You make the dumbest face when you talk about her," Selene said.

Flora tipped her head up. "Gee, thanks." Selene, tall and thin, long-faced and handsome, took after their dad. Flora had their mother's zaftig shape, her round and friendly features. Flora frowned. What weird face did she make about Gwen?

"No, like. A good dumb face," Selene tried to explain. Flora sipped her drink with her eyebrows raised. Selene went on, "Like you're *really* into her."

She was, but it just wasn't that simple. "We're keeping things casual."

"Oh, please," Selene burst out. Usually Flora loved having a sister she was so close to, a best friend but even better, someone who knew her better than herself sometimes and wasn't afraid to call her out. This was not one of those moments. Selene poked her straw in Flora's face, and sticky drops of liquid fell to the tabletop. "Nothing about that dumb face says casual."

Flora looked at her drink: a frozen strawberry daiquiri, now more a puddle of pink than a festive cocktail. She sighed. "I just don't know what Gwen wants." She couldn't insist on some kind of commitment only for Gwen to feel suffocated or trapped; then Flora would risk losing her entirely.

Gwen made her feel... as if she had been coasting. Gwen kissed her and she felt a rush of excitement and energy, Gwen smiled at her and her heart soared, Gwen— Gwen fucked her because what else could she call that, the things they did that made Flora squirm and pulse just thinking about it. She couldn't go back to coasting; she couldn't take that chance.

Selene stabbed the straw back in her drink with a rattle of ice. "And what about what you want? I know you Flora; you aren't happy with casual. Don't be afraid to stand up for what you want just because you're easygoing."

Flora swallowed a knot in her throat. "What if she doesn't want the same things?"

A group of students at the bar cheered loudly at the hockey game on the huge flat-screen TV. Selene waited out the noise, then gave Flora a no-nonsense look. "I guess you have to decide if you want to be with someone who isn't willing to meet you halfway. I mean, is 'my way or the highway' really the type of relationship you want?"

Flora stared at the scuffed tabletop and stirred her melting drink while the crowd groaned at the game. Of course she didn't want that kind of relationship, but up until right now she'd considered it the better of the two options: that or nothing.

"Anyway," Selene said, smacking her palms flat on the table. "Subject change. So Kahlil and I have decided to start trying for a baby next year. Don't tell mom and dad. I don't need that kind of pressure and meddling."

"Oh my god!" Flora had to move to the other side of the booth to squish against her sister and squeal. "Selene, that's amazing!"

She didn't really expect to see Gwen until well after she'd moved, but there she was, bright and early the next morning, moving day, with a bag of muffins and two chai teas in travel mugs. "Thought we could use some energy before loading the truck."

"Oh." Flora said, taking a cup and muffin. She sipped the tea: a touch of sugar and cream, just the way she always took it. "I thought you were working."

Gwen shrugged. Her hair was still peroxide blonde. "I told them my girlfriend was moving, and I needed the morning off. They were cool with it."

Flora watched Gwen as she tested different boxes, hefting a small one full of books against her chest. *Girlfriend.* "That okay?" Gwen said, giving Flora a concerned, suddenly unsure look. "I mean, did you just want your friends to help or..."

"No." Flora shook her head, giddy happiness or caffeine or excitement or all of them rushing inside her. "No that's—this is what I want."

18

Even after a mere four hours of restless sleep on the plane, Gwen rushes into the room, drops her bags, twirls, and takes off to check out the place before it disappears like the mirage it seems to be.

Clementine's hotel room is *astounding*. Hotel room isn't even the right name for it, it's... a fucking *palace*. Taking up the top two floors of one of Vegas's most extravagant hotels, it is not just huge, not just luxurious: it has a full living room equipped with a sectional sofa so large it takes up an entire wall, a marble fireplace, and floor to ceiling windows with an incredible view of The Strip and beyond. The dining table is made of petrified wood and bronze in swirls and whorls and variegated natural edges, and is so beautiful Gwen can't imagine doing something as barbaric as eating on it.

There are three full bedrooms with three full baths, and walk-in closets big enough to drive a car into. Nico would lose his mind over such closets. There's even a golden spiral staircase, winding up to the loft where two of the bedrooms are located. There is a *butler*.

And she thought the drive from the airport in a Rolls Royce and the private check-in with complimentary champagne was swanky.

Oh, Gwen wishes Flora were here, especially when she wanders out to the private pool deck and spots the hot tub with colored flashing lights and massage jets. They could put bathtub sex to shame out here.

The morning is already crackling with dry heat; the sun, unhindered by a single cloud, shimmers on the pool. Gwen sinks into one of the many outdoor couches under an awning, props her feet on a table, and stretches her hands back behind her head.

"You look comfy." Clementine saunters out of the glass door in a bikini with her hair up in a messy topknot.

Gwen glances over, then looks away; a flash of heat prickles across her skin. "Just enjoying a moment of hedonism." She sighs. "I'm sure my room is fine and everything."

Clementine lowers herself onto her belly on one of the deck chairs lining the intricately tiled pool's edge. "Oh god, girl. Just stay here, I know you want to."

"Was I that obvious?"

Clementine looks over her shoulder, spine curving in, chest pushing out. "You were singing 'A Moment Like This' to one of the beds. So, yeah. That obvious."

Gwen licks her dry lips, fights the heaviness of her eyelids. It's an enticing offer. Dangerously enticing. "I should probably take a nap, get some food. Call Flora." Sleep and food. Checking in with her wife. That's probably important.

"Good. Then nap out here. I'll order us some breakfast. You call Flora while we wait." Clementine reaches out with one slender arm to pat the deck chair next to hers. Her tone doesn't leave any room to argue.

"I'll get my bathing suit."

Gwen takes the golden staircase up to one of the rooms, tests out the king-sized bed and very nearly doesn't get up again. She does sing to it once more. Then she fires off a quick text— *made it here, miss you*—and descends the staircase back to the pool.

Grady is there now, after getting settled in his own room and changed into a suit that barely covers the essentials. He's all muscles and skin and wiry golden hair, his face freshly shaven, and he's eating a breakfast burrito in the chair beside Clementine's. He looks better, Gwen thinks, more relaxed; or at least he's distracted enough to look better and more relaxed.

They eat cinnamon brioche French toast and bagels with lox and fresh berries. They drink cold cherry-ginger-infused tea and freshly squeezed orange-mango juice.

"Anything else, Ms. Campbell?" *The Butler* asks, after everything has been cleared away.

"Yes," Clementine says, stretched out on her back. "If you could roll that awning out a little more." The butler hits a button on his ever-present remote. It controls nearly everything in the suite. "And," Clementine continues, flashing Gwen a grin, "we'll take a deep-tissue massage each."

In the shade, muscles relaxed and loose from her neck to her toes, the breeze from a fan caressing her back and thighs and the side of her face not buried in the pillow of her arms, Gwen mumbles, "Not becoming a country music star was the worst decision of my life." She's so relaxed and blissed-out from her massage that it's a slurred mishmash of syllables.

Clementine and Grady talk in hushed, clipped tones. Grady wants to go off on his own, and Clementine won't let him. Gwen thinks that's what they're saying, but her synapses are sluggish and she keeps slipping in and out of consciousness; she's sleep deprived and was turned into putty by an Amazon with magical giant hands named Freya.

The next thing she knows, Gwen is in the pool, and she's not alone. The heat and bright sun are making everything glimmer around her like a mirage, as if she's encased in a floating bubble with the sound muted and her vision blurred; the scene is unreal and too real, all at once. Gwen moves her body, and the water glides and swirls, a caress over every inch of her skin.

She's naked.

There's no time to worry about that, though, because Clementine is here, on the steps in her little white bikini, and Gwen is overwhelmed by urgency; she has to go, she shouldn't be here, something else is so much more important, but she can't remember what; her head feels full of cotton batting and her body is like liquid. She churns in the water but can't go anywhere.

"Are you ready?" is all Gwen can to think to say. She doesn't know why.

Clementine winks, pinches the tie holding the bikini bottom together on her hip, and reaches back to the tie for the top. "I'm always ready for you, sugar."

Clementine is graceful and slender everywhere; her breasts are round and firm and high, with small pink nipples; the rest of her body is tanned bronze. Her stomach is smooth and sloping; her legs are long, toned, and sleekly muscular. Every curve and mound and dip of her is enticingly exposed.

Gwen stares. Closes her eyes to stop staring. When she opens them again, Clementine is in front of her, pressing her fingers to the small of Gwen's back and pushing her forward, pressing the length of her body against Gwen's when she's close enough. She says, "Don't let 'em see you sweat," before kissing her.

It's rough and strange, and Gwen can't get ahead of anything that's happening. Why can't she think or speak, and why does it feel as if heat is lashing down her spine and searing her skin when she's floating in the cool deep end of the pool?

Clementine's lips are demanding on hers, her tongue spears roughly inside, her teeth catch sharply on Gwen's bottom lip, and it's nothing like kissing Flora, nothing like the love and connection and care of Flora. Flora.

"Flora," Gwen gasps into Clementine's mouth. No, no, no. This is wrong. This is—

"Hey, G." Behind her, Flora's breasts press into Gwen's back, Flora's hand slips into the space between Gwen's body and Clementine's body to knead and stroke them both.

"Flora?"

Familiar lips trace the curve of Gwen's neck, and Flora murmurs into the hot, sweat-slick skin there. "Are you happy?"

Gwen tries to twist around and kiss Flora, but she's immobilized between their bodies, trapped in the surreal suspension of the water. Instead, Clementine cranes over Gwen's shoulder and kisses Flora in the same roughly claiming way she'd kissed Gwen.

Gwen groans and her hips churn in the water, desperate for something to rub her aching pussy against, *someone*, limbs and naked slippery skin and mouths and hands everywhere.

"Are you happy?" Flora says again, in front of Gwen in a flash, hiking one of Gwen's legs up over the bend of her hip. Clementine is behind Flora now, kissing and biting on Flora's jaw and neck and ears, lifting the full mounds of Flora's breasts in her hands. Gwen watches as Clementine pinches and pulls at Flora's nipples, then slips a hand down between them, rubbing Flora, rubbing Gwen, making them both gasp and writhe in the water.

"I don't, I don't—" She can't *think* and everything is strange and hazy, and why is Flora here in Vegas, why does she keep asking if Gwen is happy, and how is this happening? But god, she's close, a tight build in her belly and groin reaching and reaching, the squelch and slap of their bodies, all three of them wet and flushed and moving together and the way Flora and Clementine looked when they kissed, Clementine demanding and rough, Flora giving herself to it so sweetly.

So, so close. If she could just—a little more. A little harder. A little faster. But it builds and builds and builds to nothing, and then Clementine is gone and Flora is gone, vanished like a hallucination. And Gwen is alone in the pool, panting and throbbing and bereft.

"Gwen?"

When she flutters her eyes open, it's to the blurry sight of Clementine's lean, sculpted stomach in front of her face. Gwen scrambles to sit up with a shocked inward breath.

"You okay? Looked like you were having a bad dream or something."

Gwen smacks her dry mouth a few times and rubs at her eyes to clear the sleep and confusion away. She's in the lounge chair. At the pool. Bone dry and dreaming about threesomes. She can feel how swollen and slick she is. She crosses her legs tightly.

"Yeah. Bad dream." Gwen goes for a chuckle but it sounds like the croak of a bullfrog. Clementine tilts her head.

"Well, if you wouldn't mind, now that you're awake?" In Clementine's outstretched hand is a bottle of tanning oil. "I want to get a little more sun before I head out."

Alarm bells go off in Gwen's head. Panicked, she searches for Grady; Clementine and Grady are close, he can slather her with oil; but he's swimming laps in the pool. His muscled body glides through the water like a torpedo.

Clementine is still holding out the bottle of oil and staring at her. Gwen takes it with shaky hands and tries to talk herself down. Clementine stretches out on her stomach in the sun, and Gwen kneels next to her.

Okay. They didn't *actually* have a threesome, she reminds herself, squirting a dollop of the oil into her cupped palm, though why she was dreaming about it, in vivid detail, may still be a problem. Gwen rubs the slippery oil onto Clementine's shoulders and neck, making her skin glisten. Fine. This is fine. She's handling this just fine. Then Clementine reaches back and unties the string of her top, and the thin fabric settles open at her sides.

Gwen looks away, clenches her jaw, and squeezes another dollop of oil into her hand. Too much squirts out, and Clementine shifts at the harsh noise, her back bows and arches, her chest lifts off the chair, her bikini top falls loose—

No. Danger, danger.

Clementine is attractive, *obviously*. Anyone with a primitive lizard brain can see that. But as far as being *attracted to her*—Gwen likes bodies, likes the variety of beauty in them, can look at Grady, even, or Nico, and enjoy their flat planes and sculpted muscles and strong jaws. She can appreciate Clementine, have a silly crush on her, can think about her body because she has to put clothes on her body. It stops there, though. It has to stop there.

It was just a dream. It doesn't mean anything because it *can't*.

"You doin' all right over there, sugar?"

Gwen looks at her oil-covered hand, looks at Clementine's naked torso, and then stands on wobbly legs and says, "I think I'm dehydrated. I'm gonna head inside."

Once inside, Gwen washes her hand with cool water, splashes some on her face and takes a long drink of iced tea. She presses the cold glass to her forehead, and still doesn't feel any less overheated.

19

"**What are you** wearing?"

"Wow, we're just jumping right into it then. Okay."

On the grainy rectangle of Gwen's phone screen, Flora shakes her head and smiles in that lovingly bemused way she so often does. Across the room, Grady is folded into a chair, one leg bent up beneath him, the other with a guitar perched on it. He picks a frantic bluegrass tune. Clementine is out at a radio interview and a private industry party. Gwen helped her get ready with shaking hands, then took a very cold shower.

"No, really, what on earth are you wearing?"

Gwen smooths her hands down the robe she found in one of the spa-like bathrooms. "Oh, this old thing?" It's gorgeous raw silk, likely cost upwards of eight hundred dollars and, on her tiny frame, looks like a beautiful, magnificent tent. Gwen waggles her eyebrows at Flora on her phone screen. "Are you into it?"

Flora purses her lips, and Gwen wants to kiss her. The dream flashes into her head again, how Clementine kissed Flora, how she kissed Gwen. After a cold shower and another nap, during which she dreamed about nothing at all, she still can't shake it.

"It kind of looks like that muumuu my Nona wears. You know the one," Flora finally says.

Gwen frowns as she picks at the robe. It does kind of look like that garishly bright muumuu Flora's grandmother wears in the mornings. "So... it's *not* doing anything for you?"

Flora laughs. She's in the kitchen, backlit by her sunny garden, where the last blooms of summer still hang on in the rapidly cooling transition to fall. In this light her hair is highlighted deep golden red, and her eyes are warm amber.

"I miss you," Gwen says. It's true, regardless of what her subconscious may have to say about it.

"I was surprised you didn't call right away." Flora shifts her phone from one hand to the other; the lag makes her face blur and freeze for a second.

"I kinda crashed. Jet lag, didn't sleep much on the plane." That's mostly true. "Oh, and Clementine's room is insane. Like luxurious to a truly ridiculous and unnecessary degree."

"So, like Vegas?"

Oh, her sweet Flora, who likes the simple, gentle pleasures of life: a long hike on a spring day, waterfalls, the perfect tomato growing in her garden, a cozy fire and a good book. She's down-to-earth and mellow, yet married to Gwen for some crazy reason.

Speaking of a cozy fire. "Flora, look. The fire is remote controlled." Gwen presses a button on the remote that's resting on the side table, and the fire magically roars to life from the black stones. She clicks it back off. Flares it up once more. "Wacky, right?"

Grady's plucky bluegrass song comes to an abrupt stop, and Gwen watches as he stands, finds the remote, and begins to flip through channels on the TV, which is as large as a mattress and nearly as thin as a sliver of onion skin.

"That's great," Flora says. "Hey listen, I need some input on the nursery. I know it's early still, but—" Gwen drags her focus back to Flora as the image of her on the screen bumps and swoops; she's walking somewhere, upstairs it looks like, still talking.

Clementine bursts into the suite, strides through the living room, and points at Gwen. "Let's go shopping, yes? Okay. I'm gonna change." And she walks right on through the dining room and kitchen, past the pool deck and into the master bedroom.

Grady is still flipping through the channels, and Gwen hears rapid, loud bursts of shows and commercials and commentary, flashes of programming so fast he can't possibly be catching what they are. The fireplace roars in the air-conditioned room. Gwen is distracted. Does Clementine want to shop for fun or shop for an event? Gwen didn't think she had anything lined up the rest of the day, but maybe she should call Nico. Oh shit, she forgot to call Nico.

Flora is still talking, and Gwen has barely caught a word. When she focuses back on the screen, Flora is in the extra bedroom closest to theirs—a guest room, but not for much longer—holding up a long sheet of paint colors. "Or this one?"

"Um," Gwen says, to stall for time. "Show me again?"

Flora sighs a little, but holds up a series of paint options for the wall. "Deep Taupe. Maple Sugar. Mystic Beige—"

Gwen mmhmms after the first two and scowls after the third. *Mystic Beige?*

"—Burlap. Peanut Shell. Oklahoma Wheat—"

Gwen starts to answer, but Grady's constant channel flipping and the heat of the fire are making her twitchy.

"Must you?" she says to Grady. He shrugs, turns off the TV, and then goes back to plucking at his guitar. "Honey, I don't—they're all beige. Don't babies need stimulating, contrasting colors for brain development or something?"

"Well, the research now suggests that babies need low-stress, soothing environments," Flora explains. "Earth colors." She flips through the paint samples. "Why, do you think it's too soothing?"

What she thinks is that they have plenty of time to decide between light beige or medium beige or slightly darker medium beige, and *Mystic Beige* which is not actually mystic, not even close, and all of them are tied for dead last on the list of what Gwen would ever paint a room. She doesn't want to hurt Flora's feelings, so she just says, "Whatever you want, okay? I'm fine with whatever."

Flora's face goes stony for just a flash. Then she looks away, just off the side of the phone screen and says, "Of course you are."

"Flora..." Gwen's not even sure what she did, but she certainly did something.

"You're busy. I'll talk to you later, okay?"

"Flora." But the phone beeps, and Flora's face disappears. Gwen sends Nico a text: *where are you?* Then she shuts off her phone, tosses it to the side, and finally snaps the fireplace back off. She drops her head back against the couch and puts her feet up on the coffee table, and Grady starts an up-tempo song. Maybe Flora could feel her guilt over that stupid dream through the video call. Flora's always been so good at reading her, better than she can read herself.

"You ever have a weird sex dream?"

Grady pauses his song and looks up, his curls spiraling down his forehead. "Sure." He starts to play again, fingers tripping expertly over the strings, and then the song slows and goes quiet. "Once I dreamed I went to a brothel, but they wouldn't let me pick just one person, I had to take all of them. Then just as we were all getting into it, they all turned into cat-people. Just stood there in a circle and stared at me while I was naked and ready to go. It was scary as hell. And I still woke up. You know. *Happy.*"

Gwen flops her head to the side to look at him. "That is definitely weird. And a little concerning."

Grady rolls his eyes in a manner so disdainful he could only have learned it from Nico. "It's just a dream. Just your brain spitting out nonsense." He strums the guitar fast, almost frantically, but seems totally comfortable talking about sex and weird sex dreams.

Gwen smashes her cheek into the armrest and watches him. Nico has to be totally shit-faced before he'll talk to her about this stuff. "Can I ask you something?"

With his lips curled, Grady nods his head to the music, slow and bluesy now.

She loves his music, always has. There's this raw, soulful quality to his songs. He doesn't hold back; he really, really means every word and note. He's like that with Nico, the way he loves him, the way he looks at him and touches him.

Grady doesn't look up or stop playing, but he inclines his head. "I'm a little afraid to say yes." His smile turns teasing.

"Nothing too raunchy," Gwen says. "Now that you're just tapping the one ass on the regular—or is it the other way around? I never got clarification on that—what was I... Oh, right, do you ever miss women? Like, their soft skin. Or the way they smell." Gwen hums and closes her eyes. "Boobs."

Grady sets his guitar down between his knees and rests his hands on the headstock. "They do smell good." He smiles; it's kind of sad. Wistful. "Nico smells good. Tastes good, too."

"I'll take your word for it. But. Okay. If you're with Nico, and you're never with another woman. Never. You're fine with that?"

Grady pushes his hair back and looks at Gwen with those intense blue eyes so steadily it makes her stomach squirm. "Think of it this way, right," he finally says. "If I'm with Nico the rest of my life—and I wanna be—I'll never be with another man. Just like I'll never be with another woman. I'll never be with another person; that's the whole deal with monogamy."

Gwen sits up and presses her fingertips to her mouth and coos, "Aw, Grady. You want to be with Nico for the rest of your life; that's so exciting."

He doesn't smile, he sighs. He picks at the tightly wound strings just below the pegs with a dog whistle-high *plink plink.* "He'll be on his way here soon, so I guess we'll see if Nico still wants that."

20

Clementine comes into the room while the air still hangs heavy and sad, puts her hands on her hips, and says, "Are you going shopping in a robe three times too big for you or what?" She snaps her fingers. "Go change, girl!"

"It's a relaxed fit, okay?" Gwen defends, then stands to untie and remove the robe, dropping it on the couch behind her in a perfectly timed flourish. "Voilà!" Gwen wiggles her fingers up and down her sides to point out that she is dressed; she is wearing red tartan patchwork pants and a white heart-print tank cut open at the sides, with a black bandeau bra beneath.

"Just let me pick some boots." As she searches among several pairs of black boots she brought—classic, studded, buckled, knee-high—she can hear Grady, hyperactive and aimless again, flipping through the channels. "You need an activity," she tells him, after finding the Docs she had in mind. "Come with us."

Clementine is at the door, dressed in stilettos and a deep plum strapless sheath more lavish—and tighter—than the dress Gwen recommended for the industry event. Where exactly are they shopping? Paris?

"Yeah, Grady. You can hold our stuff," Clementine says, with a bright smile.

The TV zaps off. "I reckon I don't have anything better to do."

"That's the spirit!" Gwen mock-punches his arm, connecting with hard muscle. She winces as they walk into the hallway, the three of them plus Kevin who was, of course, waiting right outside the door. "God, you're built like a tree trunk."

Grady chuckles and yanks her close to his chest, and this is how Gwen learns that when she's bent at the waist and tucked into Grady's solid side, she fits, just right, under his armpit.

Clementine works during the entire ride. She is either on her phone negotiating and planning or pausing to smile at Gwen, or to play with Gwen's hair, or to press her knee to Gwen's. Clementine has been hustling almost nonstop, save for a couple hours by the pool, a shower, and the ten minutes she sat on a stool at the bar in her room with her beauty team. She must run on sheer determination alone. Grady chatters and points out all of his favorite Vegas spots, of which there are many. He's energetic on even less sleep than Gwen managed, but then *he* seems to run on nothing but Mello Yello and moxie.

When they arrive at an underground, hidden entrance to The Venetian, Clementine slips her arm through Gwen's and breathlessly explains how The Shoppes is her favorite Vegas spot for high-end fashion. Gwen lets herself be tugged along. Grady is behind them, keeping pace and looking around with his hands stuffed in his pockets. Inside it's meant to look like Venice, complete with intricate, old-world Italian architecture, a canal with gondolas and gondoliers in striped shirts and red neckerchiefs, and a ceiling painted like the Sistine fucking Chapel. So ridiculous. So over-the-top. So awesome.

So Vegas.

They've attracted a crowd already, a gang of people with their phones out to snap pictures and take video that swells in number as they make their way to the store Clementine set her sights on.

By the time they get to the entrance of the Tory Burch store, it's a mob scene, a sea of people pushing and shoving and shouting, trying to get an autograph or a picture or just an acknowledgment—good or bad attention doesn't seem to matter much, as long as Clementine or Grady notices them.

"This is why me and Grady don't go out in public together much anymore."

The crowd is in a frenzy, and now there are paparazzi, too, standing around the outside of the store with their huge, long zoom-lensed cameras and professional-grade video equipment. Kevin is a vigilant shadow no less than one step away from Clementine at all times. Gwen has never been more grateful for his presence; the mob is terrifying, and grabs at them, pushing, pleading.

Gwen isn't as wary as Nico. Even now he appears in public with a grim reluctance; he accepts all the attention as part of the package, but he doesn't like it. Gwen hasn't had to deal with it in the same way he has, the intrusiveness and lies and gossip and men in bushes taking their pictures. But the mob is pushing ever closer, and cameras are right in their faces, flash after blinding flash. Gwen ducks away, suffocated and scared, and a hand grabs hers.

Long, elegant fingers, soft skin. She threads their fingers together, pulls Gwen close and sets her temple against Gwen's hair. Gwen stands, shocked and frozen in the spotlight; then Clementine squeezes her hand.

Clementine is calm and cool under fire. Grady grins and greets fans, hugs them and takes pictures; he is engaged in full-on star mode. So Gwen stands there, holds tight to Clementine's hand and turns, looks over one shoulder and smiles stiffly. It's only a minute, maybe two, but when Kevin blocks them from view with his massive body and steers them inside the empty store, Gwen can barely see for the flashes blocking her vision, can barely hear for the ringing in her ears. She's exhausted and overwhelmed; her head spins.

Only now does Gwen realize what that could have looked like back there. And she and Clementine have already been dubbed an item in the tabloids, thanks to an anonymous source.

When Clementine kisses Gwen's cheek, it barely registers. She flounces off to shop, beckoning Gwen to come with her. Grady makes himself comfortable on the counter and starts to knock a rhythm against it with his heels and knuckles, and someone hands Gwen a bottle of water. If only it were a bottle of wine instead.

"Life in the spotlight," Grady trills.

Gwen swigs her water. "It's terrible."

"You get used to it." Grady taps a quick beat. "Is what it is."

Gwen can't imagine getting accustomed to this flip side of glamour, the real price of luxury. Clementine's life is her career, and her career her life, because every single moment, private and public, is dedicated to it. Everything is calculated, intentional. Something about that tugs at Gwen. "You guys were really never together?"

"Nah." He's still drumming away on the counter, now with a pen he found. "But I think it was easier on her when they thought we were. She hates when they ask who she's dating. Like it wasn't a lie but, she could do worse than me, so she let 'em think what they wanted, ya know?" He winks and drums on his own head.

"Right," Gwen says.

Clementine breezes past again. Gwen picks out a blue and white, vertical-striped embroidered cotton caftan, a fringed jacquard knit wrap dress, a belted, high-collared linen jacket, and orange guipure lace shorts. After she hands them off for Clementine to try on, Gwen circles back to the cash register.

Grady is now sprawled on top of it with one arm dangling limply to the side.

"Having fun?" Gwen pokes his bicep.

"Barrels," he says to the ceiling. "How am I bored in Vegas? I should have brought my knitting."

Gwen props herself on the counter near his knees and jokes, "The problem is that Nico isn't here to wear you out." He frowns, and Gwen elbows his leg. "He's not coming all the way here to break up with you, Grady. He may keep the sordid details locked up tight, but I know for a fact that he's ass-over-elbows about you. He loves you."

Grady's fingers twitch, grasping at nothing. "People can love you with all their heart, and still shatter yours apart."

Gwen scans up his prone body to his sad, stormy face. "Isn't that a song lyric?"

His mouth twitches up. "Maybe."

Gwen cranes to look past the closed gates of the store where the crowd is still gathered. She can't face them again; she's barely recovered. They have today and tonight; then they take off back to Nashville. Clementine has another event or party or interview to attend after this—Gwen's not sure, really—and she has done her part for now. Anyway, Clementine's definitely being weird, and Flora is being weird, and this mall, with its canal and Michelangelo'd ceilings, is weird. Gwen's dream was weird. Vegas is *weird*.

"Hey. Let's go do something fun and crazy."

Grady lifts his head. "Yeah?"

"Sure. We're in Vegas. We both have super serious relationship stuff on the bleak horizon here. For a few hours, let's just—fuck it, you know? Relive our rebellious and idiotic youth."

Grady pushes up to his elbows and smiles slowly, cocky and satisfied. "Now you're speakin' my language, darlin'." He slides off the counter.

This is when Gwen learns that Grady can swing her over his shoulder like a gunnysack filled with feathers and carry her out of the store.

21

"**Nico can never** know about this place," Gwen says as she steps out of the cab. They've taken it about twenty minutes outside of town, down one lone road through pale sand and scrabbly trees and nothing to where the glitz and glamour and hallucinogenic hyperreality of Las Vegas turns into flat, parched land.

They've arrived at a racetrack and a hangar stocked with the most expensive and exotic muscle cars available—some are not even on the market yet. A large sign on the building reads: *Fantasy Racing.*

"I know, we'd probably end up taking at least one home with us," Grady says. Gwen falls into step beside him, and then he pauses and adds, "Or he'd take one home with him, I guess."

"Grady—" Gwen starts, but he's already moving on, taking long strides into the shadow of the hangar and only stopping to shake hands with the guy who comes to get them set up.

"You pick," Grady says, after all the introductory explanations and paperwork are finished, and charms the guy into letting them drive without an instructor. He nods at the lineup of luxury cars, all shining and sleek, red, black, and silver, even a few neon green, yellow, and electric blue.

"Oh, I don't, I don't know much about cars." Enough to change a tire and check the oil and jump the battery. Enough to know what Ferraris and Lamborghinis and Porsches and Aston Martins are, but not why she should choose one over the other.

"Just pick one 'cause it's sexy," Grady says, his voice dropping to a purr. He bumps Gwen with his elbow. "They won't be offended."

Pick a sexy car, okay. Gwen nibbles her lips and tucks her hands behind her back as she walks the rows of cars and considers them. She stops at one on the end of the fifth row, at a shining red Ferrari. It's low to the ground, not too wide but not compact; slinky curves coil from front to back, arch over the front tires, bow in the center, and then crest up over the rear.

Gwen reaches to touch the hood, pauses, and then delicately drags one finger up and around the supple round shape of one side, then over the other. "This one."

"This is the 458 Italia," Pete, who's showing them around, says. "You won't find a sexier car than this."

"That a V-8?" Grady says, and Pete pops the hood. Grady gives a low whistle. Pete and Grady discuss horsepower and rpms and torque, and Gwen nods along, but she's really just itching to get inside. She loves her cute little Mini Cooper, but this thing makes it look like a Little Tikes Cozy Coupe.

"Hey, Small Fry," Grady calls; a shiny red key fob is tossed at her head. "You're up first."

She doesn't appreciate the height joke, but when she and Grady climb into the car and he beams at her, she's just glad to see him so happy: not fake happy, not trying to be happy, not uncomfortably-hyperactive happy, but wearing that huge, sunshiny grin she's used to seeing.

The inside of the car is just as gorgeous as the outside: smooth, supple leather, a futuristic-looking steering wheel and dash with button and lights and knobs that Pete explains and Gwen vaguely understands. She slides the key into the little slot, thumbs the engine button, and breathes, "Oh, wow."

The car rumbles to life like a satisfied cougar.

"Do you need a booster seat?" Grady teases.

"*Ha. Ha.*" Gwen glares at him, then cranes her neck to look over the console. These bucket seats are a little low. Well, she's committed now.

Pete hands them both helmets, double-checks that they're strapped in correctly, and reviews all the buttons and gizmos on the wheel, as well as the gearshift, turn signal, wipers and radio controls, and the easy-to-use paddle shifter. Gwen puts it in gear, eases off the brake, and then creeps out of the hangar and onto the track.

Clutching the steering wheel tightly, her heart tapping furiously against her sternum and palms sweaty, she takes a deep breath and waits for the signal.

"You gotta give her a lil' tease," Grady says, at ease in the seat beside her. His helmet muffles his words, but his voice is loud and clear in the speakers inside her own helmet. "Play with her to warm her up."

So she flips the gear to neutral, presses down on the accelerator, and the engine snarls out a growl. "Oh my god, I'm all tingly." She does it again. Oh, that *is* sexy.

Grady smacks her helmet and laughs. "Now you get it."

The first loop around the track Gwen takes slowly, carefully, getting used to the car and the way it handles. But it's so responsive and smooth that it's easy to just let go and let loose, to go faster and faster, making quick zips around the turns and revving the engine as hard as she can through the straightaways. She's up to speeds that make their bodies press to the seats and shake with the force of it, so dangerous that one tiny mistake would end them and the car in an instant, and that just makes it even more exciting.

Her ten laps are over in a flash, and then she and Grady swap. She screams and laughs through Grady's crazy race around the track. He adds some terrifying drifts and ticks the steering wheel back and forth to wiggle the car smoothly from one side of the track to the other.

As they slow to a coasting crawl and bring the car back, Gwen wants to call Flora, wants to take a picture with this beautiful, erotic car and tell her how it made her think of her wife; and she thinks about how Flora would duck her head and hide a smile as though embarrassed, but Gwen would know she secretly loves it. And even though Flora would want nothing to do with driving this car, she would be excited for Gwen anyway, but would still worry and tell her to be careful and take the turns slower, because one of them has to be sensible.

Flora is going to be an amazing mother. She's patient, nurturing, and calm; has to be, to handle a classroom full of seven year-olds with ease. Gwen can see it in the way Flora is with her nieces, and in Flora's loving, close relationship with her own mother.

Gwen's mother has been disappointed in her since her first breath, taken ten days past her due date and after twenty-five hours of breech labor. She's heard the story a million times—as if Gwen, still in the womb, just *had* to be difficult. Her whole life she's been either crushed under the desperate need to please her parents, or openly defiant of their expectations because she will never meet them. They're disappointed in her clothes, her hair, her personal life, her lack of a college degree, and her unusual career. At best she has a tepid, distant relationship with her mother. She has *no idea* what a normal, healthy mother-and-child dynamic is.

Thank god she has Flora. Thank god she can just leave all the parenting decisions to her. Gwen tugs the helmet off and is immediately desperate for another jolt of adrenaline, to be held in a moment of *doing* where nothing else matters.

When they head back to the parking lot to wait for their cab, they're both red-faced and wild-eyed and giggling at nothing. Her hair is in sweaty spikes all over her head, and Grady's curls are smashed flat.

"That was so fucking fun," Gwen says, hopping up and down like a super bounce ball.

A cab comes into view. "All right, Small Fry, your turn to pick."

She's having such a great time that she lets the annoying nickname stay, and she knows exactly what she wants to do next.

22

"A roller coaster?"

The cab dropped them off at a gas station just before The Strip so they could get something to drink: Grady's ubiquitous Mello Yello, of course, and for Gwen a strawberry Yoo-Hoo. That's what she would always get at two a.m. to refuel after the concerts she'd sneak out to see.

"Not *a* roller coaster," Gwen corrects, keeping pace with Grady on the sidewalk and squinting against the hot sun beating down on them. "*All* of the roller coasters."

Grady takes a swig of his soda. "Not bad. All right, let's do it."

At the next corner they turn, heading first to the New York-New York Hotel and Casino for the coaster that rises from the top like a serpent, winding around and behind the fake Statue of Liberty.

"Flora and I came to Vegas a few years ago and went on this one," Gwen explains. "And afterward she swore off roller coasters for good. But then again, she thinks Great Thunder Mountain at Disneyland is a thrill ride, even though the kindergartener in front of us called it lame. She's so cu—" And Gwen cuts off her rambling with a gasp and comes to a dead stop on the sidewalk. "*Oh* my god."

"What? What happened?" Grady retreats the few steps he'd gone on ahead; his eyebrows and mouth are drawn flat.

"That's—there's… Oh my god." Gwen presses both hands to her mouth and squeaks. "There's an In-N-Out Burger, Grady. In-N-Out Burger!"

"Oh." Grady gives her an odd look, then turns. "Oh yeah, so there is. Want—"

Gwen is already dragging him toward the familiar swooping red and yellow sign on the red-roofed building a few blocks down. Inside, it smells like deep-fried grease and charred meat and *home*. She downs her Double-Double Animal Style and cheese fries like a starving gerbil, moaning obscenely several times, which earns her a few odd looks from the other customers and an amused grin from Grady.

He clears the wrappers and comes back with a hand held out. "Ready, Small Fry?"

Gwen lets him pull her up; she's deliciously bloated and slow. "Ready. But I'm calling you Double Beef if you're sticking with the Small Fry thing."

Grady responds with a loud belly laugh, and someone across the restaurant takes pictures of him in a private moment of genuine joy that feels stolen now. Gwen glances back to scowl at the nosy, intrusive stranger, but Grady has moved on, out the door and back on his way.

On the roller coasters, they climb up steep hills, careen around bends, tear around loops and corkscrews, fly down hills, and spin upside down. One coaster hangs over the edge of a high-rise resort and dangles them nine hundred feet in the open air, and one slides down a track aimed straight at the ground way below, stopping just as they're sure the car and all of its occupants will end up a mere splat on the pavement.

As they're getting strapped into a ride that will launch them, at forty-five miles per hour, to the top of the needle on the highest resort in Las Vegas, Gwen hesitates for the first time. She's lightheaded and queasy after so many rides.

Grady cranes past the padded shoulder straps to ask, "Can't handle this one? Tapping out?"

Gwen straps her harness between her thighs and responds, "How's your junk feeling? Little snug? Maybe you need to sit this one out."

Grady's reply is a wince and an "Oof," when the ride makes its first jerky jump.

Gwen cackles, then screams—up, up, up—and has to clamp her mouth closed on the sudden drop down as the contents of her stomach lurch upward.

It only gets worse at the SkyJump, a 108-story free fall off the side of the Stratosphere.

"I see your roller coasters, and raise you jumping off a ledge," Grady says in challenge. It's not as though she can back down, not with that knowing smirk he gives her just before jumping, coasting down the building on nothing but a single metal cable.

So she jumps, knees shaking, stomach roiling, heart in her throat. At the bottom, she gives Grady a shaky thumbs-up, gets unhooked from the harness, and then turns and experiences an unwelcome second appearance of the cheese fries and Double-Double Animal Style burger.

"I think I need a break." Back on the safe, solid ground outside of the hotel, Gwen burps and swallows and stumbles dizzily.

They find a bus stop bench, wave off a guy who keeps pushing flyers into their faces for a jungle-themed strip club, and melt into the splintered, paint-chipped oasis. Gwen takes long pulls of the hot, dry air and blinks at the cloudless blue sky.

If Flora were here, she'd tut and get Gwen water and something bland to eat, then point out, sympathetically, that perhaps a huge fast food meal and a dozen thrill rides are not the best combination. "At least digest first," she'd say, and kiss Gwen's forehead.

Then they'd go back to their irresponsibly cold hotel room and read until Gwen convinced her to make out for a while. She smiles at imaginary Flora. When she looks over at Grady, he's signing strip-club flyers and restaurant napkins for a group of people who stare at him as if he's a chimpanzee behind glass and they're waiting for him to do a trick.

"Hey. Shoo." Gwen stands, blocks him with her body as much as she can and waves her arms. "There's a tiger living a miserable existence at the Mirage, go gawk at him."

They don't. Instead, one of them asks Grady to take a selfie. By the time they're able to move on, Gwen's stomach is settled, but annoyance has drawn her shoulders tight, and she's walking with snappy, stomping strides. She says without thinking, "I'm starting to see why Nico can't deal with that shit. I'd run away, too."

Grady's face crumples before he's able to get ahead of it and plaster on a fake almost-smile instead.

"Shit, Grady, I'm sorry. My mouth works independently of my brain sometimes, I didn't mean—"

"Don't worry about it," Grady says, in a tone that clearly means he doesn't want to talk about it, *at all.* And then, even among the clanging slot machines and shouts of the flyer pushers, the honking horns and the streaming crowds of people hyped up on indulgence and sin, there's a palpable quiet between them.

They march forward because they're marching forward. It's getting dark now; all the harsh lights and signs flash on-off-on like strobe lights—or camera flashes. They stop at a crosswalk, far enough down The Strip that they wait with just a few stragglers for the cross signal. Beyond that is, of course, a strip club.

"Hey. I have a joke for you." She lifts to her toes and inclines her head toward the white building. Its sign advertises a topless cabaret. "A lesbian and bisexual walk into a strip club..."

And there's that reluctant, tugging grin again. The light turns green, and the crosswalk signal flips to go. "Well, what's the punch line?" Grady says, striding up onto the curb.

"Oh." Gwen scratches the side of her head. "Um, the bartender says, 'Hey, why the long face' because strips clubs actually make me very uncomfortable?"

"Not your best joke, Small Fry." Grady tucks her roughly under his armpit, gives her a squeeze, and spins them around in the direction they just came from.

"Where the hell are we going, Grady?"

"I have no idea."

They head back, in a comfortable quiet now, Grady's arm heavy and comforting on her shoulders so Gwen is safe against his solid side. She gets a text from Clementine. *What are you crazy kids up to? Meet me at the Hyde in two. XOXO*

Two more hours to kill. She is most definitely through with thrill rides for the day, her inner ear canal feels permanently off-kilter, her neck hurts, and her stomach is still burbling its discontent. The shine has worn off of living the highlife and Vegas, here at the very end of The Strip, as if the carpet has been lifted and the filthy, ashtray-scented, skeevy crumbs swept beneath it are on horrifying display.

"I used to go to places like that all the time," Grady confesses. "Those strip clubs. I was kind of an ass back then."

They pass a door with a yellow and orange dragon painted on it. "I used to hang out at these a lot," Gwen says. The tattoo parlor is tucked among a Walgreens, a frozen yogurt place, and a discount souvenir shop with half-price show tickets. "I miss having piercings."

Grady glances at her, then at the shop. "So get one."

"Nah. A few of them got infected." And once she got her belly button ring caught on a loose-weave sweater and ripped it clear out of her skin. That was traumatizing.

"So get a tattoo," Grady says offhandedly. Gwen laughs and laughs.

"It would be less dramatic if I just murdered my mother straight away." Rebecca Pasternak has a line, a point of no return, and that line is tattoos.

Grady looks around left and right and up above the crowd, and even cups a hand over his eyes to indicate a long look into the distance. "I don't see your mama here. Do you?"

"You're a terrible influence," Gwen tells him.

"I will if you will."

"Like I said. Terrible."

Two hours later, one side of her ribs is taped with gauze and oozing ink and blood. It feels like a smoking brand. She's trembling with excitement and the rush of pain endorphins, waiting in the front of the tattoo shop for Grady to finish. What will her mother say? What will Flora say? Will it matter that she got the little purple violet that curves gently around her ribcage for Flora, and that violets always make Gwen think of her, beautiful and sweet and shy, that she really actually loves the tattoo and doesn't have a single regret?

Grady comes from the back, a little pale with spots of red high on his cheeks. His hair is in curly clumps as if he's been holding on to it for dear life.

"What did you get?" Gwen asks after he pays and tips his artist, then gets an aftercare package of soap and antibacterial cream that he tucks in his pocket.

"Swallows." They stop at the mirrored door.

"Hold on, so many raunchy jokes just popped into my head."

Grady laughs, then lifts his shirt. "*Swallows.*" On his chest, inked into the muscled rise of his pecs, Gwen can just make out the outline of two birds beneath the white gauze. Grady looks at his chest in the mirror. "The artist said sailors used to get them at the end of a long journey to show they had survived. That they could survive anything. And it means—" He pauses, letting sadness pass over his features without pushing it down and away. "I wanted something that means loyalty. Swallows always return to the same place. The same person."

"That's really sweet, Grady." She helps him tug his T-shirt back down. "When is Nico getting here? I bet he'll love it."

Grady shakes his head, just one quick dismissal. "He's not answering his phone, but I left him a message and told him not to come." He pushes the door open; it chimes cheerily.

"Why?"

Grady steps into the darkness, holds the door open and says, "This was always where we were headed, wasn't it? People leave, Gwen. They always leave in the end."

23

Grady walks to the Bellagio with all the ease and speed of a running back or a wide receiver or whatever football player position takes the ball and runs it down the field like a dancer the size of a refrigerator. Gwen walks behind him, then jogs behind him, then panics when she loses him on the crowded sidewalk that's lit up in carnival lights.

Gwen catches sight of him again on the other side of the choreographed water spouts; she sees the bounce of his curls as he goes inside. She yells for him, but either he doesn't hear her over the blast of "Billie Jean" and the gush of the fountains, or he's ignoring her.

"Hey, there you are!"

Gwen barely notices the elegance of the exclusive club: low purple lights cast in slanting lines onto long leather couches; a sleekly polished wood bar with every top-shelf liquor imaginable, and many Gwen has never had the privilege to hear of; an all-VIP clientele; bouncers around the perimeter. Clementine is wearing a dress so tight it's a second skin.

It doesn't matter, none of this. She doesn't feel special or VIP; she feels out of place. And Grady is slipping through her fingers, falling faster than she can catch him. What happens when he slips away for good? "Grady," Gwen wheezes, and pokes at a stitch in her side; the tattoo is still burning on the other. Damn her short legs.

"Relax, he's right there."

And he is, on a couch, with an expression so blank it makes Gwen's heart squeeze. *People always leave in the end.*

That may be true of Grady's life so far, but Nico didn't—well, he *did*, but not like that. Unless he did leave like that? Like Gwen left Flora. Why is she here if she isn't running away, too?

"Hey, come dance with me." Clementine pushes a drink into Gwen's hand and holds Gwen's hip, pressing close and swaying to the beat.

The dance floor is small, with spotlights that sweep across tangled bodies. Gwen throws back her drink too fast; her throat clamps down on the sting of strong alcohol. Clementine raises her hands above her head and shimmies.

Gwen looks past her. She recognizes some of the faces on the couches and lingering at the bar; she's seen them on TV and in movies and magazines. Bouncers are everywhere, on the dance floor, at the bar, at velvet ropes, and in hidden elevated booths. This is a place where people who are always being watched can let loose and do the things no one will take from this room. She's only here because of Clementine, and because Clementine wants something from her, or to do something with her that no one can know about. Gwen has known that from the start, hasn't she? She saw the offer to come here for what it was—an open door, a different path.

Clementine brings her arms down over Gwen's shoulders and wiggles her hips against Gwen's hips. She grinds up and down Gwen's body, presses her chest close, holds her mouth next to Gwen's ear and breathes, hot and frantic and rasping.

Is Grady right? Everyone comes into the world alone and goes out of the world alone, and everything in between is a stopgap measure against the clawing, empty loneliness? Are they better off without her, Flora and the baby? She's here because she can't possibly be the mother her child deserves, so she'll get out now before she mucks it all to hell, before she has to look at the face of the woman she loves—whom she wants to make happy above all—and know she's let her down the way she always knew she would?

Clementine's cheek is warm on Gwen's cheek; her body is slinky and writhes all along Gwen's. A bass line thumps through her bones and rattles against her skull. She's still flipped around a loop-de-loop, all upside down, sideways, and scrambled, and she can't get her bearings. What is she doing?

Stop. Think. Is this how she wants it to end?

Gwen leans back on one heel to find Grady again—Grady, who spent the day getting mixed up and turned around with her—and that's when she realizes Clementine's lips are one trembling breath from her own.

"Whoa." Gwen releases Clementine's waist and steps back.

For a split second, Clementine's eyes widen. Then the look of shock and guilt is gone, replaced by the same toothy smile she gives her fans who come to her in pushy mobs. "That was fun! I'm gonna get another drink. You want?"

Gwen blinks and shakes her head. Everything is so surreal and glittery, and purple-pink-blue flashes of light make her head spin and her vision tip from side to side as vertigo narrows the world to Clementine's shining locks, bouncing as she walks. At the bar, Clementine bends over the counter to order, looks back over her shoulder, and gives Gwen a very clear come-hither look: hair tossed, eyelids lowered, lip bitten, long throat stretched in invitation to take whatever she wants.

On some level, in this place of "what happens here stays here," this place of "all that matters is this moment," Gwen does want; she can admit that now. Clementine is sexy and pretty, confident and brash and determined. Gwen could step right into her glamorous world of A-list parties and a waiting list of top celebrities begging to work with her. She could take trips to the real Venice, or anywhere else she wants, with a snap of her fingers and a private jet on call. Her life would never be boring, would never be anything less than busy and thrilling, with any luxury she could ever want. She would never disappoint anyone, because her life would be hers alone.

All she has to do is walk across that dance floor, and it can all change in an instant.

It's Grady who pulls her from her twirling, multicolored, club-remixed trance; his golden curls are cast in purple, and then shadows, as he makes a quick exit from the club.

Her choice is easy, watching Grady, who is so sure he's already been left behind that he's taken himself out of the equation—as if that didn't break him into jagged bits. As if she could ever do that to Flora or to herself. As if Nico would ever do that to Grady.

The bubble has burst. Vegas is bizarro-land; she needs to get the hell out of here and take Grady with her. The only problem is, now she has to find him again. She runs, calling his name.

She checks the bathroom first. Nothing. She checks the spa and salon, the dozen or so restaurants, all five pools, the casino, the art gallery, the botanical gardens, and the cavernous, ornate lobby.

By the time she's outside of the Bellagio, an entire kingdom unto itself, the fountains are still and quiet and waiting. She's out of breath and her feet hurt. She wheezes and presses against the stitch in her side, then winces when she remembers. She got a tattoo.

Gwen doesn't know what else to do, so she lets the flow of people on the sidewalk sweep her away; it's so loud and chaotic and crowded with lights and people, so many people, everywhere. *Where else could he be?* Every single hotel is a rabbit hole of possibilities and just as strange as Wonderland. It's impossible.

One of the pushy flyer guys follows her for a foot or two, waving an orange flyer in her face and yelling things she can't understand through all the other noise.

If Grady's as mixed-up and messed-up as she is, he could be anywhere by now. She pictures him at a seedy, dark bar, all alone and brokenhearted, only this time the glass in his hand is full of fiery clear liquor, and at his feet are the tattered remains of everything he worked so hard for.

"Piss *off*," she finally snaps at the flyer pusher, angrier at herself than anyone else. She was supposed to be helping Grady, not making things worse. She and Flora are supposed to be a team, and her running off like a rebellious, snotty teenager while Flora takes on the burden of everything else is shitty.

An orange flyer hits her face and flaps to the ground, and Gwen stops and stares at it. *Club Ammunition* is written across it in sharp black letters, and it shows a woman clad in only a gun belt and a bandolier of bullets with a smoking pistol in one hand. She's advertising a strip club with a thirty-foot pole, three floors, and three dozen exotic dancers. Gwen takes off at a run.

She knows exactly where he is. She just hopes she's not too late.

24

The strip club they passed earlier is dark inside, creepily so, and Gwen can't tell if Grady is there; she can't really see much of anything but the topless, G-stringed dancers moving under hot stage lights. The music is loud and fast; the dancers are skilled, flexible, and captivating. Gwen's eyes adjust, and she squints not at the strippers, but at the men watching. She doesn't see Grady. Another glance around and she notices the private back rooms with black curtains hiding exclusive "services." She approaches the bar with a sense of sinking dread and a desire to crawl out of her skin.

"Have you seen this man?" Gwen flashes her phone at the red-haired, buxom bartender in a leather bikini.

"No, but I'd like to." She winks.

Gwen snatches her phone back with a scowl. "He is *taken*, okay? Happily so. Does no one have *any* respect for *commitment?*"

The bartender pouts her red, red lips at Gwen. "Do you need a drink, cutie?"

Gwen's shoulders slump. "Oh my god, you have no idea." It has been a *day*. She shakes her head. "But no. I really have to find him."

The bartender's face shifts from professionally flirtatious to honestly sympathetic. "Good luck. I hope you find him."

Gwen thanks her and steps outside feeling both relief and dread. She's glad to be out of there, but has no idea where to try next. Clementine might know, but spending time with her right now is not a good idea. Still, she'd want to know Grady is—

"Gah!" She runs face-first into a wall that appears out of nowhere. No. Not a wall. "*Kevin*. Where the hell did you—no, wait. You're a wizard, right?" It's the only explanation. How else could he know she was here? How else did he arrange for a car to be waiting outside?

"Is Clem..." Gwen nods at the darkly tinted windows of the black SUV.

Kevin shakes his head.

"Do you know where Grady is?" Kevin's chin dips just slightly. Gwen gets in the car. "Just tell me," she says to the back of Kevin's head as they drive. "Tracking device? Are you the Terminator? You can trust me."

Kevin is silent, and the car slows. Gwen taps her fingers on the armrest.

A deep, soothing voice says, "Miss Campbell asked me to keep an eye on Mr. Dawson. And you. She wanted to ensure your safety. I'm very good at what I do, Ms. Pasternak."

"Oh." Gwen squints. "That... makes more sense." Then she adds, after another silent moment, "Thanks, Kevin."

The car stops in front of a quaint little blue triangular building that's right in the middle of the grand hotels and loud casinos, the billboards and clubs and insanity. It has stained glass windows, a carved front door, and a white cross on the gable. It's a chapel.

"Oh, no." Gwen bolts from the car, bangs open the heavy wooden doors, and yells, "Grady, don't join a convent! Things aren't that bad, I promise!"

Her voice echoes through the peaceful sanctuary. It is a real church, with an altar, prayer candles and even an organ. And in the back, sitting in the center of one of the long wooden pews, is Grady.

"Not becoming a nun," Grady says when she sits next to him. "I don't think they allow men." He glances around the sanctuary. "Anyway, I'm pretty sure this church is Episcopalian."

"It's possible I jumped to the wrong conclusion." She fidgets on the hard bench. Should she kneel or say a prayer? She's never quite sure. At the events she's attended for Flora's family—weddings, baptisms, and funerals, the big three Catholic life events—it was easy enough to stay distracted by the activities, but this church is hushed and empty and filled with soft light.

"You a churchgoer?" Grady asks, hands clasped in his lap, head tilted up.

"Not in practice, no. My dad is an agnostic in his rare, more hopeful moments, and my mother worships at the altar of pragmatism." She lifts her shoulders against the hard backrest. "Sometimes I wonder if they're more dismayed that I married a woman or a practicing Catholic."

Grady nods. "I don't go much anymore. Went to that Buddhist church Nico's parents go to? I liked that. Felt welcome." He looks around thoughtfully. "I never really managed that whole good-Christian thing."

Gwen isn't exactly an expert on the subject, but, "Isn't their whole thing forgiveness, though? Like you just have to ask, right?"

He doesn't answer. Gwen wiggles. Should she light a candle or page through the waxy, thin pages of the Bible for something to quote at him?

"I think maybe," she says, sliding a hand across the buffed, shining wood on the pew in front of them, "forgiveness is more about getting right with yourself and the person you wronged and less about eternal salvation."

Grady looks at her. His face is anguished, his throat works, and his eyes are wet. "It's been six years today."

Gwen scrunches her face in confusion. Six years since... She knows his first big breakout hit is coming up on six years now, but that can't be it. What came before that was a mess of hard work tempered by hard partying, and for a while after that, too, until he got sober. Something bad, she knows by his shattered expression, something devastating.

She takes a stab. "Your grandmother?"

He presses his lips together, gives a shuddering breath, and confesses, "I had played a show that night, a back corner of a pool hall, but I was *playing*. Getting paid. I had just been signed to a label. I was all caught up in *my* moment, you know? All hyped up and high, and she called me. Left a message and said she was feeling ill and could I come home." He drags a hand through his messy curls. "I didn't. I was too busy getting wasted and bein' full of myself."

"Grady..." Gwen sets a hand on top of his hands, which are still folded as if in prayer.

"When I got home, she was..." He drops his head. "It was too late."

"Grady, it wasn't your fault. Even if you had been there—" It was a massive stroke, Nico told her when he filled her in on his first visit to Grady's hometown in rural Tennessee. "Unless you were a nurse who knew exactly what to do, Grady. You can't take on the burden of her death like that."

He shakes his head and looks away. "I should have been there. At least she wouldn't have been alone." An elderly man shuffles into the sanctuary, lights a candle, and kneels in front of the flickering light. "That thing you said about forgiveness? She always forgave me. And I never deserved it. She forgave my mother. And my grandfather. She was a good person. Kind. Always gave and gave and let us hurt her over and over again and for what? To die alone in her trailer. At what point does it stop being forgiveness and start being a crucifixion?"

Gwen spares a glance at the cross, at the old man still on his knees. "I don't know," she admits. "But I do know that holding on to guilt like that will poison you from the inside out." She gives his hands another squeeze. "You have to forgive yourself. *For* yourself. Because you're a human being who makes mistakes. So am I. And so is Nico. I can certainly relate to being caught up in a moment and forgetting that the rest of the world keeps spinning on anyway."

His mouth tips with a hint of a smile. "I always think maybe it won't hit me so hard this year, and then it always does."

"Well, next year maybe keep in mind that you don't have to do this alone." She pats his hands. "Our little family may be a patchwork of weirdos, but we've got each other's backs, and that counts for something."

Grady chuckles, slinging his arm behind Gwen's on the pew. "Family. I like that." He releases a relieved breath. "Clem brought me here because she thought I could use the distraction. But I'd really just like to go home now."

Gwen tucks into his side. "Yeah, me too."

The elderly man finishes his prayer, heaves himself up, and shuffles out; his candle is still burning.

"What happens when the three-legged race has gone off course and you both trip and fall in the mud?" Grady asks.

"You help each other up and you keep hobbling along out of love and stubbornness," Gwen says. "Even when it's hard. Even when it looks impossible. Otherwise you wind up at the finish line all by yourself." She stands, tugs Grady to his feet with a grunt. "Shall we hobble?"

"I will if you will."

25

Grady suggested one last trip to In-N-Out, but Gwen has well and truly purged In-N-Out from her system so they get salads and smoothies and eat them in the car that was waiting for them, though Kevin has vanished once again. When they arrive at the hotel it's well past midnight.

As the elevator doors slide closed, Gwen hesitates at the rows of buttons. Staying in Clementine's suite again doesn't feel right, not when she hasn't talked to Flora, who is most certainly fast asleep.

Tomorrow. Talking, going home. *Home*—it took being away from Nashville to realize that she does think of it that way, because that's where Flora is, that's where her life is, and she misses it.

First, she needs to get Grady safely to his room. She'll find somewhere to crash.

"What's your floor?"

Grady mumbles an answer; his accent is so thick when he's exhausted it's as if he's speaking through a mouthful of wool. She pushes the 8. He looks seconds away from falling asleep right here against the walls of the elevator; so his go-go-go energy does have a limit. When the elevator dings and the doors slide open, she yanks his arm and gets her shoulders under him. "Come on, Double Beef. Let's get you to bed."

His room is nice, not lap-of-luxury nice, but upscale-hotel nice with a pristine queen-size bed and a large bathroom, all clean and crisp and modern.

"No penthouse suite?" she asks, depositing Grady on the bed.

He stretches and smiles and purrs, "I'm a simple man with simple needs."

Gwen unties his boots, tugs one off, and thumps it on the floor. "So you say that stuff, and people take their panties right off, just like that. Amazing." She thumps the other boot to the floor. He laughs and winks, then rolls to his side. "Okay, you." Gwen says, as seriously as she can manage right now. "Stay here. Sleep. We'll take off and make things right in the morning."

She turns to the door and Grady mumbles, "Where're ya sleepin'?"

Gwen waves off his concern. "If they don't have anything here, I'll find one of those pay-by-the hour joints." She crosses her fingers in the air. "Here's hoping they have a dungeon-themed one."

Grady sleepily pats the bed next to him. "Get on in here."

"Okay, but no funny business."

"Yes, ma'am," Grady drawls.

In the bathroom she strips to her tank top and underwear, removes the bandage covering her ribs to start the airing-out and healing phase, according to the care sheet, and cleans the tender tattoo. She cleans up with the hotel-provided toiletries, then insists Grady do the same, shoving him from the bed with all her remaining strength and energy.

She's drifting and sluggish when Grady falls back into bed and cuddles close, arms and legs flung over her. She feels as if she's being snuggled by a hot-blooded giant squid.

"I usually sleep naked." His chin is set on the top of her head. "But I kept on a shirt and underwear."

Gwen wheezes out from beneath him, "I appreciate you staying partially clothed for me, Grady."

He chuckles and rubs his fuzzy legs against hers.

"You're crushing me, you big lug; roll over," she whines.

He does. Then tosses and turns and flails and huffs like a squid flopping around on the shore. She sighs and flips over, winds her arms around his chest, and curls her body against the shape of his. He stills, huge and tall and thick in her arms.

"I feel like a human backpack," she says against his too-warm skin. She wiggles and shifts closer. It's just not right, all hard flat planes and bulging muscles. "Are you actually sculpted from marble? You're too hard for cuddling."

He laughs and flexes his pecs under her hands. "I haven't had any complaints."

"This is me complaining." She moves her hands down around his ribs. That's not any better. She yearns for Flora's soft, giving curves.

He twists around a bit to look at her. "This really doesn't do anything at all for you?"

It's late enough that she decides to indulge his obvious fishing, and she's spent long enough in this industry to recognize that the need for external validation is vital to the process of an artist. She yawns first, waits for him to turn back around and stew for minute. "It's like a pair of six-inch, platform, spiked Louboutin stilettos. Fun to look at, but not really something I want to put on and break my ankle with."

He mulls this over. "I'm confused. What part of you is your ankle in this scenario?" Grady asks with a yawn of his own.

"Oh, I think you know."

They go quiet, the mismatched pair of them thrown together in the dark, but Gwen is really glad she's not alone tonight, and she knows Grady feels the same way when he relaxes against her and breathes slowly and peacefully. He'll be okay. They both will.

When she stirs awake, it's to sunlight breaching the cracks in the heavy curtain. Grady is still in her arms, and she has the unsettling realization that someone has been staring at her while she struggles to consciousness.

"Go away, Cheese; it's not food time," she snuffles against Grady's broad back. He groans and stretches and mumbles, "Cheese?"

A new voice says, "There's a reason you two aren't allowed to hang out alone." Arms crossed, one impeccable eyebrow raised, lips twisted, hair artfully tousled, and dressed to the nines in Alexander Wang black-on-black tropical-printed board shorts, a slim-fit, black and white chino and matching black lapel jacket, black boots, and a black and white scarf to tie it all together: "Nico," Gwen says.

"Nico?" Grady is up in a flash. "You came?"

Nico's face softens into his Grady look. "Of course I came. Did you really think you were getting rid of me that easily?" Grady comes closer, and Nico brushes a spiraled lock of hair from his face. "I'm sorry it took me so long. There were storms over Dallas, and I got stuck on the tarmac with a dead phone. I barely made my connection, and the clusterfuck of morons known as the United gate at JFK could not get its shit together, and I may be banned outright from Charlotte-Douglas International, can you believe they flag you as a security risk and hold you in a room with no phone signal or Wi-Fi just for threatening *one* person with shoving that goddam intercom up their—" He opens his arms for Grady; his look of annoyance slips away the moment they touch. "Anyway, I'm here."

Grady sighs, crowds into Nico's space, and tucks himself into Nico's body. Much better. They look like a perfect fit. "God, I love you."

"I love you, too." Nico sinks one hand into Grady's hair, strokes the nape of his neck with the other, breathes him in, and closes his eyes. "I'm so sorry. About the apartment, and taking off, and not being here yesterday. I tried to so hard to make it, because I know how difficult it is for you. You shouldn't have been alone."

Grady sniffs and holds him tighter. "It's okay. We're okay. I'm sorry, too."

Still ensnared in the sheets and duvet and barely awake, Gwen presses her hands to her cheeks. "Aww, you guys," she coos.

Grady lifts his head from Nico's neck to smile at Gwen. "I wasn't alone, though."

"Mmm," Nico says. "And how much trouble did she get you into?"

"*None*," Gwen says, defensive. Here she kept Grady safe and sound, searched all over Nashville *and* Las Vegas while he was off burying himself in work and what thanks does she get? None.

But then Grady smirks and says, "Kind of a lot."

"Grady." Gwen throws a pillow at him. "You're such a tattletale, gosh."

He bends to whisper something in Nico's ear, and Gwen doesn't miss the way his lips drag and linger on the shell of it, or the way Nico's breath catches and his eyes roll back. When Nico lifts Grady's shirt and traces around the tattoos with reverent fingers,

Gwen takes that as her cue to extricate herself from the bed, put on some pants and go fetch her luggage.

"'Kay, you guys have fun and make sure to change the sheets when you're finished."

"Wait." Nico tugs Grady's shirt down. Then he goes to the case he always has nearby. "You have trouble of your own, Gwen. Thought you might want to know about this."

Gwen catches the magazine and folded-up papers he tosses her way: screen grabs from a few entertainment websites printed out in black and white.

> *Is This Clementine Campbell's Girlfriend? Our source says, "It wouldn't surprise me."*
>
> *Clementine and Gal Pal Definitely More Than Pals Sunning On Vegas Pool Deck.*
>
> *Our exclusive source and close confidant of both says: Clementine's married girlfriend "would cheat for sure. She was always touching her. There's been an energy between them from the very beginning."*

There are pictures: of her rubbing sunscreen on Clementine's bare back, which looks far steamier in a fuzzy long-range picture than it actually was; a picture of them from the back at the store in the Venetian, with their hands clasped and Clementine curled in close, her lips on Gwen's cheek; and most damning of all, the two of them grinding together at the VIP club at the Bellagio just last night. "I don't—" Frantic and confused, she flaps the magazine and printouts in the air. "What is this? This isn't—Nico, I didn't, I *swear*."

Nico holds both hands up. "Hey, I am well aware of the slander of tabloids. I get it." He gives her a sympathetic look. "I'm just not sure Flora is going to."

"Oh god." Gwen grips the short strands of her sleep-spiky hair in both hands. "Shit, this not good. I'm—" What else? Who else can she possibly go to right now? "I need to talk to Clementine."

There's an energy between them.
Always touching her.
She'd cheat for sure. For sure.

Of course I was always touching Clementine, Gwen fumes, shifting from foot to foot as she waits for the elevator. *It's part of my job.* And then it clicks. Of course. Of *fucking* course. The elevator arrives, and on the ride to Clementine's private top-floor suite, Gwen jabs out a text message to Spencer. It has to be him. But why? She liked him, she *defended* him. She gave him a chance that he clearly didn't deserve.

Gwen: So you ran off to L.A. to become a rat I see.

She glares at the numbers flashing over the door while she waits for a reply. *9...10...11...12...13...14...15...*

Spencer: I didn't say anything that wasn't true.

Her jaw clenches, her nostrils flare, and she clutches her phone so hard the edges dig into her skin. *16...17...18...19...* A gray text bubble pops up next to Spencer's name with the scrolling ellipses that mean he's typing. It disappears. Comes back. Disappears. Finally, he sends something.

Spencer: It's hard out here. I needed money.

Gwen shakes her head and goes back to glaring at the numbers as the elevator gets closer to the top floor. Of course it's hard to make it as a new stylist with barely any experience, and that's *why* they gave him an internship in the first damn place, but too late now. He's burned his bridges; he can sink on his own. That's what she should say.

But she remembers being young and impatient, tired of being told what to do and who to be, figuratively and literally giving the entire world the middle finger. Hell, who is she kidding? She still does that; she's been doing it all weekend.

And she also knows what it's like to have someone who saw her as she was and as she could be. Someone who believed in her. She stops in her tracks and calls Flora first, but it goes to voicemail. "Hey, Flora, I, um. I'm coming home. I just... I love you, okay?"

Then she replies to Spencer.

Gwen: I really see potential in you. A fearlessness and a shrewdness that can't be taught. But you do need to learn things. Most importantly...

The elevator doors open and she steps off.

Gwen: Most importantly that connecting yourself to— and relying on—other people is not a weakness. It is vital to success.

He doesn't reply, not even an indecisive text bubble. She hopes that maybe she planted a seed, at least. Bridges can be rebuilt with care and thought and patience. She has some she needs to get working on. Gwen speed-walks down the hall, no shoes, no makeup, hair a mess, and wearing yesterday's wrinkled, smelly clothes, only to encounter the solid wall of Kevin blocking the door to Clementine's room.

"Excuse me, Kevin, I just need to—" Then she notices her luggage at Kevin's feet. "What—"

"Miss Campbell," Kevin intones, "has requested that I inform you there is a jet waiting to take you and Mr. Dawson back to Nashville." His expression, always so staid and stiff, seems pitying. "Whenever you're ready to leave, Ms. Pasternak."

26

Six years ago...

It was the cats that finally spooked Gwen. On a bright Sunday morning they'd gone grocery shopping. It was the perfect day people move to Southern California for: sunny and warm with clear blue skies and just enough of a breeze to keep the heat pleasant instead of suffocating. They drove with the windows down; cheesy pop music that Gwen had long given up pretending she didn't like murmured in the background. She sang along or chattered excitedly about work, and Flora could see their lives stretching on like this for miles and miles.

"You know Nico, that hairstylist I was telling you about?"

Flora pulled into a space near her apartment, next to the dumpster. Someone had ditched a broken particleboard bookshelf next to it. "The pretty one that you have a crush on?"

Gwen scoffed, jabbing the button to release her seatbelt. "I do not." She tipped her head and reconsidered. "The man has presence."

"It's okay," Flora said, getting out of the car. "I'm not the jealous type. You can think he's pretty." She popped open the trunk and pulled at one of the cloth grocery bags.

Gwen grabbed two bags and they walked across the parking lot, weighed down with their first load, as Gwen continued. "Anyway, he and I were talking about how the salon has a lot of celebrity clients, and I mentioned that I really wanted to get into fashion styling, but don't really have funds to start up my own firm."

They dropped the groceries on the kitchen counter and went back for the second load. "And he said he had the money his parents set aside for college still because he never went, and that we should go into business together."

Flora pulled out the last bag and slammed the trunk closed. "Wow."

"Yeah." Gwen scuffed her boots along the cracked pavement of the parking lot. Flora's apartment was nicer than Gwen's, but on a first-year teacher's salary, not by much. "Is it crazy?" Gwen asked, then decided before Flora could answer. "It's crazy. Honestly, it's so hard to make it as a new styling firm, and neither of us have interned—"

"Gwen." Flora stopped just past the rancid sour milk smell of the dumpster. "I think it's a fantastic idea. You absolutely have what it takes."

Gwen rose up on her toes, smiled, and walked backward to ramble, "I mean. Between my fashion knowledge and his cool in the face of bratty celebrity demands, at least we—" Something in the dumpster squeaked. Gwen set her bag down. "What was that?"

"I don't know." Flora moved closer, holding her breath at the stench. *Goodness, what died in there?* They waited and waited and...

A cry. A miserable mewling cry.

"Oh! A kitten!" Gwen was halfway into the dumpster, using the wobbling broken bookshelf as a ladder, giving no thought or care to the stench or the fact that she was *climbing into a dumpster.*

"Let me go get a net or something—Gwen!" Too late. Gwen hauled her other leg over and dove in. Just the bright blonde top of her head was visible as she dug around.

"It's okay, oh, I won't hurt you, *shit.*" From the sound of it, Gwen dove for the kitten and missed. Flora took a breath, held it, and craned up to see. "Is there meat or something in one of the grocery bags?" Gwen whisper-shouted, sunk to her hips in reeking garbage. "It's terrified, but it looks so skinny. I bet it's hungry."

Flora rushed to the bag, found lunch meat and fumbled with it, and finally managed to tear off a corner of a slice. She handed it to Gwen and could see the kitten's wary green eyes hiding behind a black bag that was oozing something orange and lumpy from a tear in the middle. Flora grimaced and called, "I hope you've had a recent tetanus shot, Gwen."

As disgusting as it was, and it really, really was, watching Gwen coo to and soothe this terrified, emaciated kitten in a dumpster, heedless of her own comfort or safety—or smell—only concerned for this cat and its well-being, made Flora's heart glow with affection. Gwen would make a wonderful mother.

And then. A louder, more demanding meow. "There's another one!" Flora called. The second kitten, its orange fur matted with dirt and grime, came out of hiding, falling over the uneven piles of trash to get to the shred of turkey Gwen held out. It came close enough for Gwen to scoop it up and hand it to Flora. With some patience and after a few grabs that sent it running back behind the slimy black bag, they managed to get the other little orange cat, too.

Flora sent Gwen off to shower and change while she put the groceries away and called a vet. The kittens were secure in a box with a blanket and water in a custard cup.

"We can take them in tomorrow; for now we should probably go get some kitten food." Flora said when Gwen emerged. She hadn't bothered to blow-dry her hair or put on makeup, just crouched over the box with her hair dripping on the collar of her shredded Union Jack T-shirt. "Hey, do you want chili tonight? I can throw it in the crockpot now."

"Sure." Gwen reached into the box, and tiny nails skittered on the cardboard. "So scared, poor babies. Hey, so how do you want to split this?"

Flora looked up from washing a green pepper. "Split this?"

"Yeah, like—" She was sitting cross-legged next to the box, one hand placed very still inside. "Should I take one and you take one? Or we keep them together and share custody." She looked up with a silly smile. "You take them to school during the week, and I can be fun weekend-mom."

Flora put the pepper on the cutting board and dried her hands on the tea towel that hung from the oven handle. Gwen had picked out the towels; they had mermaids printed on them. "Gwen, when was the last time you actually slept at your own apartment?"

"I—" Gwen's face pulled together. "I was just there... to get more clothes..." She frowned down at the box of kittens. "Huh."

And perhaps it wasn't the kittens so much as what Flora said next *because* of the kittens. "Your name may not be on the lease, but we live together, Gwen. So the cats can stay here and we can all be a happy family unit." Flora sliced the peppers into strips. "So, meatless chili or—"

But Gwen was up and moving toward the door and avoiding eye contact as she said, "I should, um, go get ready for work. I'll see you later." Then she left. And Flora was alone with two filthy, hungry dumpster kittens, a kitchen full of food, and one chopped green pepper.

She made spicy chili verde and went shopping for the kittens while it cooked. She bought food and bowls and a little bed and toys and tiny collars with tiny jingling bells. She ate one bowl of piping hot chili and froze the rest of it. Gwen never came back.

Later, Flora was tucked on the couch with Band-Aids and antibiotic ointment on her arms—she'd decided to give the kittens a bath. After all that trauma, she figured she might as well name them: Mac and Cheese. She was reading a novel and sipping tea, with the kittens curled up in their box, asleep, when her phone rang.

"Hello?" She was hopeful, expecting to hear Gwen's voice.

It was mostly background noise, though, talking, glasses rattling, music playing. A bar. "Hey, Flora! I was calling to see if you and Gwen wanted to come out, but Gwen is already here! You guys good?"

Brianna. One of their nosiest friends in common. Flora didn't set her book down, just kept her thumb where she'd left off. "We're fine." Maybe they weren't, but Flora wasn't ready to jump to the worst-case scenario. Even if she had been, she certainly wouldn't tell Brianna of all people.

"Really?" Brianna's voice was heavy with disbelief and barely-contained delight. "Because she's looking awfully cozy with this rando chick at the bar."

Against her better judgment, Flora found out where they were and went. She trusted Gwen and she *wasn't* the jealous type, but Gwen was acting so weirded out and Flora just—she wanted to see for herself. She couldn't focus on her book after the phone call, so the night was a wash anyway.

What she saw was Gwen leaning into the space of a skinny, black-haired girl with tattoos everywhere and a leather jacket, who looked as if she were fresh from some clichéd biker bar. Gwen's hair was a blunt asymmetrical chin-length bob, her latest style, and Flora couldn't see her face, just a swaying fringe of blonde. But her body language was flirty and open, her skirt was micro-short, and she was wearing what Gwen herself called her "Fuck you, fuck me" thigh-high boots.

Flora went sick and cold all over: skin clammy and heart heavy. Still, she walked over. Still, she refused to just turn and away and let this happen, because she was not a doormat. Her kindness was *not* weakness. She tapped Gwen on the shoulder. Gwen turned; her face went cartoonish; her eyes bugged out and her mouth gaped on soundless words. Flora held up her hand. Gwen's mouth snapped closed. The wannabe biker chick glared at both of them.

"I just want you to stop and think," Flora said. "Really think about if this is the way you want it to end, Gwen." Gwen started to speak again, and Flora shook her head. "Stop. Think."

Then she was the one who got to leave.

Gwen called her that night and again the next morning. She called while the kittens were getting an examination, shots, and flea and ear mite treatment at the vet. She called while Flora was teaching and studying and at home. Flora needed space and time, and Gwen could wait. And if she couldn't, then...

"So did she cheat on you?"

Flora was stretched on her couch; it was dark outside and mostly dark inside. One of the cats, Mac, was warming up to her. He'd settled on the armrest with his eyes half open and his fuzzy little body crouched, staying there even when she'd scratched at his ears. The vet said that they were on their way to being feral and would probably always be shy and skittish.

"I don't know." Flora sighed, her breath rattling through the phone's speakers. "The bigger point is, I can't be the only person in this relationship. I want commitment. I want a future. Gwen knows this. And if she doesn't, I'm not going to force her. She needs to want it too." Flora may be calm and nurturing and gentle, but she refused to be stomped all over, "fuck me" boots or no.

"That's very reasonable and mature, Flora," her sister replied, not without some bemusement. "You're also allowed to be sad. Or angry. Or to go out and find a biker chick of your own."

Flora huffed out a laugh. Mac startled and moved closer to the wall. "No thanks." She scratched gently under Mac's chin. "Enough about me. How are you?"

"Ugh," Selene groaned. "Big as a house. Constant heartburn. Thinking about moving into the bathroom I have to pee so much. Mom calls me every fifteen minutes to ask if my mucus plug came out, *my god*. I am so ready for this kid to vacate the premises."

"Soon," Flora reassured. As miserable as Selene sounded, Flora was a little envious. She wasn't sure if kids were even in the ten-year plan for her; she didn't know if Gwen would be in the picture for the next ten minutes. "I can't believe I'm going to miss baby Evie's birth."

"Me too. But you'll be here right after. And... You know you can always come back out this way and teach." This was not the first time Selene—or one or both of their parents—had brought this up.

"Maybe someday. Or at least somewhere closer than across the country." A knock on the door caused Mac to bolt to another room. "Hey, can I call you back?"

Flora opened the door, and a frantic, sallow-skinned, bruised-dark-circled-and-bloodshot eyed Gwen rushed in. "I had to say this in person."

Flora braced herself. "Okay."

Gwen took a breath. "I act out and screw up on purpose because I know that I'm going to screw up eventually. And you look at me and you don't just see me, you see the person that I can be *and* the person that I am. No one looks at me like that. No one has ever believed in me like that, and I am just waiting for you to realize what a terrible mistake you've made."

Flora watched her push off the door and stand in the center of the living room. She looked even smaller than usual with her bony shoulders hunched in and her head ducked, wearing ratty sneakers and clothes that looked as if she'd picked them up off the floor. It was unsettling.

"So you figured you'd just get it over with?" Flora said, arms crossed.

Gwen laughed a little. "See? That's exactly what I mean. You know."

Flora summoned all of her courage and said, "If you've come to break up with me, just do it. You should know that I'm keeping both of the cats and I've named them Mac and Cheese." She doesn't want to separate them, and anyway, she likes their quiet, standoffish company.

"No, Flor—" Gwen shook her head and dug a hand into the pocket of her wrinkled pants. "Well, I guess you don't know everything. I should be more open with you, and I will. Because somehow, despite all my efforts to be a disappointment, I got you. You look at me and you see something to believe in, and I don't understand why or what you could possibly see, but I want to be that person. You make me want to be better, but you also make me proud to be who I already am." She held something out between her thumb and index finger, a glint of metal and stone: A ring. "I want to spend the rest of my life with you."

Flora blinked at the ring, then up at Gwen's hopeful, nervous face and back at the ring. "Are you seriously asking me to marry you right now?"

A raised eyebrow. An impish grin. "I did a lot of thinking like you said. I left the bar right after you and cried in my bathtub for like three days. And then I hocked some of my vintage albums and sold some plasma and took some extra shampooing shifts at the salon. And bought this. Because you're the best thing that ever happened to me. And I'm sorry I had to freak out a little before I realized that."

Flora just shook her head and laughed and dropped her arms loose at her sides. "What am I going to do with you, G?"

Gwen shrugged. "Marry me?"

27

"You're really bringing 'travel chic' to a whole new level today, Gwennie."

Gwen lifts her chin, smooths the puffy layers of her black tulle skirt, tugs at the mesh and leather crop top, and crosses one metallic silver, rhinestone-encrusted heeled boot over the other. "Last night I went straight from jumping off a building to vomiting into a recycling bin to getting a tattoo to making sure your boyfriend got back to the hotel safe and sound, *you're welcome,* and I didn't get a chance to wear my club look." It's not the most comfortable outfit for flying, but, "Indulge me."

Nico purses his lips and raises a sharp eyebrow. He flicks a finger at her. "I have a black lace pillbox hat that would be perfect with it."

In Nico-speak, that means: "I missed you" and "Thank you for being there" and "Fine, I'll indulge you."

"I was thinking a skull headband," she says. Nico frowns. "Kitten ears? A tiara!"

Nico puts his thumb on his bottom lip and sighs. "I feel like I've been gone so long that I can't even tell if you're messing with me or not." She is messing with him; it's just so easy. Nico rolls his eyes at the teasing look she gives him, then turns to the seat next to him. Grady conked out almost immediately after boarding; he's dropped sideways on his oversized chair with his head pillowed in Nico's lap.

Gwen slept okay last night, and Grady did too, as far she was aware, though she has a feeling Grady is now making up for a two-week sleep deficit. "He's like a Labrador."

Nico runs his palm up Grady's arm, then into his hair. "A golden-doodle."

Gwen snorts a laugh. "Totally. I had to practically lie on top of him last night to get him to stay freaking still. So now I need to know, after you tie him up for fun, do you leave him like that or... I mean how else do you keep him still?"

Predictably, Nico glares. "*Anyway*," he says, changing the subject. "Is he—I mean, you spent a lot of time with him. Other than getting into some mischief, is he okay?"

Mischief. Is that all it was? What felt like rebellion and escape was just a little naughty impish fun? As if that was all they needed, as if it was that easy to shake off the chains and start fresh. Until next Vegas weekend.

Unless Flora has been uncharacteristically reading tabloids, and believes them. Unless Flora now thinks that Gwen is cheating on her with Clementine, and has already left.

"Yeah, he's okay." Gwen smiles when Grady drools on Nico's designer dry-clean-only pants. "Are you guys okay?"

Nico twirls a curl around his index finger. "Yeah. We will be. I think I just needed to freak out a little? Winding your life around someone else's so completely is a little scary. Particularly when it's Grady's life." He twirls and twirls Grady's hair, then shakes his head. "I just keep treating him like he's made of glass because I'm afraid of hurting him. And then I hurt him anyway."

Gwen stares down at her puffy tulle-covered lap. She's all dolled up for a night out she never had in an imaginary life she never really wanted. She's been holding back, too, treading around Flora as if she really is a fragile, wilting flower, so that one word of concern or disagreement or confession of unhappiness will destroy them both. She's been holding back because she's afraid of how Flora will react, but more afraid that the places where Gwen falls short will open a chasm between them that can't be bridged.

"I'm not going to be a good mom," Gwen says to her lap. "I'm not selfless enough. I'm not nurturing. What if my kid has to grow up with a mom who is just as cold and distant and disapproving as mine? That's all I know."

Nico responds with one of his most epic eye-rolls yet. "Oh, please."

"Nico, I'm serious. I'm freaking out. I almost—" *Had an affair with Clementine Campbell?* Did it get that close, did she really go that far? "I almost really fucked up. And I called Flora fifteen times before we got on the plane, so maybe I did really fuck things up and I—" She fluffs her skirt even fluffier. "I was trying so hard not to hurt her and I hurt her anyway."

Nico's face relaxes. He smiles down at Grady and brushes his knuckles along Grady's jaw. "If he's taught me anything, it's that no one is defined by their mistakes. We're defined by the choices we make after that to try harder. To do better." He looks at Gwen, sharp and serious. "You are audacious and bright and bawdy and so determined, and I know you like to think of yourself as this punk rock rebel, but honestly…" He cocks his head and smiles. "The fiercest thing about you is the way you love. No way will you be a cold, indifferent mother. That is the opposite of who you are."

"Aww, Nico." She doesn't care if he stiffens and does the awkward back-pat thing, she launches herself at him and hugs him tight.

"Okay, okay." He hesitates, pats her back a few times, and then pulls her closer.

Smushed between them, Grady says, faintly, "You're suffocating me."

Gwen squeezes even tighter. "Good."

She spends the rest of the flight with a sense of weightlessness, aided by the soaring wings of the plane and the wispy white clouds. She goes over the looks and inspirations from Nico's trip to L.A. and listens to the jaunty, upbeat songs Grady sings not quite under his breath. Weightlessness lasts until the plane touches down with jolt and then screams to a stop. Gwen checks her messages and missed calls right away—six hours on a plane and still not a peep from Flora.

She blew it. She flirted with disaster, and disaster won. Gwen turns her key in the lock and drags her suitcase in behind her. The downstairs is empty and muted by the somber twilight outside. Cheese doesn't come to greet her and beg for food. The kitchen doesn't smell like spices or baked goods. The floors and tabletops are neat and clean and cleared of clutter.

Has Flora gone to her sister's place in Maryland? Her parents in Virginia? Has she seen the tabloids and made up her mind? Are there even any beams left to reach across the gap Gwen made by leaving? Any faith remaining to anchor a bridge? Can they rebuild, if there's nothing left for Flora to steady herself on?

Gwen climbs the stairs with not even the cat to keep her company in the independent and unshackled life she thought she wanted—just briefly, but long enough to destroy what she had and took for granted. Gwen pushes open the door, and all her breath leaves her lungs at once.

"Hi."

"You're here."

"It's seven o'clock on a Sunday night. Where else would I be?" Flora squints at her. There's a red pen between her teeth and a pile of tests is on the bed in front of her. "I didn't expect you back until later."

Mouth agape, Gwen just looks at her. "I called. Like *dozens* of times. I thought—god, Flor."

Flora's eyebrows pinch. "Huh." She searches the bed, moves papers, and lifts the covers. Then she drops to the floor to check under the bed, calling "Ah-hah," as she emerges with her phone in hand. "It died this morning, and I forgot to charge it."

Gwen breathes, in and out, and pinches the bridge of her nose to get a grip on the situation. "I have to tell you some things, but what I say hinges quite a bit on what you already know."

Flora sits on the bed, tucks one leg beneath her, and stacks the tests in a neat pile. "Already know about what?"

"Right." Gwen climbs onto the bed, crosses her legs Zen-style, and settles the layers of tulle over them. "I wasn't honest with you about why I went to Vegas."

Flora looks up. "Okay..."

"I was kind of freaking out about the baby and I wanted to get away."

Flora sets the pen down, brows knit together, her mouth a straight line. "Okay."

"And someone saw me and Clementine and made up a story about us dating."

"Okay." Flora shakes her head and smiles.

Gwen presses her hands together in front of her chest, takes a deep breath and rattles off, "I drove a Ferrari on a racetrack, and then I rode every roller coaster and thrill ride in Vegas, and I jumped off the top of the Stratosphere, and then I puked in a recycling can, and I feel terrible for the earth, but they are not going to be recycling those bottles anymore, and then I got a tattoo, and then I went to a club and my makeup was probably melted off and my clothes were all wrinkled and I'm sure I smelled funky, but I danced with Clementine, and then I lost track of Grady, and I thought he was at a strip club and *then* I thought he was joining a convent but he was sad about his Memaw and Nico, so we cuddled and he's wiggly like a puppy, and his butt is really firm, it was weird and oh, Clementine tried to kiss me." She breathes out in a gust. *Wow, that feels better.*

Flora just blinks, sits and blinks and doesn't move. "I—that is a lot to take in."

"I know. It was a crazy weekend." Gwen lifts her shoulders, going for affable. "Vegas, you know."

Flora brings her braid forward over her shoulder and tugs at the end of it while she mulls everything over. "What was that last one, again?"

"Oh. Yeah, Grady's butt is really toned. He must do a thousand squats every morning. Like two ripe honeydew melons." She makes a squeezing motion with both hands in the air to demonstrate.

"No. No, no." Flora closes her eyes, clearly drawing on her last vestiges of patience. "After that one."

Right. The, uh, Clementine thing. Gwen was hoping they could skate on by that one, but no luck. "She tried to kiss me? And maybe more?"

Flora eyes narrow, her jaw clenches, and her nostrils flare like a bull going for the red cape. "She did what, now?"

Flora is made almost entirely of sweetness and light, kindness and generosity and compassion. But not completely. No. "It wasn't just her. I knew she was flirting, I knew there was something there. And I didn't put to a stop to it."

Flora deflates. Anger, confusion, and sadness war for position across her face and body. "Why? Gwen, what has been going on with you lately? And don't say 'nothing' or 'it's fine,' because I know it isn't. Please stop hiding and running away and avoiding me. Tell me the truth."

The truth. She got spooked and, as she has done so often in her life, she dove right off the deep end into black uncharted waters instead of stopping and thinking and *being reasonable.* The truth has never been difficult for Flora. She would see right through anything else. *Does* see through anything else.

"I'm having second thoughts," Gwen says to the ruffles of her skirt.

Flora shifts on the bed. Cheese glares, upended from her comfortable spot next to Flora's legs. Flora blinks and blinks and inhales. "About—about me or the baby? Or?"

Gwen shakes her head. "No, Flor—about me. If I can do this. All I've ever wanted is to be creative and successful and to make you happy, and I don't know how to deal with adding more to that. I don't think I can do it."

"Gwen," Flora says, tugging at her braid. Her eyes dart as she takes in Gwen's confession. "I want you to really think about this. Do you have feelings for her?"

Gwen doesn't need to think. "No."

"Because I would rather you tell me than just—"

"Flora, no." Clementine is fun and feisty and beautiful, but it was never her, not really. She was just a convenient, indulgent, glamorous escape. "I don't; I promise."

Flora nods, round dark eyes fixed on Gwen's. "Okay, I believe you." There's a hush, only the distant background noise of suburban life carrying on: the rustle of leaves, dogs barking several doors down, car doors closing, children yelling and laughing, garage doors cranking open and closed. "I know you're freaking out. You've been freaking out since we signed the deed to this place. No one is holding you captive here, Gwen. I am not your warden."

Is that how she's been making Flora feel? As if Gwen is only here until she can escape in the dead of night as soon as she gets the chance? "I know," Gwen says, moving closer on the bed, hooking her pinkie over Flora's. "I do want to be here, I—you know how I get. It's like I have to do something the wrong way first and then I can do it right. I went off course a little. I'm sorry."

Flora huffs, "G, you don't have to apologize for freaking out; I'm freaking out too."

"Really?" She's so steady and steadfast, so sure. Gwen hasn't stopped to remember that below the stillness can be churning chaos; Flora just keeps it quieter than she does.

"Yes, really." Flora drops back against the headboard. "We're having a child. That is terrifying. I worry that I can't do it, too, you know. That I'll be overwhelmed, juggling too much and dropping the ball on everything. And then I think," Flora says as she flips her hand over to lace their fingers together, "thank god I have Gwen, who grabs life by the balls and gives it a squeeze just for fun." Gwen smirks and tightens her hold on Flora's hand.

"Because I know you'll step in when I get overwhelmed. I know that you'll stop me from being a total softie pushover," Flora continues. "That you're my partner in this and that we can do anything together. And I know that you'll love this baby with a fire and fierce determination. There's no one else I want to do this with." Gwen tugs Flora's wrists until they move to cup her neck and skull, their foreheads lean together, and Flora whispers, millimeters from her lips, "We're a team. A damn good one."

"Everything is going to change," Gwen says softly, her lips brushing Flora's.

"Yes." Flora's lips curl against hers. "And I can't wait for our next adventure."

They stay just like that for several comforting breaths, with everything out in the open, honest and connecting and feeling a palpable relief. Then Gwen opens her eyes and means to say something about how much she loves Flora or how lucky she feels or how perfectly matched they are, only Flora is wearing a tight ribbed tank top and the generous swell of her cleavage is just *right there.*

"So you wanna, you know. *Make up.*" Gwen glances up, then back down, then back up. Lifts her eyebrows a few times just to be sure Flora gets the memo.

"You have such a one-track mind."

"Is that a—oh." She's flipped suddenly to her back. Flora's hands are now tight on Gwen's wrists, and she hovers over her. Gwen swallows and asks, "Are you, uh, feeling okay, then?" She hasn't even asked about Flora's morning sickness and exhaustion and sore, tender breasts.

"Yeah, I feel great, strangely enough. Like it's gone away?" It is strange, or maybe Flora has adjusted to the changes in her body, but Gwen can't think about that for long, because Flora's lips drag up her throat and she asks huskily, "Should I remind you who you belong to now?"

Gwen shivers and flexes her pinned-down hands. Flora is so rarely possessive or jealous. Their faith in each other is a point of pride for them both, but, god, if it isn't working for her right now. "Yes," Gwen hisses.

Flora's lips barely brush the line of Gwen's jaw, her ear, the exposed sides of her collarbones beneath the skimpy leather halter top, and finally Gwen's mouth, just a tease of pressure and then gone, moving over to breathe in Gwen's ear, "I don't care who Clementine Campbell is. She can want you, but she can't have you." A bite to Gwen's earlobe and Gwen wriggles and whines. "You're mine."

Gwen thrashes her head to get at Flora's mouth with her own, but Flora has moved away and is now leaning back and looking down, biting her lip shyly. "That was too much, right? Is this weird? This is weird."

She is seriously so cute. Gwen surges up as much as she can with Flora still holding her down, more tentatively now, and reassures her with a hard, off-center, eager kiss. "Not weird. So hot."

Flora flashes a grin that's far too angelic for the heat building low in Gwen's belly. Flora leans down for a peck, says, "Okay then," and then puts more pressure on Gwen's wrists. She drags tongue and teeth back down the stretched skin on Gwen's throat, her shoulders and stomach, and then moves to her sides.

"Can I?" Flora says, touching Gwen's side with the new tattoo, the petals of the violet etched there hidden under her shirt, just the green stem poking out from beneath the fabric.

"Yeah. It's still healing, though." It's still flaky and crusty, though the care sheet assures her this is normal.

Flora plucks at the hem of the halter set snug against Gwen's sternum, and together they untie it and lift it away. Gwen's nipples stand stiff and hard, but Flora bypasses them, settles across Gwen's hips and skims fingertips up her ribs. She traces around the flower petals, her touch so gentle and soft that Gwen breaks out in goosebumps across her bared chest.

"Beautiful," Flora says.

"You like it?"

Flora scans Gwen's chest, her face, and smiles. "I do." Then her jaw sets, a wicked look appears in her eyes, and she says, "Now where were we?"

Flora shifts to the side, keeping a hand flat on Gwen's bare stomach; her hips and legs press Gwen's lower half into the mattress. Flora shoves her thigh between Gwen's, and Gwen instantly clamps her legs tight, rubbing against her in a slow build of arousal. Flora makes a teasing path around one of Gwen's breasts; her parted lips drag around and under, dot kiss after kiss in the space between, then move on to the other side.

She blows a cool stream of air on one nipple, then the other. Gwen grunts and grinds against Flora's leg, but doesn't voice a single demand. This is Flora's show, and Gwen wants to let her run it.

She moves up to kiss Gwen with a promising flick of her tongue. When she bites down on Gwen's bottom lip, Gwen whimpers; she drags her sharp teeth down Gwen's neck, and Gwen arches and gasps; she sucks a nipple into her mouth, takes it between her teeth, and flicks the tip of her tongue against it. The frantic push of Gwen's hips with too much fabric in the way isn't nearly enough to relieve the ache.

Gwen only has one hand free. The other is held captive beneath Flora's shoulders; she can't do much more than wriggle some space to shove her own hand under the waistband of her fluffy skirt. Flora catches her wrist just as she gets two fingertips into her own underwear.

"Don't," Flora commands.

"Okay," Gwen agrees easily, and moves Flora's hand down instead. She pulls it away with a laugh. "Relax, G. I've got you."

She does, Gwen knows. She always has. So Gwen tucks her hand behind her head and trusts that Flora will get her there.

Flora shifts again, moving her thigh away and pushing Gwen's legs wide. The ridiculous tulle skirt is bunched up in a heap of ruffles and completely in the way, but Flora doesn't take it off. She ducks back to Gwen's breast, cupping and squeezing, and sucks hard on her nipple, sending shockwaves of pleasure coursing through Gwen's body with each sharp clamp of teeth. Gwen thinks she might come just from this, eventually, with pulse after pulse of wet heat between her legs pulling arousal so tight she could snap like a bowstring.

Then Flora finally flips the layers of tulle up and slips Gwen's underwear off, pushes two fingers inside, and bends to take Gwen's clit into her mouth. She licks and sucks and pushes her fingers in relentlessly, until Gwen's body arches up off the bed, her breath catches in her lungs, her skirt flips down over Flora's head, and pleasure shatters through her in waves.

Gwen floats back down to earth, catching her breath and spreading lax across the bed. Flora's not done with her, though. She's tugging the puffy skirt off, drawing circles and lines and zigzags across Gwen's now exquisitely sensitive pussy. Every pass over her clit is like a jolt of lighting in her belly, bordering between too much and just right as moan after moan spills from Gwen's lips.

"You're mine," Flora whispers.

Gwen jolts and gasps, "Yes. Oh god, *yes*."

Flora drags wetness from Gwen's opening and rubs a tight circle in a spot that makes stars flash across Gwen's closed eyes. Gwen comes with another rush, comes again after that, shuddering and shaking, and once again with nothing but a sigh as her blissed-out body and brain refuse to do anything more.

She tries to speak and pull Flora up, but manages only a mumble and the uncoordinated flap of one hand. Flora laughs and kisses Gwen's forehead.

"I missed you," she says.

"Mmph," Gwen replies, assuming Flora will know what she means. The bed dips and bounces as Flora gets up, water runs in the bathroom sink, and Flora returns to the bedside with a glass of water.

Gwen's brain comes back on track enough for her to say, "Get naked and get up here." She sprawls and smiles lazily.

"Making me do all the work," Flora tuts, stripping off her pajamas and crawling up Gwen's body.

Gwen kisses her, runs her hands all over Flora's soft skin, her dizzying full curves, from knee to thigh to ass to hip to stomach to the heavy, full sway of her breasts. "You ravished me, and now I'm useless."

Flora legs are spread wide over Gwen's shoulders and she grips the headboard. "Not *completely* useless, I hope."

Gwen hums, pulling her down and in until she can lick at the hot center of her with her neck craned and her mouth sealed tight over her pussy. She pulls back to press her tongue flat and let Flora ride it with quick rocks of her hips, then switches to pointed circles when Flora's thighs start to shake and she lets out little huffs of air above her.

Flora is close, but not quite there, building but not cresting, and Gwen's neck is getting sore. She moves her hands higher, kneads the swell of Flora's ass and then rubs between her cheeks, her hole, and then her slick opening and Flora goes still, silent. Gwen continues to suck on and lick her clit and finally, Flora shudders and comes.

They lie together naked. Flora is curled behind her, soft and comfortable and exactly right. "What about dark brown for the room," Gwen muses hazily. "Really dark. Really, really—"

"We are not painting the baby's room black," Flora says mildly, arm resting loose on Gwen's waist.

"Black and red. With an anarchy symbol spray-painted on one wall. It'll go perfectly with the baby's tiny safety pin pants and Mohawk," Gwen teases. "Or do you want our baby to be another cog in the machine, Flor? Is that what you want?"

"You're ridiculous," Flora says, rubbing her nose along Gwen's neck. "The baby Mohawk sounds cute, though."

"Doesn't it?" She was also sort of serious about the safety pin pants. "Sid Vicious works well for a boy or girl's name. Think about it."

Flora shoves at her. "Go get ready for bed." Gwen gets up, snags some underwear, and throws Flora a disgruntled look before heading to the bathroom. She catches Flora whispering to herself— "Sid"—as if she's trying it on for size. Giddy and effervescent with happiness, Gwen closes the door.

The mood stays through her bedtime routine, stays when Cheese nuzzles up to her, remembering that she isn't a stranger but someone who will feed her, and winds around Gwen's legs until she does so.

She stays light, joyous, and content; she is home. Settled in Flora's arms, she drifts to sleep and dreams of wispy, brightly-colored nothing.

Sometime in the dead of night, she wakes to their pitch-black room and finds the other side of the bed cold. Flora is gone. From the bathroom comes a steady *drip, drip, drip.*

Something is wrong. Gwen stumbles, confused and concerned, to the bathroom, every step heavy with dread. She pushes the door open—

Something is terribly, horribly wrong.

It's like a sick cosmic joke when they get the news they were dreading; both of them were afraid to speak it aloud, as if that would compel it into being. They knew, when Flora was curled in on herself in the bathtub shot through with crimson, the steady drip of the faucet punctuating Flora's pained gasps. They knew in the quiet of the car ride. They knew in the waiting room and during the exam. Their terse silence didn't matter, and Flora's whispered prayers didn't help; it happened anyway.

"I'd been gardening," Flora says, ashen and crying. "Without gloves. Could it—"

And Gwen confesses, her throat tight, "I was out of town, she had to change the litterbox, and she was stressed, maybe—"

The doctor is brusque yet kind, busy but willing to sit and softly reassure them. "This is no one's fault," she keeps telling them. "Miscarriage in the first twelve weeks is very common."

There's good news, and Gwen can tell the doctor means it as a comfort; there is no need for any further procedure, since it was so early the baby was probably never viable. Flora is healthy, and after she rests and recovers, they can try to conceive again right away. The echo of that squeezes like a fist around Gwen's heart.

They don't want *a* baby. They wanted *that* baby.

Try again, the doctor says, and all Gwen hears is the universe mocking, "Oh, now you want this baby so badly? Too late." She's haunted by the idea that her indifference caused this, that if she'd been there, if she'd only done something differently, if she'd talked to Flora sooner about her fears—

Too late.

Only this time, she speaks her fears, her hurt, her late night panicking. They work through it together. Terrible things happen to good people for no reason, and there's nothing to do but walk through it and hope tomorrow's sunrise eases the empty space a little.

Flora rests. The days are crisp and colorful, but their world feels covered with gray muslin: empty and quiet, permeated with heartbreak. Gwen waits on Flora hand and foot, offers all of her favorite foods, sea-salt caramel chocolates, massages and baths with lavender-scented bath salts, cheap and predictable paperback mysteries that she wrinkles her nose at, then devours in an afternoon.

One afternoon Nico and Grady back into the driveway with a truck bed full of plants and dirt. Grady hugs Flora tightly and murmurs something in her ear. Flora brushes a tear away.

"This is at my mother's insistence," Nico says as Grady yanks open the tailgate. "She says you have to 'connect to the earth and sun to heal.'" He pitches his voice high and clipped at the end. "And Flora, she's also concerned that you aren't getting enough iron."

Gwen knows it's not just from Nico's mom, though, not when he hands her a pot of flowers with delicate pink petals and says sadly, "I wish there was something more we could do for you."

The plants with blooms will stay inside for the fall and winter, decorating the house with a blush of color and life. Outside, they find a spot in the yard to all crouch together in the cool dirt, planting bulbs and wildflower seeds that will lie dormant until spring. When Flora goes inside, Gwen stands to stretch her legs and watches Nico and Grady pull each other up.

"As soon as we find our place," Nico says, wiping a smear of dirt from Grady's cheek, "we should plant a memorial garden like this for your grandparents."

Gwen can see Grady's quick intake of breath. "*Our* place?"

The dirt is gone from Grady's face, but Nico continues to stroke the spot, a steady back and forth. "Yes. Ours."

Flora returns with a candle her parents left after their recent visit—along with a fridge packed with food—a tall glass votive painted with a serene portrait of the Virgin Mary. She places it in the garden's center, where the flowers will soon bloom. "You don't have to pray with me," she says, lighting the candle. The three of them crouch behind her, and Grady folds his hands together. Flora bows her head and whispers, "*I have called you by name. You are mine.*"

Together, they watch the smoke curl and rise and disappear into the air when Flora blows the candle out.

"There's a tradition, in Japan" Nico says after a quiet moment, "for lost infants. They're called *mizuko*: water child. The idea is that a soul comes into existence like the flow of water, drop by drop, instead of all at once. So a soul is never really gone, it just flows inward and outward, like a single wave returning to the ocean."

Flora takes his hand and smiles. "That's really lovely, Nico."

Gwen isn't much for prayer or religion or souls flowing into existence, but after that day in their new memorial garden it seems as if the weight on their hearts starts to lift.

Nico gives her another week off, but two days in she's driving Flora crazy. The constant doting has become smothering, Gwen is listless and bored and starts reorganizing things: the spice rack, the pantry, the Tupperware cabinet with its frustrating refusal to stay tidy, magically spawning container-less lids and lidless containers that never match. She culls off-season and out-of-date styles from her own closet. When she starts on Flora's and casually mentions that Flora should try working in peplums and pencil skirts, Flora demands that Gwen go to work.

"No dressing me. Rule number one. It was in our vows," Flora says, handing Gwen her purse and shooing her out the door.

"Was not," Gwen protests, though it probably should have been.

She doesn't want to leave, but Flora seems to be okay, and some of her teacher friends are coming over. Gwen is never sure how that crowd feels about her, or her more off-color humor, so she goes, for the sake of marital harmony and avoiding disapproving schoolmarm flashbacks.

When she arrives at their office, Nico is at his desk, on the phone and clicking at his laptop. His mouth sets in concern as she sits at her desk.

"Distract me," she says, when he hangs up, puts his phone down, and spins his chair in her direction.

"I have a stack of packing slips that need to be entered into a spreadsheet."

It's perfect. Menial and irritating and requiring just enough focus to keep her from thinking about anything else. "Yes, please."

He's finishing prep here, then joining Clementine for the first leg of her tour. Grady has more work in the studio, then he's coming along as well. She doesn't know where things stand with her and Clementine. It's a path she isn't quite up to traversing right now.

"How are you and Grady lately?" Gwen asks, anxious for someone else's happiness to ease the bruising of her own heart.

Nico considers. "We're getting there." He moves his chair from side to side and looks out the window. "Decided to sell the apartment and Grady's house. Option C, you know? Try something else." He pulls at his bottom lip. "We test-drove a Ferrari 458 Italia."

Gwen enters a return shipping receipt for a six thousand-dollar alligator clutch that Clementine never used. "Did you buy it?"

"No," he says, then his mouth fights off a smirk. He doesn't look at her when he admits in a secretive hush, "We had crazy hot sex in the dealership's bathroom."

Gwen pauses her itemizing, puts her hands on her chest, and says, "Nico. You shared the salacious details of your life with me and you aren't even shit-faced. I'm touched."

He rolls his eyes. "Well, you slept with my boyfriend so I think we're there."

"He has a really firm butt," Gwen says, going back to the stack of invoices. Solid gold seven-band cage ring. Worth: twenty-one thou.

Nico hums and says in a tone of voice he usually reserves for statement blazers or his first cup of coffee, "Oh, I know." He scoots back over to his desk. "Are you and Flora—are you doing okay?"

Gwen considers. They're devastated and unsure of where to go from here, but minute by minute, hour by hour, day by day, they're healing. They're moving forward because there is no other way to go, navigating around the emptiness instead of tumbling headlong into it.

Life marches on, whether or not they'd like it to.

"We're getting there," Gwen finally decides.

October becomes November. Flora goes back to work, Nico leaves, and Gwen keeps busy with short-term clients in Nashville while Clementine is gone and Grady diligently puts down tracks for his next album. He stops by sometimes for dinner because Flora likes to feed him. Grady is always complimentary and charismatic and makes Flora blush and giggle. Gwen likes to keep tabs on him, but he seems okay. They're all climbing their way up to being okay.

For Thanksgiving they host both families. Flora's family is effusive and warm and boisterous; Gwen's parents are buttoned-up and stiff. Flora's nieces run around the house and terrify Cheese so badly they don't see her for three entire days after they leave and resort to sliding food and water under their bed, where nothing but a pair of glowing yellow eyes in the corner reassure them she's still alive under there. They spend a busy Christmas in the warm embrace of Flora's extended family in Virginia.

Gwen gets an email from her mother a few days after they get back home. The fridge is stacked with leftovers, and on the counter are five fractional pies covered with plastic.

> *Gwen,*
>
> *I never offered my condolences. I lost a baby when you were two years old. I don't think I've ever informed you of that. I understand what a difficult time this must be. Your father and I would like to extend an invitation to a traditional holiday celebration next year, though I am aware of your disdain for traditions of any sort.*
> *Mom.*

"She was so close," Gwen says, chin on her fist, resting on her stomach on the bed while Flora works on lesson plans.

She leans forward to read over Gwen's shoulder and scratches through the newly buzzed hair of her undercut, which is freshly trimmed and highlighted in silvery lilac. "At least she's trying. And they came all the way here just for Thanksgiving dinner. That counts for something."

"I guess," Gwen muses. "It's an excuse to go back to L.A. for a while, at least."

Flora mmhmms and writes something with her caustic-smelling marker. "You know, I was thinking. We could start spending our summers there. If you pick up some L.A. clients and Nico doesn't mind. Maybe get a little condo." She shakes her head at something on the curriculum guide at her knee. "I know you miss it still."

Gwen agrees, and sends a brief affirmative reply email. It would be a nice compromise. And it would work even when their kids are in school.

They still haven't talked about it, what's next. Occasionally, one of them points out that they still have two samples of sperm left, that maybe they should make an appointment, and that they can try again now. It just never seems to happen. It never seems like the right time.

The Sunday after the temperatures first drop below freezing overnight, their doorbell rings unexpectedly. Gwen answers the door with one rubber glove still on, not terribly upset at being interrupted mid-toilet-cleaning.

"Clementine?"

30

"**Aren't you in** the middle of a tour?" Gwen opens the door just a crack, just enough to see Clementine in a belted cashmere trenchcoat buttoned up to her chin with her hands buried in the deep pockets and pink blooming across her nose. Gwen hasn't had any communication with Clementine these past months; it's all been filtered through Nico, and even then, all business.

"What are you doing here?"

Clementine tucks her windswept hair behind her ears. "We're heading up to St. Louis from Atlanta and I wanted to stop by." She looks over Gwen's head, then pats at something in the inside breast pocket of her thick coat. "Actually, is Flora here?"

"Um." Gwen hesitates. This could go very badly. "Well, she—"

"Gwen! Why are you letting all the heat out; it's wasteful." Flora walks past, dirty dustrag in hand, wearing sweats, her hair twisted up and held back by a colorful scarf. "Oh."

"Hey, Flora." Clementine wiggles her fingers in a wave.

Flora looks at Clementine, then looks at Gwen. "Hi, Clementine. Come on in; it's freezing out there."

They all stand awkwardly in the entryway until Flora offers to make tea and Gwen grabs a tin of cookies, and then they all sit awkwardly at the dining room table.

"I'm sorry I didn't call ahead," Clementine says as soon as Flora sets a hot mug of peppermint tea down in front of her. She doesn't remove her coat, and her face is still flushed from the cold. "I... honestly kept chickening out, so this was sort of last-minute. Kevin insisted I come. I think he was tired of listening to me rehearse what I wanted to say."

"It's fine, we were ju—"

Clementine interrupts Flora right away. "I'm sorry to interrupt, it's just if I don't go ahead and say this I'm afraid I never will." Holding tight to the mug, she shakes her head and closes her eyes. "I want to apologize, Gwen. And to you, too, Flora. For the way I behaved in Las Vegas. I am... so embarrassed." Flora stays quiet, thoughtfully watching her as she steels herself for the rest. "What you two have, I want. Not..." She glances at Gwen. "Not *you* specifically, Gwen. I mean you're cute and all, but you could have been anyone."

Gwen squints one eye at her. "Thank you?"

Clementine chuckles softly, staring down at her tea. "It was more like, I wanted to see how it felt because I, I don't think I'll ever have the kind of love you have. And I thought maybe—even if was fake, even if only other people believe it, I could have it, just a little bit."

Clementine glances at Flora, then at Gwen. "Sometimes my ambition gets the best of me, and I forget that people aren't business strategies or things that I can accomplish just because I want them. I am really, truly sorry."

"It's okay." Gwen reaches out to her and then thinks better of it, leaving her hand half-outstretched on the table. "I've sure as hell let my career compromise my personal life and judgment." She never has quite figured out how to balance them both; maybe there is no such thing. "But wait," Gwen pulls her hand back. "I get how being connected to Grady made sense, but me? Wouldn't that be bad for your career? A woman? And not even a famous one?"

Clementine's spine straightens, her shoulders are set high, and that cool, confident ease permeates her body and expression. "A little controversy has always been good for my career." With a wry smile and a flash of excitement in her eyes, she says in a newscaster's bombastic tone, "What will she do next?" She switches back to her own lilting voice and says, "I like keepin' people on their toes."

Flora stays quiet, holding tight to her mug with both hands, but not drinking. The clock in the kitchen ticks like a countdown. Gwen nods, crosses and uncrosses and recrosses her legs, and slurps her tea. Finally, Flora speaks, her tone even and measured. "It takes a good person to own their missteps and make things right. An almost-mistake, a lapse of judgment, is not something you should beat yourself up over. We all fall short sometimes." She glances at Gwen. "I know I do."

Clementine turns the tea mug around and around in her hands. "I expect better of myself. One stupid mistake could end my career. That's why I try to avoid relationships in the first darn place." She's solemn, until suddenly she sits up straight and her eyes light up. "Anyway! I didn't come here to bring y'all down or dump my woes on you. I said what I wanted to say, and I've brought you something." She unbuttons her coat and pulls something from the inside pocket.

"Clementine, you don't have to bribe us with gifts, we totally forgive you—oh my god, a kitten!" Gwen reaches immediately for the wiggly little meowing ball of orange and white fuzz. "Flor, look at the baby!" Gwen holds the kitten nose to nose and it meows loudly.

Flora is melting and trying not to melt, Gwen can tell—an obvious internal war.

"Don't worry," Clementine says, looking at Flora's knotted brow and pressed-together lips. "I have a backup home for her, just in case. But we were coming up from Jacksonville, stopped for gas and Kevin was uh, relieving himself in the woods."

"Classic Kevin," Gwen tells the kitten.

Clementine smiles at the pair of them. "And he happened to see these little kittens in a box, just left there in the woods. So we brought them onto the tour bus and found homes for the others, but this little gal reminded me of your Cheese."

Gwen turns her tiny kitten body around. She has the same coloring and similar striped markings, but also a little splotch of orange next to her nose. Gwen bops it with her finger. The kitten mews at her.

"Flora... Look... The baby..." Gwen singsongs, moving the kitten through the air toward Flora, who is rapidly losing the battle to keep a reasoned and safe emotional distance.

"Oh, fine. Give her here." The kitten cries a few more times, and then Cheese appears, staring at them from between the spindles of the stairs, not daring to come any closer. Flora tucks the kitten against her chest and she immediately snuggles into the softness of Flora's breasts.

"I feel a deep spiritual connection to this kitten," Gwen says. She can hear the kitten purring away in contentment while Flora scratches at her teeny little head.

Clementine looks pleased and much more at ease. "I'd keep her, but I'm gone too much. And now Cheese doesn't have to be all alone."

"That's really sweet Clementine, thank you." Flora reaches across the table, hands Gwen the kitten and takes Clementine's hand and holds it long enough for the air between them to go clear and light. "However, if you try to kiss my wife again you *will* be sorry."

Clementine chuckles again.

"Oh, she's not joking," Gwen says. The kitten is gnawing on her hand.

"No," Flora says, flat.

Clementine nods. "Understood." She gives the kitten a parting pat as she stands. She clears her throat and says in a clipped tone, "I hope we can resume our working relationship now, Gwen."

"Uh, I don't think so," Gwen scoffs. Clementine tilts her head. "Because we're friends," Gwen clarifies, standing to walk her to the door. "Friends who don't care about luxury weekends away in a penthouse suite. Friends who want you to know that you definitely aren't all alone."

"Yes," Flora says opening the door, "Come by anytime." She pulls Clementine into a hug. "And don't give up on love so soon. You never know who might end up capturing your heart for good."

Gwen rises on her toes to join the hug. Scents of honeysuckle and wood polish and peppermint swirl in the biting cold air. "You'll find a girl who loves you back, and likes you, just you. I know it."

When they pull away, Clementine wipes her eyes, smiles at Flora and Gwen, and turns the collar up on her coat. "Or a him, or a them, or..." She shrugs and steps onto the porch. "I'd like to keep my options open. I never did like settling for the status quo." She winks and jogs down the steps, hair sweeping and shimmering, skin glowing and eyes bright. "I'll see you gals soon!"

Gwen closes the door and looks at Flora in stunned silence.

"That was—" Flora says.

"Yeah."

"She is really—"

"Yep."

She really is something else, Clementine Campbell. Gwen is just glad to be an ally and not an enemy in Clem's inevitable world domination.

They name the kitten Crackers.

They're in the bath together that night when everything clicks into place for Gwen. She's washing Flora's hair, kneeling behind her with rivulets of flowery-smelling suds running down her arms into the bathwater. Crackers the kitten watches from the tub's edge, batting occasionally at the bubbles.

It's so odd how things end up, what choices or mistakes or near mistakes led them here, the fragmented pieces of a puzzle that needed to come together just right.

"Did you know Grady was raised by his grandparents?" Gwen works the shampoo through her hair, rubs at her scalp and temples.

"Mmhmm." Flora is loose and loopy; sex and a bath and hairwashing, and she becomes the purring kitten.

"What do you think would have happened to him, if they hadn't stepped in?"

"Mmm, foster care, I guess?" Flora passes back a cup so Gwen can rinse and start with the conditioner.

"Yeah, probably so."

Here they've been so focused on option A—when they'd be ready again, if they'd be ready again—that they haven't even considered other paths. "Hey, Flor?" Gwen piles her conditioner-slick hair on top of her head. "Have you ever thought about adoption?"

31

"**Why are you** showing me this?"

The next morning, Gwen pulls up a tabloid website while they eat spinach and mushroom omelets in the kitchen. The window is clouded with cold dew, the gardens and yard outside are brown and barren, and the trees are spindly skeletons. It's the very first picture of her arm on Clementine's waist; the one that started the rumors.

"She was trying to get away from this pushy photographer. It was terrifying," Gwen explains, feeling a pang of sadness for Clementine. It's part of the deal, but sometimes Gwen isn't quite sure why. Everyone should be allowed moments that are for themselves and not for show. "Anyway, that's not what I wanted to show you. It's this." She points to a banner in the corner of the photograph. It's blurry, but "Hope for Children" is legible in swooping yellow letters.

Flora chews her omelet. "And that is..."

"I only read a little bit of the brochure, but they help children in foster care find families, and help couples or individuals who want to foster or adopt. Classes and trainings and support groups. Counseling, events to meet waiting kids. Stuff like that." Gwen opens a new tab on her browser and loads the Hope for Children page. "It's like Nico said about the water spirits. Maybe there's a little soul already out there, just waiting for us."

It's as if she can feel it, this connection, fragile and invisible, but tugging at her. "I can go ahead and call, see what our first steps would be?"

Gwen searches for a piece of paper and pen nearby and settles for using the back of the water bill envelope. She scribbles down the main number, the fax number, email contacts, and the street address for the main office.

Flora is quiet, watching Gwen click and write and transfer all the pertinent info into her phone while Gwen's breakfast and tea go cold and untouched. "You're really excited about this," Flora says, sipping her tea with a small smile.

Gwen looks up from entering all the upcoming foster-to-adopt intro classes. "Yeah, I—" It's not that the pregnancy, or the loss of it, was the wrong path. She's still heartbroken over it, may always be so. But this feels like those times in her life when she took a sudden detour, like dropping out of college to work as a lowly part-time personal shopper's assistant at Nordstrom's and working at a salon to pay the bills—the salon where she met Nico, the store where she honed her eye for styling; locking eyes with the girl she never thought would give her a second look, much less a second date, and certainly not a lifetime; moving away from L.A.; going to Vegas in a panic and coming back with a fresh perspective and closer friendships. All these were things she never expected to work out the way they did, all were things that could have gone wrong, but instead led her to the exact place she needed to be.

"It feels right," Gwen says. Of course, she won't do it without Flora. "Don't you think?"

Flora sips her tea and scans Gwen's face. "I do."

The orientation they attend answers all of their questions and brings up several sets of new ones, and a ton of paperwork with even harder questions: What about a child with special needs? Or with a history of abuse? Prenatal drug exposure? Would they be open to a group of siblings? Older children?

They sip watery coffee in paper cups in a church classroom, chatting with other hopeful adoptive parents, all of them excited and nervous. The couple who led the meeting, a college professor and his photographer husband who adopted three elementary-aged siblings last year, stay behind to offer seasoned advice.

"Adopting from foster care requires two things," the photographer husband says, "Faith and fearlessness."

Gwen turns to Flora. "Between the two of us, I think we have that covered."

Soon, though, they discover that more than anything, it requires waiting. Waiting for their next class or training, for the paperwork to go through, to be assigned a social worker. Making appointments for background checks and medical clearances and CPR certification. Then waiting for the home inspection and, after that, waiting for the results.

Flora has years of calm in the face of long, difficult days under her belt from being an elementary school teacher, and Gwen has put in her fair share of drudgery while working her way up from coffee fetcher to respected stylist. Through it all, drudgery and paperwork and impossible choices and endless waiting, it's something they're doing together, not a strange phenomenon that is happening to Flora while Gwen watches, anxious and unsure, from the sidelines.

They chug along with the certification process while winter continues in full force. Crackers is hyperactive and destructive, running around the house as though possessed, climbing curtains and bookshelves and Flora's skirts and harassing Cheese. She makes up for it all by curling into their laps whenever they sit down, rumbling like a motor, and meowing to be held, petted, and loved.

Spring comes and Crackers grows into a lanky, demanding adolescent. She eases off Cheese, though, and they finally start to get along: sunning in the square patches of light in their entryway, grooming each other, cuddling together under the bed.

The miscarriage comes up in unexpected ways, as when they're filling out the age range they'd prefer. "Do you think we'll regret never bringing a newborn baby home?" Flora wonders, late at night when they confess their fears and worry to each other in the dark, held safe in each other's arms.

"I don't want this kid to feel like a replacement," Gwen counters. "We need to want *them*, not the baby we lost." Still unsure, they mark down an age range of newborn to age three.

And it comes up in expected ways: while painting the nursery in dark, rich browns and greens with a forest mural on one wall; while buying toys and clothes in a variety of age ranges and sizes, including newborn, just so they're ready; when they put together a crib, knowing there was once someone else they were preparing for.

Flora spends a long time smoothing out the fitted sheet on the crib mattress, getting every possible wrinkle out. Gwen stacks half a dozen packs of diapers by size in the closet.

"You okay?"

Flora frowns and rests her hand in the center of the empty crib. "Yeah, I think so." Crackers bounds into the room and winds around Gwen's legs, then Flora's, then hops right into the crib. Flora tsks and scoops her up. "You are not actually a baby, you know that, right?" Crackers purrs her loud-motor purr and nuzzles her fuzzy head against Flora's chin.

On an evening when it's finally warm enough to turn off the heat and crack a window open—all the waiting and preparation has led to them sitting around in the evenings, staring at their phones and willing them to ring—Gwen finally has enough.

The cats are at a window watching the crickets and birds outside, and Gwen is watching them, slowly going mad. "I can't take this. We should go out. See a show." What is the point of living in the music capital of the country if they never go see any music?

Flora gives up pretending to have any interest in her book. "Okay. Should we see if anyone is free?"

Nico and Grady are back in town, but still looking for a new place. Clementine is finishing a press junket now that her tour to promote her new album is over. Some of Flora's teacher friends are probably available, but—

"Let's just go out, me and you. We haven't had a date night in so long."

Flora hums, then runs the back of her fingers on Gwen's thigh. "That sounds nice. And I'll even let you dress me."

"Really?" She stands, and Gwen, mind racing with possibilities, scampers upstairs after her. She never gets to do this anymore, *never*. Oh, and she has the perfect dress in mind.

"Nothing low-cut," Flora adds at the top of that stairs.

Gwen freezes with one foot in the air. "What? Oh come on, that's just cruel!" Flora laughs and disappears into the room, so Gwen races up the stairs in case she changes her mind.

Gwen zips Flora into a slim, clingy dress. She brushes her silky dark hair with long strokes, clasps a delicate necklace around her throat, and then cups her chin and swipes lipstick the color of dark ripe cherries across her plush lips. She gets down from the counter and says, "Beautiful," with all the reverence and awe Flora deserves.

32

The club is stone-walled and tin-ceilinged, and warmly lit in muted oranges and yellows like a sunset. The stage is small; the acts are all singer-songwriter types. Gwen and Flora sip wine and eat appetizers and enjoy the sort of easy, comfortable company Gwen has come to appreciate.

It's no hot-spot Vegas nightclub: no bouncers at the door, no celebrity clientele, no techno music thumping away the functionality of her eardrums. It's the life she chose, not the life she flirted with. She's grown since Vegas, she likes to think. Flora is not something she needs to rebel against, and Vegas—or somewhere else—is always there should she need to go a little crazy again. That's not a life, though, at least not one she has any interest in living full-time.

The second act leaves the stage, and Flora looks at Gwen across the table, sips her wine and chuckles.

"What?"

"I was just thinking about our first date and what a disaster it was."

"Oh god, I was so nervous," Gwen groans. She is never going to live that picnic down. "I couldn't believe that you actually called me and I was trying so hard to make a good impression."

"So you spilled illegally procured champagne on my skirt." Flora tips her wine glass at Gwen.

"In my defense, I really wanted you to take your skirt off."

Flora laughs, then sets her glass down, drops her chin into one hand and gazes at Gwen with a grin. "I thought you were adorable."

"I was trying to be cool, not adorable."

"When I first saw you," Flora says, still gazing at Gwen with heavy-lidded eyes and quirked-up cherry-red lips, "I thought you were so cool and badass. All those piercings and that blue hair, dressed head to toe in black. That black lipstick you wore!"

Gwen shakes her head. "If could I go back in time and tell myself that sometimes less is more..." Live and learn.

"And then, you took me on a date," Flora continues, "And you were so fumbly and adorable and you spilled wine everywhere. Then on our next date you spent half of it lecturing me all about the history of corsets, and I knew for sure, then..." She takes Gwen's hand across the table. "That you were actually a huge dork."

Gwen pulls her hand away with a mock scoff and wrinkles her nose. "Corsets have a really fascinating sociopolitical background, okay?"

Flora laughs again. "Dork."

After one more act, they head home, swinging their hands between them on the way to the parking garage. The night is cool, the trees along the sidewalk are budding with new leaves: the hope and promise of spring. Downtown is buzzing with energy and neon lights and music. Nashville isn't New York or L.A., or even Vegas, but it has a vibrancy and character all its own.

"I thought I was a rebound," Gwen confesses, walking at the flash of the crosswalk. Red lights spill onto the street where they hurry across. "That you'd go back to Imani, and I'd never see you again."

Flora stops them under the pink and green dotted awning of a children's boutique that's closed for the night. "Let me tell you about Imani," Flora says, winding Gwen close. "She was stunningly gorgeous and brilliant and well-read and—"

"Is this supposed to be making me feel better?"

"I was getting there, hush. *And* I saw absolutely no future with her. She was right on paper, but nothing else. You were nothing that I expected and everything I needed. And when I looked at you, when I was with you…" Flora runs one hand up the back of Gwen's head. "I saw forever. And not just that, I was *excited* about our forever."

Gwen brings her hand around, kisses the center of her palm and lets her lips linger there to say against her skin, "No wonder we work so well; I'm a huge dork and you're a giant sap."

Flora smacks at her hip, and they continue on. "You know, Imani is still single," Flora teases when they get in the car.

Gwen backs out of the space and onto the street. "Maybe we could hook her up with Clementine." She's joking, but that's actually not a half-bad idea.

Back at home they make out on the couch the way they did the first time Gwen brought her home, only the place is much nicer and the furniture isn't a bare mattress she found on a corner, and Gwen isn't quite as shocked to be kissing Flora. She's straddling Flora's lap, one hand down Flora's shirt and the other up her skirt, creeping past the waistband of her panties, when her phone rings.

It's probably Nico, with either a fashion crisis or a "Grady and I will never agree on a house and we're going to live in the bed of his truck at this rate" crisis. She lets it go to voicemail and continues on her mission.

Gwen pushes the sleeve off Flora's shoulder, wiggles her fingers deeper—

Flora's phone rings. She cranes from under Gwen to check it. "Hello?" Gwen drags her tongue along the slope of her shoulder, dots kisses along the curve of her clavicle, and nips at her mouth. "Thi—mmm. This is she, yes."

Gwen moves her lips down Flora's neck, sucking and kissing, to the hinge of her jaw, her earlobe. She doesn't need Flora's full attention to have fun. Then Flora stands, upending Gwen right onto the floor.

"Ow." Gwen pouts.

"What? Yes, of course. Okay. Okay. Thank you." Flora hangs up the phone, turns to Gwen with eyes widened and the phone clutched to her chest. "A baby," is all she can say.

They don't know much about him. He's eleven weeks old and was born nearly three months premature. Birth mom had no prenatal care; he has "probable" continuing medical and developmental complications. His first placement fell through at the last minute. He has a shock of thick black hair, light brown eyes, and soft skin a few shades darker than Flora's. And in less than twelve hours after the phone call, he is home.

His name is Cayo.

33

Parenting, Gwen quickly learns, is the opposite of beige drudgery. It's not for the faint of spirit, or weak of stomach, and there's no sense of stability or normalcy at all for those first few topsy-turvy days. Flora's parents and sister and nieces come to visit, cuddle and spoil Cayo, give Flora and Gwen so many baby care tips they could fill an encyclopedia, take a million pictures, and leave them with more food than they could ever eat and a mountain of tiny clothes.

Clementine sends them a gift basket of luxe baby items from a boutique in France. Nico and Grady come by with a slick, black, Armani leather diaper bag stocked with supplies and a wicked space-age stroller.

"Top of the line," Nico says in his "I'm extraordinarily pleased with myself" voice, "all-terrain wheels with a reversible seat and twelve-inch wheels with settings for sand or snow. One-handed operation and folding, five-point harness for safety, and we even threw in a parasol, snack tray and cupholder, and a cozy wool seat liner."

"You can take this baby off-roading," Grady adds, his arm settled proudly around Nico's waist. "Oh! Dibs on taking him for his first four-wheeler ride!"

They babble at the baby sleeping in Flora's arms, and then Grady holds him and sings to him and Nico keeps a pleasant and polite distance.

Gwen's parents send a gift card.

"Okay, I'm just gonna be up-front with you: I have no idea what I'm doing." Flora is at work, finishing the last few weeks of the school year, as it was easier for Gwen to get time off at a moment's notice. Flora's family is gone, all the visitors are back to their daily lives, and now it's just Cayo and Gwen. It's as if she's standing on the roof of the Stratosphere again, taking a breath and jumping with blind stupid courage all she has to cling to.

Easing him carefully onto the changing table, she struggles with the little snaps on his onesie and tries to remember all the advice swimming around in her brain: Get everything ready before starting; keep one hand on his belly to keep him from squirming off the table and cracking his head on the floor; put a washcloth over his little baby firehose penis or she will get sprayed. Don't use diaper cream every time. Or was it *do* use diaper cream every time? Or *never* use diaper cream? Or was it baby powder? Which one causes cancer? She can't remember...

Cayo kicks his feet, dislodges the washcloth, and starts to fuss. "Okay. All right, I—" Gwen blows out a frustrated breath. "Everyone seems to have faith in my ability to do this, but I think they may be wrong. Lucky for you, I'm all about the doing and not so much with the thinking." She opens a clean diaper and starts to slide it under him. "Or maybe unlucky for you, depending. At any rate, we're gonna do this, and if I screw up then we can both be thankful that your long-term memory has yet to develop."

Cayo scrunches up his whole face, kicks his feet, and squawks.

"Exactly," Gwen tells him.

It takes a few tries, some mismatched buttons, and a little frustrated crying on both their parts, but they manage. Then she has to figure out how to dose him with his reflux medicine and warm a bottle while he ramps up the crying with his little fists balled and his legs kicking furiously.

By the time they make it to the couch and he's pulling on the bottle with greedy little grunts, one hand gripping the front of her shirt, Gwen is exhausted. And it's only midmorning. She hasn't had a shower yet, hasn't eaten. The cats ate, at least; they made sure of that.

"Right, where were we?" she says as he sucks with his eyes half closed in the cradle of her arms. "I think we left off at the Industrial Revolution at around three in the morning, right? So, with the advent of factory technology, interest in fashion took off in the middle class and even working classes. Style was no longer a luxury for the wealthy, Cayo. This is where fashion design and innovation gets really inter—"

A text from Flora interrupts the lesson.

Flora: How is he? How are you? Is he still sniffly he seemed sniffly this morning.

Gwen sends a picture of him eating and reassures Flora that he's fine and doesn't seem sniffly.

She puffs out a breath so hard it makes the stringy hair fly up from her face. Great, now she's worried about him being sick. She drops her head back against the couch and watches him eat. At twelve weeks old he is still roughly the size of a newborn, still mostly acts like a newborn. The doctor they've seen a few times already assures them that this is normal, and it takes time but most preemies catch up eventually, more or less.

The hospital released his medical records to them, and they learned a little more: He'd been on oxygen for months and had some hemorrhaging in his brain that caused some vision loss, though to what extent they won't know for some time. His digestive system is still immature, so he has to eat special formula very frequently, day and night.

Gwen has never been so tired and less sure of her abilities. And when she looks at him—eyes only open to drowsy slivers, his eyelashes like butterfly wings, tiny feet and chubby cheeks, and his little hand holding on to Gwen as if she's his safe harbor in this crazy world—she has never been more in love.

She had no idea she could love someone this much.

So she is completely out of her depth and still convinced she's going to screw this up one way or another. She still sees Flora and the way she held Cayo for the first time: it was as if the mothering switch flicked on. Gwen is still waiting for that to happen, if it ever will. But she would stand in front of a speeding train for this boy without needing to give it a second thought, and that has to count for something. She loves him right now, exactly as he is, and she wants only his happiness. It seems so simple and so tremendously impossible.

After his bottle, Cayo slips off to sleep, milk-drunk and messy. Gwen carefully wipes his chin and mouth, eases him to her shoulder to burp him, and has just decided to try him in his little bedside bassinet and go back to sleep herself when her phone rings. Cayo startles, and she settles him back to sleep by bouncing and pacing as she answers the phone.

"Mom?"

"Gwen. Hello. Your father and I were discussing coming there to meet the baby at some point in the future."

Gwen fumbles with the phone, almost dropping it when Cayo shifts in her arms. "Let me put him down, hold on." She drops the phone on the couch next to his empty bottle and the soiled burp cloth, swaddles Cayo and puts him in his crib, and then has to find and sanitize a pacifier for when he wakes. She gets him settled again and does not expect her mother to be waiting when she remembers where she left her phone.

"You still there?" Her mother gives a noise of affirmation. "Sorry. I'm completely frazzled right now. What were you calling about?"

"I remember those days," her mother says. "You were a very difficult baby."

Gwen is raw from lack of sleep and an overwhelming roller coaster of emotions, so she snaps, "I'm sorry I've been such a disappointment and source of misery for you since birth."

Her mother says nothing. Gwen leans against a wall and presses her thumb and index finger against her glassy, bloodshot eyes. She starts to apologize.

"Gwen," her mother interrupts. "I've been thinking a lot. And I, I'd like to start fresh, if we can. I know we haven't always seen eye to eye—"

Gwen snorts; delirious exhaustion has reduced her very thin layer of self-preservation to nothing at all. "Sorry."

"However," her mother goes on, ignoring Gwen's outburst, "you are an adult now, and your father and I are both very proud of the life you've built for yourself. Even if it isn't the one we would have chosen for you. I guess you know now how your children are never quite what you'd expect."

Gwen smiles at the surprising journey that led them to Cayo. "Yeah. 'Expect the unexpected' is the key to parenting successfully, I think."

Her mother hmphs disdainfully over the phone. "A couple weeks in and you're a parenting expert? You still have plenty to learn, Gwen."

Gwen lifts her eyes to the ceiling, but manages to contain her heavy sigh. *Baby steps*, she thinks. They can exchange vague pleasantries and surface-level affection, and she can start fresh, let things roll off her back like water off a duck's oily feathers. Speaking of oily—she touches her hair and curls her lip in disgust. She really should take a shower while she can.

"You guys are welcome here whenever. I'd like to start fresh, too, Mom." She covers a yawn with her elbow. Nap first, then a shower.

"In that case perhaps we'll go ahead and book a flight."

Gwen blinks. "Wait, for real?"

Her mother has switched to no-nonsense mode, the one Gwen is most familiar with. "Yes, I'd like to meet my grandson."

Gwen hadn't been sure they would accept Cayo at all, if they would ever truly consider him family. "Really?"

"Of course. Now we should discuss getting him on a schedule. He's not too young to learn discipline, Gwen—"

Cayo starts to cry, and Gwen still has to shower and eat and nap, and as she heads up the stairs the cats hop in front of her, begging for food. Perfect timing, really.

"Baby is crying; gotta go." Gwen hangs up before her mom can continue the lecture. She can laugh about it, though. She picks Cayo up and rubs his back soothingly. Her mother may be trying, but some things never change.

They spend most of the summer in Los Angeles, subletting a little condo near the beach while one of Flora's teacher friends house-and-cat-sits for them. It gives Cayo a chance to get to know his West Coast family and roots. Gwen picks up clients with no problem, and she and Flora take Cayo to all their old spots: the cafés serving fresh California produce; the hiking trails and gardens; Flora's old school and favorite library; Disneyland; and downtown, where Gwen spent much of her time, patronizing and then working with clients who were appearing at the clubs there.

Cayo won't remember any of it, but L.A. will be woven into the story of his life.

The last day there, they sit on the beach and stick his little feet in the Pacific Ocean. After a visit to Ocean City, Maryland with Flora's sister and her family, Cayo has now been to both coasts.

"I don't miss it the way I thought I would," Gwen says, as a wave slides up around them. "Like finally coming home again, but it doesn't feel that way."

"No?"

Cayo is curled up on Flora's lap, his skin is sand- and sun-kissed, and he's fast asleep. The low tide glides in as far as Flora's crossed legs, but doesn't reach the baby safe in the cradle of Flora's arms.

Gwen smiles at them, the dual tugs on her heartstrings. "I guess *home* really is just a state of mind." Cayo's little bare, wet-sandy feet stretch out and push against Gwen's knee, and his hand rests high on Flora's chest. Wherever she wanders, Gwen knows where her home is.

34

Three months ago...

Flora's ideas about destiny weren't quite the same as Gwen's; Flora believed in choice, like Gwen, and that choices rippled out like falling dominoes or waves of energy or, sometimes, an avalanche. Unlike Gwen, she did believe in a higher power, a guiding force, the whisper in her gut that said, "This way."

That was what had brought her to California on a scholarship, and to Gwen—to staying with Gwen even through the bleakest moments. That was what had told her it was time to move on from L.A. and that Tennessee was right—what made her *sure* that Gwen would never betray her trust, despite what those terrible magazines had to say about it.

She believed that fate was what had brought her to Cayo; and fate was choices guided by destiny. How else to explain that the moment she laid eyes on him, she knew without a doubt that he was her son, and that they had been waiting for each other?

But losing the baby... No. That wasn't predestined. That wasn't meant to be. It was terrible and heartbreaking, because life is sometimes terrible and heartbreaking. The courage to try again, to take Gwen's hand and trust in Gwen's bravery and her own faith, to take the jump together—that was meant to be. They had found a new path, together.

Though destiny, of course, was not quite as simple as arriving at the proper place and time and then all was as it should be.

For all of Gwen's worry about being a terrible mother, she certainly dove right in anyway. Flora knew she would, but still, the absolute chaos of those first several days; it was as if the settled quiet of their life as a couple was suddenly shot from a cannon, landing them in this exhausting new reality of a baby who was learning to eat, learning to settle and sleep, learning everything. The diaper changes and baths, the late nights and early mornings, deciphering what his cries meant and how to soothe him, family in and family out and friends in and friends out...

Gwen thrived in the insanity, while Flora was overwhelmed.

Then finally, they found a routine; a settling into their new normal. Flora was relieved. And Gwen was restless, which brought them to their compromise: a cozy apartment in Marina Del Rey for the summer. It wasn't much bigger than Gwen's first place near the university, but considerably nicer, with nautical decorations of ship's wheels and seashells, blue and white stripes and anchors and old-timey maps. It was crisp and bright, with the taste of salt in the air. She and Cayo spent most of their time in a rocking chair by the big sliding glass door. Cayo ate and slept and blinked wide-eyed at the world around them; Flora fed and soothed and watched. Watched him, watched the boats in the marina drift in and out. Watched the waves bump against the docks. Watched the seagulls spiral and screech and heard the palm trees rustle in the brined ocean breeze. She'd always loved the ocean; she found its power and mystery soothing.

Gwen worked, taking on jobs that required the hustle and vehemence and kick-in-the-teeth that Nashville just didn't. They'd found their stride, for now.

"He's getting so chunky! I love it. The girls can't wait to get their grubby hands on him again."

Flora tucked the phone between her right ear and shoulder and spoke softly. Cayo was heavy with sleep and limp in her left arm with his bowed little mouth slack, eyes darting behind his eyelids. She marveled at how much he'd changed already: His skin had darkened in the California sun, his cheeks were now round and fat, and his thighs were adorably squishy. His hair remained thick and black with a mind of its own; there was just more of it now.

Selene continued as Cayo snoozed away, "How is he doing?"

"Mmm, well. He's six months old, but three adjusted. He's hitting milestones slow and steady. In his own time, you know?" Flora wasn't worried because their pediatrician wasn't worried, and of course she'd read every book and article and blog and message board that had ever been published about both adoption and preemies. Gwen remained adamant that he was a rebel determined to do things his own way, and that worked for Flora.

"And how are—" Something crashed in the background on Selene's end of the phone call. "Nyla! Outside with that!" During a brief back and forth, Flora watched Cayo's little mouth curl and pout and suckle on nothing. "Sorry," Selene said, "I cannot believe Dad thought it was a good idea to get her a bow and arrow set."

Flora laughed and Selene scoffed, "Just wait until he gets Cayo obnoxious presents, and then we'll see how funny it is."

"Oh gosh." Flora groaned. "He's already way too excited about having a boy to roughhouse with. I can't even imagine..."

"Maybe Cayo will be a gentle and sensitive child like you, with an interest in fashion like Gwen, and you'll be safe."

Cayo grunted and kicked out his fat little legs, scowling the way he did when he was gearing up to scream for food. "I kind of doubt that will happen."

His NICU nurse had called him a fighter, while he squalled thorough her demonstration of the specific way he liked to be swaddled and the exact angle to hold him for a minimum of reflux vomiting and how to keep him awake through a feeding without upsetting him so much that he'd scream instead of eating—take off his socks and tickle his feet; still not a guarantee.

Cayo grunted again, louder, fists balled and legs stretching. Flora dropped a bottle in the warmer and stroked his soft cheek. She hoped for Cayo that he'd have Gwen's headstrong bravery and Flora's unshakable faith, ending up with a fiery tenacity that would serve him well in his life. She hoped many things for Cayo. The whole world at his fingertips and a life stuffed to the brim with happiness wasn't too much to ask, was it?

"It's... I love it, being a mom. I do."

Her hesitation must have given her away. "But..." Selene said, her tone nudging Flora to continue.

"But I—" Flora shook her head. She shouldn't complain, she's so *lucky* to have everything she does: Cayo, Gwen, this amazing little family of theirs. "Nothing. I'm just tired, I think."

Selene tsked. "Flora. Come on."

"I don't know." Flora sighed, hauling herself up with the phone tucked on one shoulder and the stirring baby on the other. "Every choice feels so monumental. Should I stay home with him in the fall even though I'm already going stir-crazy? Is he sleeping enough? Are pacifiers bad? Is thumb-sucking bad? Is swaddling bad now, too?" Once she started talking, all her fears and worries tumbled out as if floodgates were thrown open. "Is it too soon to start solid foods? But then if we wait it might be too late. And Selene, I nicked his little pinky finger when I was cutting his nails and he *bled*. I cried harder than he did; it was horrible. Then a few days ago this old lady at the grocery store yelled at me because he wasn't wearing a hat, but it's hot out. Maybe she meant a sun hat? Should he always be wearing a hat, Selene? I don't know! I don't know the infant hat rules!"

She looked down at Cayo as he blinked his eyes open. "I've failed the first tests of motherhood. I really thought I'd know what I was *doing* by now." Flora's eyes filled with tears just as Cayo let out his first cry for food. Selene laughed. She *laughed*.

"Oh, thanks." Flora sniffed.

"No, it's just. Oh, Flora. I have two kids, one in elementary school, even, and I don't know what I'm doing. This is the secret to parenthood that no one tells you until you're in the club: We're all just making this up as we go along."

"Really?" Flora checked the bottle, which was still a little cold. "Because Gwen looks at me like I'm some reincarnated Mother Earth and I keep thinking I *should* be. Shouldn't I? I read books and articles and chatted in message boards. I babysat. I am a *teacher*, for heaven's sake."

"Not the same," Selene said. There was another crash. "I *swear* to—listen, I have to run; my house is in shambles. I mean more so than usual. Just—parenthood is boot camp, Flora. You have to slap on a helmet and some waterproof boots and pray that no one gets a concussion. Do your best. Love him. There are no hat rules, I promise. You're fine. Be kind to yourself when you mess up, because you will. And if you feel overwhelmed, tell Gwen. You don't have to stoically handle everything without a peep of complaint, okay? You and Gwen are opposite sides of the same stubborn coin, I swear."

Flora sniffled again. "Thanks, Selene."

"Anytime." Selene, already in the middle of sending someone to timeout, ended the call.

Finally the bottle was ready, and it was once again back to the rocking chair. He ate quickly, one hand gripping her braid tightly as usual, legs kicking, feet digging into her stomach. The view outside the window behind him was a boat, getting ready to undock and head out to sea; the flaps of sails unfolding, rudders flapping and making little rippling waves on the flat surface of the water.

Cayo didn't like being put down. He seemed to need twenty-four-hour physical reassurance that someone was there. But after a meal he was usually satiated enough for Flora to use the bathroom or eat or, if she were very fast, shower.

Today, however, Gwen only had one fitting later in the day, and Flora had a leisurely morning for once. She took a bath and ate hot food, called her dad and mom, and then called Selene. So she was content to hold Cayo after the first bottle, marvel at him, and smile at him when he looked up. He smiled back at her, and she could float right away into the clouds at the surge of love she felt every time he did.

She didn't know. She had no idea. She'd had plenty of love in her life. But this. As if her heart could crack down microscopic fissure lines from the intensity. "I love you. Always. Forever."

Cayo grinned another drooling, gummy grin: the most beautiful smile to ever be smiled.

"Okay, hand him over." Gwen rushed in with a racket of dropped bags and the double slam of the door rapidly opening and closing. Flora was thankful the baby wasn't sleeping, because he certainly wouldn't have been after that, but she couldn't fault Gwen for being so anxious to see him.

In fact, the look on Gwen's face when Cayo directed a gummy smile her way made Flora's chest tight with joy. Watching Gwen fall head over heels in love with their son had brought a surprising new depth to their relationship; she got to watch the person she loved fall in love.

Flora stood for a quick kiss, and then passed Cayo into Gwen's impatient hands. "We're doing okay. The three of us?" Her voice wavered, wanting to be sure it was true.

Gwen sat down and set Cayo across her legs so she could make funny faces at him and circle his little legs as if he were riding a tiny, invisible, upside-down bicycle. "I think so." Face pinched with concern, she looked up at Flora.

"I just—" Flora picked at a scratch in the rocking chair as she confessed. "I'm so afraid of messing it up." She's supposed to be the one who was ready for this, who would take to mothering naturally as if she'd finally fulfilled her destiny. And here she was, crying over not putting a hat on her baby when she should have.

"Aw, Flor, hey." Gwen tilted her head to the side, indicating she wanted Flora to sit on the couch with them. "We're gonna mess up," she said, once Flora tucked herself against Gwen's side and let

Cayo grasp her finger. "I mean, that's why some people have more than one of these, right? Practice kid."

Flora scoffed, shaking her head and sniffling a laugh.

"The fact that it matters so much to you to get it right means you're an amazing mom. And I know that no matter what, you will love him and accept him for who he is, and always stand by him…" She ran her hand down Flora's braid and smiled. "But I already knew that."

"We're doing okay," Flora said, this time without the waver of uncertainly in her voice.

"Well," Gwen said, pumping Cayo's fist in the air like he's at a rock concert, "we do make a pretty kickass team."

35

"**I hope none** of you were expecting a home-cooked meal," Gwen says, carrying a stack of pizza boxes from the kitchen into the dining room. She passes Nico and Grady, who are at the front door wiping their feet and removing light coats. She plops the pizzas on the table where Flora and Clementine—who is on a brief stopover in Nashville before she begins her international tour—are chatting and making goofy faces at Cayo.

"Bubba's been teething and not sleeping very well." Gwen ruffles Cayo's wild hair. "Bah!" he says and bounces like a jack-in-the-box in his high chair. "And with Flora back to work now, we're eating all of our meals from takeout containers or while standing in front of the fridge." And usually with the baby on her hip while he tries to grab anything within reach.

Clementine is in a delicate white lace sheath dress that is expensive and dry-clean only, and she's dangerously close to Cayo with his fists that go from his drooling mouth to whatever he can get at.

"You should have said! I'd have had something catered." She tickles Cayo's belly, and he flaps his arms and giggles.

"Catered dinner in the three hours you're in town?" Gwen passes plates around.

"I'd have handled it," Clementine dismisses.

Gwen doesn't doubt it. Nico and Grady join them, and there's chatter and updates: they've been gone and Clementine's been on tour; Grady's been in the studio and Nico's been here and with Clementine and back out to New York and L.A.; and finally they're all in the same place at the same time. The weirdness with Clementine has faded to a wisp of a memory. Gwen looks around the table, at this odd hodgepodge of people, of family, and is content that Gwen and Flora's home is the beating heart in the center, not because of where it is, but because it's where they all are.

"Oh, I finished little man's blanket, finally." One arm draped over the back of Nico's chair, Grady is working on a slice of pepperoni. "It's in the truck if you want it."

"Uh, yeah." Gwen takes a bite of her veggie pizza, then spoons a blob of sweet potato mush into Cayo's mouth while she chews. "About time," she teases. Grady makes at face at her and pops back outside.

"How's the house-hunting going?" Flora asks, taking a turn feeding Cayo.

Nico scrubs a hand through his hair; he's frustrated. "I think at this point we're going to end up with more than one. Which is insane." He shakes his head. "My life is insane."

"I have more than one," Clementine points out, nibbling her artichoke and sun-dried tomato slice.

"Making my point for me," Nico dismisses with a jut of his chin. "But you know, Grady needs room to roam, and I need to be around civilized people, and we need a home but—"

"Sometimes you just get a little bit restless, a little more reckless." Gwen finishes.

Nico dips his head as Grady bangs back into the house, wipes his feet, unfurls a blanket, and says, "Isn't that a song lyric?"

Clementine raises her hand. "It's mine."

"Oh, Grady, the blanket is beautiful!" Flora says.

Cayo smacks his hands on his high chair tray and yells joyfully.

The blanket is zigzagging blocks of colors: brown, dark green, and light blue, repeating toward the center and ending with a bright, bold strip of orange. It matches Cayo's room, it matches their house, it matches them.

"Memaw always made a blanket for new babies in the family. Felt right to keep up the tradition."

Gwen takes the blanket and presses it to her cheek. It feels as if it were made from fairy wings, it's so soft. "You're gonna make me cry, you jerk."

Grady winks, settles next to Nico, and places a kiss behind his ear.

"Bubba, look!" Cayo reaches for the blanket when Gwen gets close enough, but then she thinks better of it. "I'll show it to him later. When he isn't covered in sweet potato."

Clementine leans over Cayo's messy tray carefully. "He *is* a sweet potato, isn't he?" Cayo slaps one wet, orange mush-covered hand on the pristine sleeve of her very expensive dress. She bolts back. "Oh!"

"Oh no! I am so sorry." Flora dips a napkin in her water, frantically dabbing at Clementine's sleeve. "We'll pay for your dry cleaning!"

"It's fine. I knew I was in the danger zone. Not like I've never been around babies." She glances up at Flora, then Gwen, then over to Cayo. "I might even want one of my own someday."

"Is that so?" Flora says, looking up from Clementine's sleeve with a knowing grin. "Haven't given up on love after all?"

"Eh, we'll see." She waves her other arm dismissively. "Maybe after I'm the top-selling country artist of all time and get that spot in the Hall of Fame, I'll fall in love and other such nonsense."

"Ah, romance isn't dead after all," Nico deadpans.

"Sure isn't." Grady kisses his cheek, his jaw and down his neck. Nico's prominent ears go red.

"Anyway," Clementine continues, "not like I'm all alone or anything."

Gwen chews a bite of pizza. "Kevin, right? A real-life Whitney Houston and Kevin Costner bodyguard love affair, I knew it."

"More like that three-headed hellhound she calls her hair and makeup team," Nico chimes in.

"Or she really is with that one actor she stood next to that one time. The tabloids are never wrong, you know," Grady says with his half-cocked grin.

"All right," Clementine says with an imperious purse of her lips. "I was going to say I'm not alone because I have y'all, but I'm changing my answer now."

Cayo interjects with a loud string of babbling. Flora wipes him off, cleaning his face and hands and the soft folds of his neck, which he loudly protests. She unties his bib and lifts him from the high chair. "What about you two? Kids?"

Nico clears his throat and shifts away from Grady to gulp some water. "I think we'll just live vicariously through you guys." He lifts his eyebrows at the sweet potato massacre left behind on the high chair, at Cayo squirming and squawking in Flora's arms. "On occasion."

Grady takes a big bite of pizza and says, "Oh, you should let us babysit! Have a night out. Or a nap. *Alone* time." He winks again. "Whatever you need."

Gwen has a brief, indulgent, sexy fantasy of her and Flora in some absurdly soft hotel bed with high-thread-count sheets and a feather duvet, of her body curved into Flora's body with the late morning sun blocked by heavy curtains. They sleep and sleep and sleep. For *hours.*

"Oh my god," Gwen groans. "That would be amazing, Grady." Then she adds, joking as she starts to follow Flora to change Cayo before his bath and bedtime. "Nico, if you don't marry him, I will."

Flora laughs and hikes Cayo higher on her hip. "I never thought I'd say this, but I could be into that."

"Grady's insidious charm knows no gender or sexual orientation," Clementine adds with an undignified snort.

"Okay, okay," Grady drawls, his crooked smile and graveled laugh joining in.

Nico sits silent, his face neutral, thinking. This is the way he looks when he's carefully considering a client's request to go braless and strapless when it's ninety-five degrees out and humid. Is the stunning gown worth the risk of letting melting double-sided tape be the only weapon against a sweaty nip-slip?

He tilts his head as he does when he's made a decision, sips his water, and says, mildly, "You're right, I should."

Everyone stares at him. Even Cayo goes quiet.

"I'm sorry," Grady says slowly. "What should you do now?"

Nico places his glass back on the table, turns to Grady, and takes both his hands tightly in his own. He dips his head to catch Grady's eyes. "How does a fall wedding next year sound?"

Grady's mouth flaps without sound; his eyes blink as if he can't quite believe Nico is sitting there in front of him. "Did you—are we—are you really—" He shakes his head and laughs, then tugs their joined hands to his chest. "Lord Almighty, you are gonna end me one of these days."

Gwen recognizes the look of thrilled incredulity on Grady's face. She'll never forget that night she stopped and thought and realized for herself what it meant to make a choice, to be in charge of her own life and her own destiny. How it felt to put herself on the line, to take a risk even if it meant being rejected. What it was to look into her own future and know for sure that whatever else happened, it was Flora she wanted right there, walking it with her.

"Well?" Clementine finally broke the silence. "Don't just leave us hanging! I have a flight to Toronto in one hour, boys. Chop, chop."

Gwen can't wait until Clementine starts dating. So much drama, so much passion, so many juicy details.

"Of course I'll marry you," Grady says. They stand and kiss and hug, and then everyone hugs in a big clumsy circle, and then Cayo cries because he needs a fresh diaper and sleep.

Maybe the key to a good relationship, Gwen thinks as she steps around the cats to get upstairs, is not only teamwork and compromise and commitment, but just enough reckless gambling to keep things interesting.

ACKNOWLEDGMENTS

Thank you to my family for putting up with my long absences, both mental and physical, and giving me the space I need to chase after my dreams. To my parents for their unwavering support. Thanks to my best friend for her enthusiasm; you're probably the only person who thinks I'm cool, and I appreciate that. And to my siblings who definitely do not think I'm cool: thanks for keeping me humble. A special thanks to my IP family: the incredibly talented artist behind my beautiful cover, Victoria S, and my fellow authors who make my writing life so much richer. If writing is an island, I like to think that we're all on it together, and that someone brought cocktails. To Annie, Candy, Choi, and Lex, too. There isn't enough gratitude in the world for the belief, support, and encouragement you've given me, so: Thank you. I hope that's a good start. Finally to every reader: Thanks for reading along, this journey would certainly be much lonelier without you.

ABOUT THE AUTHOR

Lilah Suzanne has been writing actively since the sixth grade, when a literary magazine published her essay about an uncle who lost his life to AIDS. A freelance writer, she has also authored a children's book and has a devoted following in the fan fiction community.

She is also the author of the Interlude Press books *Spice*, *Pivot and Slip*, and *Broken Records*.

BLENDED NOTES
by Lilah Suzanne

COMING IN
2017

Grady Dawson's future looks bright. He has finally left behind his difficult childhood and tumultuous young adulthood. He's at the top of his music career and planning an intimate wedding with Nico, his stylist turned lover turned love of his life. He has a close-knit group of friends who have become family: Gwen and Flora who are raising a sweet little boy named Cayo, fellow country star Clementine who always has his back, and former assistant Spencer who keeps things interesting. Until his past suddenly shows up on his doorstep, the news of his upcoming nuptials gets leaked to the media, and if that weren't enough, when his record company starts making demands that challenge Grady's integrity both as an artist and as a person, the foundation Grady has built his new life on starts to crumble fast. Can Grady continue making music if it means comprising his convictions? Can he have a future if he's still haunted by his past? And will he have to make the ultimate choice between his private life with Nico and the public demands of his career?

Grady's earliest memory of his mother is watching her leave. It wasn't the first time she had dropped him off at Memaw and Granddaddy's house, and the remembered moment itself is unremarkable: He's standing by the road; a cloud of dirt from the driveway into the trailer park lingers; he can see the taillights of her car lit red at the stop sign. The right one blinks a signal, the car turns, and she's gone. Memaw came to collect him soon after, and he doesn't recall what he did next—whatever rambunctious five-year-old boys like to do. Maybe he got on his bike and tore around the neighborhood, training wheels be damned. Or maybe he found a squirrel to harass with a makeshift slingshot of forked stick and rubber band. Maybe Memaw plunked him down in front of their old jumpy television.

"Sit down for five seconds, Grady. Land's sake!" She'd say.

He doesn't remember crying over Mama leaving then, or any other time. It felt normal, the calamity she brought to their lives, and no one in that trailer ever talked about it. Memaw and

Granddaddy didn't know any more than he did about where she was going, what she was doing, or when she'd be back. So they carried on as usual, and it's only in retrospect that Grady's connected the dots between her leaving and his getting in trouble at school or at home or, later on, turning tail and running whenever his personal relationships got difficult. He's still fighting that reflex now.

"Even if I did know where she was, she wouldn't show," Grady explains, in the office of their new house.

Nico is at the old-fashioned rolltop desk in a state-of-the-art ergonomic chair. The realtor described this house as city-sleek-meets-rustic-charm, and that about sums it up for the house and everything in it, including them. Nico taps a neat pile of robin's-egg blue envelopes even neater.

"Okay, but don't you think she'd at least want to know? Whether she shows up or not? We're keeping everything so hush-hush, she won't find out otherwise."

She gave him two birthday presents during his entire life: A metal Tonka truck and a pair of snakeskin cowboy boots. The boots she brought in person when he was nine. She took him to McDonald's for lunch and let him pick anything he wanted to eat, and then he opened the present right there in the plastic booth. He remembers feeling as if he were filled with his soda's fizzing bubbles, giggly and giddy, as he admired the boots. When he looked up to thank her she shook her head.

"You look just like your daddy," she told him. "God help us all."

In the office, Grady gives up trying to get comfortable in the oblong molded fiberglass rocking chair—he still has a hard time wrapping his brain around furniture that's really decoration and decoration that's really furniture—and stands behind Nico.

"I don't know where she is," he repeats, instead of providing an answer to the question of whether or not his own mother would care that he's getting married. He doesn't know. She very well may not; and that's something Nico can't quite understand.

"How about your dad?"

Grady laughs, and Nico gives him a sharp look that either means something very, very good or very, very bad. It's fifty-fifty. "Sweetheart," Grady says, and rubs at the tense pull of muscles across Nico's slim shoulders. "I appreciate what you're trying to do, but it's not necessary. I'll have my family there. Clem, Flora and Gwen and Cayo. My band. Spencer." Nico's shoulders pull tighter at Spencer's name. "Your mom and dad and brother," Grady continues, massaging the knotted tendons at the base of Nico's long, graceful neck. "Soon they'll be my family *officially*. I'm not sad or upset about anyone missing." Other than Memaw and Granddaddy, but of course that's a different kind of missing.

Nico's shoulders relax. "Okay."

"Okay." Grady's fingers drift up Nico's neck to brush the shell of his prominent ears. They've been wedding planning for hours, hunkered down in the office checking things off lists, and it's making Grady restless. But when he bends to caress Nico's neck and ears with his lips, Nico catches him by the chin.

"Hold that thought. If I don't get these invitations addressed and out today, I will lose it."

Grady pouts and stands up. "Anything I can do?"

Nico uncaps a pen with decisive force. "You can stand there and look handsome."

"Done." Grady wanders to the bookshelf. In the corner he spots a ukulele that went missing a few weeks ago and strums a bit of his new single.

Once in a life, a boy comes along.
And blows your world apart.

It would have been better if she had just disappeared. His grandparents were dedicated and loving, even though he had been dumped on their doorstep. They didn't have much, but he never went without, never felt lacking or unstable. Then his mother would blow into town like a storm—or more rarely, his father—and he'd be shaken to pieces. And the very worst part is that when Mama was present, not just there but sober, she was wonderful.

With a love that burns so bright.

Lily was infused with light: bright and fun. She took him to Pigeon Forge once, just the two of them, to Dollywood. They ate ice cream and went to the shows and on all the rides, the big scary ones too, where she held his hand so he wouldn't be afraid. He remembers singing and laughing and raising their hands up high at the peak of a roller coaster. At age eleven Grady knew what it felt like to be Icarus.

It shines a light.
Through the cracks of your broken heart.

He always got burned, yet he never could convince himself that he was soaring headlong into the flames. *This time*, he'd think, *this time she'll stay.*

Grady's song trips into a minor key, so he sets the instrument down; there's nothing more depressing than a sad ukulele solo.

"Actually," Nico says, addressing an envelope in his careful, precise handwriting. "If I could see your contacts list… I don't have addresses for your band members."

"Then can we be done?" Only half paying attention, Grady thumbs through his contacts, then drops his phone onto the desk and slumps over it with a pleading look.

Nico cocks his head and arches a sharp eyebrow; it's dead sexy. "Good things come to those who wait."

Grady lets his voice slip low and dragging, "I do like the sound of that." He slinks closer, but is thwarted again when Nico leans away, intentionally out of reach.

Six months out and Grady is fed up with wedding planning. He'd suggest they elope, only Nico's mother would be heartbroken, and Grady would never forgive himself for hurting that dear, sweet angel who loves him like her own. Besides, there is the honeymoon to look forward to: a private bungalow in an isolated tropical paradise that Grady's half-convinced they may never leave. That suits him just fine; he can make music anywhere, anytime, for anyone.

Two weeks later the RSVPs have been trickling in. They've kept the invitation list small, limited to people they can trust to not spill the beans to a tabloid, or in other words, not Spencer.

Grady is heading to a meeting at his record company to finalize the new album; he's running out the door when a certified overnight envelope tips into the doorway. He doesn't think much of it until he starts to fling the letter inside for Nico to deal with and catches the name on the return address.

Clay Dawson.

To Be Continued

also from
lilah **suzanne**

Broken Records

Los Angeles-based stylist Nico Takahashi loves his job—or at least, he used to. Feeling fed up and exhausted from the cutthroat, gossip-fueled business of Hollywood, Nico daydreams about packing it all in and leaving for good. So when Grady Dawson—sexy country music star and rumored playboy—asks Nico to style him, Nico is reluctant. But after styling a career-changing photo shoot, Nico follows Grady to Nashville where he finds it increasingly difficult to resist Grady's charms.

ISBN (print) 978-1-941530-57-3 | (eBook) 978-1-941530-58-0

Spice

In his Ask Eros advice column, Simon Beck has an answer to every relationship question his readers can throw at him. But in his life, the answers are a little more elusive—until he meets the newest and cutest member of his company's computer support team. Simon may be charmed, but will Benji help him answer the one relationship question that's always stumped him: how to know he's met Mr. Right?

ISBN (print) 978-1-941530-25-2 | (eBook) 978-1-941530-26-9

Pivot and Slip

Former Olympic hopeful Jack Douglas traded competitive swimming for professional yoga and never looked back. When handsome pro boxer Felix Montero mistakenly registers for his yoga for Seniors class, Jack takes an active interest both in Felix's struggles to manage stress and in his heart and discovers along the way that he may have healing of his own to do.

ISBN (print) 978-1-941530-03-0 | (eBook) 978-1-941530-12-2

One **story**
can change **everything.**

@interlude**press**

Twitter | Facebook | Instagram | Pinterest

For a reader's guide to **Burning Tracks** and book club prompts,
please visit interludepress.com.